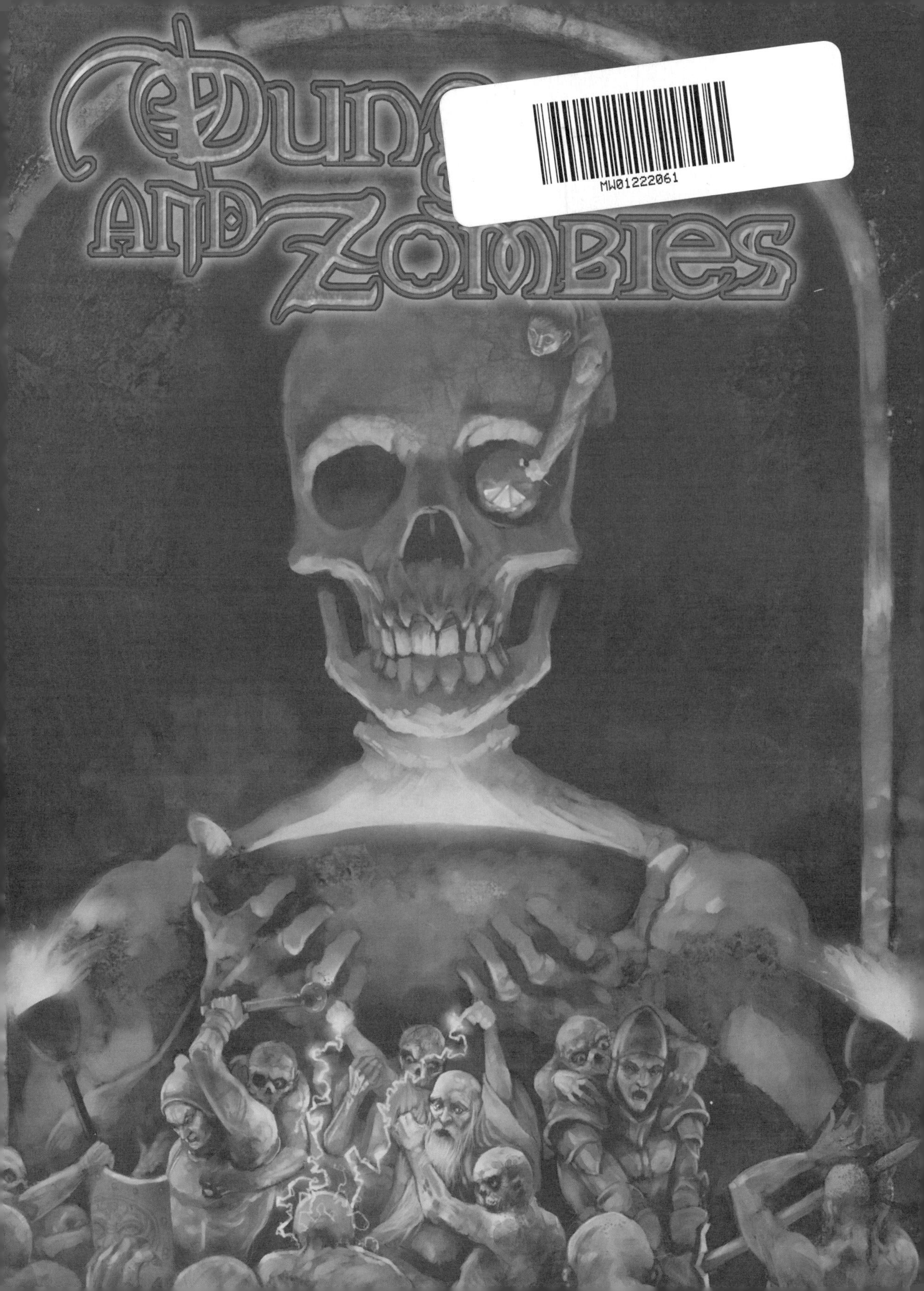

Dung
AND ZOMBIES

EDEN STUDIOS presents A SHY/VASILAKOS production

Dungeons and Zombies™

Produced by EDEN STUDIOS Directed by GEORGE VASILAKOS

Written by JASON VEY

Additional Material by ROSS A. ISAACS

Edited by ROSS A. ISAACS

Proofing by M. ALEXANDER JURKAT DAVID CARROLL DANIEL R. DAVIS SHAWN THERRIEN

Director of Photography GEORGE VASILAKOS

Visual Effects by C. BRENT FERGUSON TRAVIS INGRAM JOHNATHAN KIRTZ GREGORY PRICE DAN OROPALLO CARY POLKOVITZ GEORGE VASILAKOS KIRAN YANNER

Cover Art by JON HODGSON

Playtested by SAM ANDERSON ANDREW CIOTTI CHRISTINA COOK WAYNE CURRY DANIEL R. DAVIS CHARLIE VONESCHEN ERIC FERM ALEX GOLDMAN JULIETTE GOUIRAND SHARI HILL ERIC C. KIEFER KALIE OFCIARCIK THOR OLAVSRUD BOB RUSSELL JASON J. RYDER GERRY SARACCO E. SIERRA CLINT STOELTING DEREK STOELTING ROB STRATMAN MIKE WALLACE

Ross thanks Anthony Franchini for his help with all things dungeon. Jason thanks Derek Stoelting for selling him on the Unisystem in the first place.

Based on the Original Concept by

CHRISTOPHER SHY and GEORGE VASILAKOS

WWW.ALLFLESH.COM

Eden Studios
6 Dogwood Lane, Loudonville, NY 12211

Produced and published by Eden Studios, Inc.
The Unisystem™ is used under exclusive license.

Comments and questions can be directed via the Internet at www.allflesh.com, via e-mail at edenprod@aol.com or via letter with a self-addressed stamped envelope.

First Printing, November 2004
Stock EDN8010 ISBN 1-891153-35-8
Printed in the U.S.

ZOMBIES

Table of Contents

CHAPTER ONE

"GAH! You bit me!" Carlos lopped off the zombie's head, tore it free, and cast it aside. He'd never known pain like the thousands of burning needles now shooting into his brain. For a second he was blinded by it, which almost cost him as more zombies pressed in. Carlos recovered in time to throw a high kick, catching a zombie in the face.

Things were bleak. There were hundreds of them, everywhere. The mausoleum was their only hope. Carlos could only trust they'd all make it. He hacked his way towards Karrak. To his left and slightly ahead, Xavier adopted the same plan. If they could regroup, they might get out of this.

Suddenly, a booming voice split the air. "By the power of Mitra, back to hell!"

A blast of flame cut a clean path up the hill. As the zombies were forced back by the flames, Carlos could see Bennik, hands stretched forth, flames issuing from his fingertips. After a few seconds, the flames died down, and the dwarf dropped to one knee.

"That's it," Bennik said. "I'm spent."

"Let's go!" Karrak cried. Diminutive Squeaks scrambled off of the minotaur's shoulders so Karrak could carry the dwarf up the hill. Within seconds, Carlos and Xavier were there and the party made for the mausoleum. Behind them, the zombies shambled closer, but with their lumbering gait they had little chance of catching the companions.

"Just wait till I find out who's behind this," Carlos grumbled. "I'm going to shoot him in the face with my crossbow." He shivered with a sudden chill as the words left his mouth.

As though in answer to Carlos's challenge, a flash of lightning lit up the sky and illuminated a tall figure standing atop the mausoleum. The man wore a black cloak and looked down at the group with malicious glee. His features were gaunt and pale, and unholy light gleamed in his eyes.

Carlos sneered and drew his crossbow. "No, wait!" he cried. "Don't jump! We're gonna shoot you down!"

The man laughed, whipped his cloak around . . . and vanished.

"You should've saved the quip and just shot," Bennik croaked from Karrak's elbow.

"Bite me," Carlos said, and shivered as the door to the mausoleum creaked open before the party.

"Put me down, you blasted cow," Bennik cursed at Karrak. "I'm strong enough to walk on my own."

DELVING DOWN

"Out of the frying pan, and into the furnace," Xavier said, tying his hair behind his elven ears as the companions entered the darkened building. The door swung shut behind them with an ominous bang.

* * *

Bennik's eyes slipped into the infrared spectrum, allowing him to see the patterns of heat in the room. The others weren't so fortunate; Karrak and Xavier could see a few feet with their nightvision, but it was too dark for that to help much. There was a shuffling of packs rummaged through, Xavier whispered an incantation, and the room was bathed in the light of torches held by Carlos and Squeaks.

"Much better," Karrak said. The sound of his voice echoed off the stone walls and startled everyone. The room was far larger than it looked from the outside, and featureless, save two iron doors on the far wall.

"At least we're out of the rain," Squeaks said.

"I'm not so sure that's a plus, all things considered," Carlos said. "Anyone else notice that this place is a lot bigger inside than out?"

"I don't want to talk about that," Karrak said.

"A hot bowl of stew and a lusty companion would be perfect right now," Xavier said.

"For once, my friend, I'm in total agreement with you," Bennik muttered. "Which way?"

"One looks as good as the other at this point," Carlos said. "We've really no way of telling if there's a better way." He shrugged. "Let's go left."

Karrak tugged at the left door and it swung open. He took a deep breath and stepped through. Carlos went next, Squeaks at his heels. Before Bennik and Xavier could follow, however, the door slammed shut. Bennik pulled, yanked, kicked, and cursed to no avail.

"Wonderful," he said. "Now we've lost them."

Xavier tugged on the right hand door, which opened easily. "Seems we've been separated deliberately," he said. "The question is—was it the gods or whatever evil power runs this place?"

"I'm going with the evil power," Bennik said, and uttered his umpteenth prayer to Mitra, for good measure. "Not much other choice. Let's go." And he clumped into the darkness. The elf followed, close at Bennik's back. Neither flinched when the door closed behind them.

* * *

Squeaks pulled at the door, squealing. Carlos, then Karrak, then the two of them in tandem also tried. The door wouldn't open. Further along, a narrow staircase beckoned them, but Karrak wasn't willing to just leave without his friends. He gave one final, great yank, and let out a growl. "Dammit!" he spat, took a few steps back, and lowered his head for a charge. Carlos held up a hand to stop him.

"Probably not a good idea, Karrak. You'll just hurt yourself. I think we've been deliberately separated from Bennik and Xavier. Our road lies ahead, not back. We can only hope that they're okay and that we'll meet up later."

Karrak didn't like it, but Carlos was good at being cool under fire and was probably right. Karrak pawed the ground, snorted, turned, and climbed the staircase. Squeaks looked ready to burst into tears. Carlos laid a hand on her shoulder.

"It's going to be okay, Squeaks. We'll get through this, and we'll find them. C'mon, let's go."

A sudden chill crept up Carlos's spine and he realized he'd broken out into a sweat. His arm burned. He ran his fingers over the bite mark and shuddered again. Have to see a cleric when this was all over.

The staircase wasn't long and ended in a solid wooden door. Karrak shot a glance over his shoulder, reassuring himself that Carlos and Squeaks were still there, and tried the handle. The door swung open with a loud creak. The minotaur took a deep breath which was echoed by his two companions, and stepped through, sword in hand.

The square room was about twenty feet to a side, decorated by a red velvet curtain along the right wall and a wooden table and benches in the center. The rock walls looked solid and well kept. Torches burned in sconces along the walls and candles burned on the table. Carlos shivered again and Squeaks looked up at him in concern.

"You okay, Carlos?"

He waved his hand. "I'll be fine. I may have come down with a bug, but it can wait till we can get to a healer."

"You're sure?"

"I'm sure. We'll get out of here, I'll get healed, and we'll head for the local tavern. I'm so hungry I could eat a horse."

"So now what?" Karrak asked.

"Now we see what's behind that curtain," Carlos said.

As though on cue, the curtains parted and a familiar figure stepped forth. He flipped his black cloak away from his fine traveler's garb, and leaned upon a cane topped with a silver wolf's head. Teeth glittering in the dim light, he grinned and bowed.

"So," he said to Carlos, "Still going to shoot me down?"

"You bet," Carlos said, and in one fluid motion he dropped his swords, drew his crossbow, and let fly.

* * *

Bennik huffed. He cast a sidelong glance at Xavier and said "I've said it before, I'll say it again—good things don't happen to us."

"Bad luck? It must change eventually. Let's figure out how to get out of this cursed place and find the others."

A short, narrow staircase stretched up before them, ending at a large wooden door. The elf and dwarf made their way up the stairs, where Bennik threw the door open with little regard for what lay in wait on the other side. As the dwarf stomped through the door, Xavier started channeling Essence again, building his reserves.

The room was dimly lit by torches and black candles. Mirrors stretched across the wall to their left. Directly across the room stood a marble altar with a statue of a giant, four-armed, fanged woman behind it. Rubies gleamed in the statue's eyes, and gemstones adorned its knuckles. A priestess stood at the altar, incense burning in a dish on her right. The fumes stung Bennik and Xavier's noses, and made their eyes water. The priestess held aloft a jeweled, kris-bladed dagger, offering unseen sacrifices. Her eyes were rolled back and she swayed in ecstasy.

"Kali," Bennik growled.

"Who?" Xavier said. "Her?"

"No. The statue. I'm betting she's a high priestess."

The priestess' eyes snapped back and she lowered the dagger. She smiled wickedly at Bennik.

"Greetings, Priest of Mitra," she said. "I have been expecting you."

"It was you who brought us here?" Bennik said.

"No, the Mother of Life and of Death called you here to meet me."

"Please," Xavier said. "She's not my mother."

"You would do well, dwarf, to silence your impertinent elven friend, before I take displeasure with him."

"You'll have to go through me first," Bennik said.

"Come," the priestess said. "Let us talk."

"I've nothing to say to you."

"Surely you've no fear of a conversation with a rival priestess?"

"I never said I was afraid."

"Then where is the harm?"

Bennik chewed on his lip for a moment and cast a glance at Xavier, who shrugged. Finally, the dwarf stomped to the altar. He had to crane his neck to look the priestess in the eyes, but did so with a dignity and defiance that belied his small stature.

The priestess calmly drew the blade of her knife across her palm, and held it up for Bennik to see. A thin line of blood leaked onto her wrist. The smell of incense was dizzying. Something was very wrong. Bennik raised his sword to strike, but the priestess thrust her hand forward and cried out, "*Osak'aro Aashlem D'khashiyn!*"

A strangled cry sounded behind Bennik and he glanced back. Xavier lay upon the ground, stiff as death.

"Harlot!" he cried, spinning back to the priestess.

"He is not dead," she said, holding up her bloodied palm once again. "But he could be. I hold his soul in my hands. Will you gamble with that, or hear me out?"

Bennik frowned and turned his sword point down, hands folded over the hilt. "Speak," he said simply.

"Do you see this?" she cast a loving glance at her blood-soaked palm. "This is all that my goddess asks of us, a small sacrifice for absolute power!" She turned and caressed the statue—a trail of black blood marked its surface.

"You're going to have to do better than that," Bennik said. "I have yet to hear of a god who doesn't make such promises, and yours has overrun our world with demons."

"You don't understand. But you will . . . when you join me."

Bennik laughed, a booming and stony sound few humans ever heard from a dwarf. "You're as insane as you are lecherous."

"That is the second time you've referred to me as wanton," she said. "I will not let it pass a third. Your other three friends are about to die at the hands of a zombie lord under my command. I can choke the life out of the elf there with a mere thought. I would advise you to mind your manners."

"What do you want with me?" Bennik hissed.

"Join me. Kneel and pledge your allegiance to Kali and together we shall take her message to the dwarven nations. Together we shall raise an army to rule the world! Do this, and I shall set your friends free. Do it not, and you all die, here and now . . . starting with the elf."

Bennik growled. Her promises all rang clear in his mind. A small sacrifice and his friends would be free to go. Trembling, he came around the altar and dropped to one knee. His sweating hands wrung the grip of his sword. He bowed his head and whispered, "Milady, I would ask one favor of you."

The priestess laid her hand on his head and asked, "What boon would you ask?"

"I would ask that you burn in hell, braggart!" He cried and slashed out with his sword.

He wasn't quick enough. The priestess jumped back from his swing, suffering only a minor cut but dropping the kris-blade. Her eyes turned as black as night. "So be it," she said, an unearthly echo in her voice. "The elf dies."

Xavier howled in agony before a blast of white-hot flame enveloped his entire body, consuming it in seconds. Bennik cried out in rage and sorrow, and spun on his enemy.

"I warned you," she said. "All you had to do was kneel, but you have chosen the path of destruction instead, for you and your friends."

"I think they'd all rather die than see me kneel before you," he hissed. "Come, bitch-priest! Let us see who wins the day!"

"Yes, let us see!" She stepped backwards, into the statue, which shifted and groaned. The stone glowed and oozed around her, engulfing her as fast as the flames had consumed Xavier. As the statue embraced her, a look of nirvana spread across her features.

She was gone, and the statue stepped forward, flexing its four arms, which groaned and banged deafeningly. It swung once, catching Bennik with a glancing blow that launched him across the room. He hit the wall and slid down, then climbed to his feet. He was dizzy, but kept sword in hand to face down the deific horror that charged him.

"Mitra help me now," Bennik muttered, prepared for his final battle.

* * *

Carlos launched a bolt for the zombie lord's heart. The monster stood completely still but for its forearm, which snapped upward and caught the crossbow bolt. He raised the bolt and examined it, then looked to Carlos.

"Nice shot," he said. "Too bad it's never that easy."

The creature whipped the bolt back at them. Squeaks let out a scream and clutched at the bolt embedded in her shoulder. She fell backwards—there was a sickening *crack* as her head struck the ground.

Carlos looked at her, horrified, and a single thought entered his fevered mind: *We're out of our league here*. He dropped to one knee, letting his crossbow skitter across the floor, and took hold of his twin blades again, intending to charge the zombie lord.

His gaze was drawn to Squeaks, lying so still on the ground. So helpless . . . so innocent and sweet.

"Squeaks . . ."

On the other side of the room, Karrak was pawing the ground and snorting, glaring at the zombie lord. "You're going to pay for that."

"Am I? And who is going to make me?"

"You're far outnumbered," the minotaur said.

"And how do you count that?" the zombie lord said, gesturing at Carlos.

Karrak gasped. Carlos's skin had turned a sickly yellow blotched with red, his gaze blank and staring, all semblance of humanity gone. His chomping jaw was buried in Squeaks's shredded throat.

"By the gods!" Karrak cried. "Carlos, stop!"

Something registered in the zombie at the sound of its former name, and it lifted its blood-soaked face from its meal. It cocked its head to the side in curiosity, and examined the warm creature calling to it. Fresh meat. It lumbered clumsily towards Karrak, who stumbled backwards in terror.

"You did this to him!" He screamed at the zombie lord, "Turned him into this thing!"

"Actually, one of the undead outside did this to him. Have you noticed the bite on his arm? I simply hastened the process."

Karrak squinted at the Carlos-zombie. There was a festering wound on its arm, and Karrak cursed himself for not noticing earlier. "I'm sorry, Carlos," he said and charged. The minotaur bowled over the pitiful creature, catching the zombie in his meaty fist and slamming its head into the wall with all the force he could muster.

Carlos dropped to the floor, a wet trail of blood and gray matter on the wall. Karrak looked at the body, wracked with sorrow. Suddenly, a mighty blow struck the back of his head, sending him reeling. He struggled to focus through the spinning haze, and saw the zombie lord standing over him, brandishing his cane.

"All you've done, minotaur, is to trap his soul in the netherworlds. None shall rest so long as Ahriman and Kali rule. Congratulations; you've sent your friend to Hell and you're going to follow him."

Karrak's head thudded back to the floor and lolled to the side, his jaw slack, unconscious. The zombie lord smiled and called to Squeaks. "Arise, my child."

Squeaks's eyes popped open, glazed and yellow. The new zombie pulled itself to its feet slowly, head hanging to the side, barely supported by its torn throat. But the spine was intact; she was functional. The zombie lord patted his creation and it purred like a kitten. He led her by the hand to Karrak and she rolled her eyes between the two, hungry but questioning.

"Yes, my pet. It's time for you to feed. It's time for you to . . ."

The zombie lord's eyes popped wide and blood spewed from his mouth. The Squeaks zombie fell back as its master staggered away, a short sword driven clear through his chest. Karrak stood, wiped his blood-soaked hand on his tunic, and sneered.

"Next time, make damned sure your enemy is truly down before you gloat." He charged, lowering his head as he did. The zombie lord lunged clumsily to the side, trying to dodge. But the impalement had weakened him, and Karrak struck, twisting his head to drive one horn through the collarbone, and the other through the zombie lord's face. With a flip of his massive shoulders, Karrak ripped the zombie lord's head off and sent it across the room to splatter against the wall above Carlos's body.

He then turned his attention to Squeaks, still looking feral and hungry, but terrified. A single tear rolled down his cheek as he walked towards her, his hands out gently.

"Squeaks," he said, "come here. It's okay. Come on."

The zombie took a few halting steps towards Karrak, who reciprocated, careful to remain unthreatening. When the distance closed, Karrak reached out to caress Squeaks' pallid cheeks. Suddenly, her nose twitched and the confusion was replaced by animal hunger. Her jaws opened and closed impotently, her head lolling on few tendons holding it in place.

With a sob that echoed throughout the room, Karrak tore his friend's head from her shoulders and watched through a haze of tears as her body collapsed to the floor. He stood there for a moment, staring at the head in his hands, then dropped it and collapsed to the floor, his head buried in his hands.

"Indra's clouds, what have I done?"

Through all he'd endured in the arenas of the human empires of the world, he'd never seen anything as brutal as the events of this day.

A quiet thumping from behind the velvet curtains brought the minotaur to his senses. This wasn't over yet. There was still Bennik and Xavier to find. Karrak prayed that they had fared better. He retrieved his sword, walked to the curtains, and threw them open to find a tinted window into another room. His heart leapt when he saw Bennik, scrambling about the room on the other side of the glass. Xavier was nowhere in sight. Had the same fate befallen the elf as Carlos and Squeaks? He began feeling about the glass for a switch, some sort of lever that would operate a hidden door and grant him access to the room.

Another movement caught Karrak's attention and he snapped his gaze back to the other room. Bennik wasn't alone—an enormous four-armed statue of fanged woman charged the dwarf. Bennik shifted his sword from his right to his left hand and back again, bouncing on the balls of his feet in a battle stance across the room.

Karrak took one last look for levers or switches, then muttered, "To Hell with it." He hopped backward and charged, shoulder down and face away from the mirrors to shield it from flying glass. He hit the window and it shattered, sending the minotaur spilling into the room beyond. He pulled himself to his feet and nodded at Bennik. The statue was between the two of them.

* * *

Bennik bounced in a fighting stance. If he had to die, let it be with honor and with Mitra's name upon his lips.

Suddenly, the mirror on the far wall shattered, and an enormous form tumbled into the room. Bennik's heart sank at the thought of another enemy entering the fray, then leapt for joy as the familiar minotaur pulled himself to his feet, sword in hand, and nodded to him.

"Karrak! Where's Carlos and Squeaks?"

"Dead," the minotaur said. "along with the Zombie lord murderer. Xavier?"

"Dead. This abomination's priestess!"

"Then let's send it screaming to Hell with them!" Karrak bellowed and charged.

"He's direct, I'll give him that much," Bennik muttered and charged as well.

The Kali-thing allowed its foes to complete their charges. Chips of stone flew as their blades struck, but the avatar didn't even flinch. It picked up Bennik and Karrak by their throats and hurled them effortlessly across the room in opposite directions. Bennik bounced to his feet quickly; Karrak slower. The Kali-thing strode towards Karrak, but the dwarf was there, scaling its back like a mountain goat. He dodged and wove around the flailing arms, and hacked away with his sword. He scarred the stone face to an unrecognizable husk, but couldn't slow the beast. Desperate, he struck at the eye-rubies. A shock ran through the dwarf's body and a blinding light threw him again across the room.

The statue grabbed Karrak with all four arms and caught the minotaur in a crushing bear hug. The sound of snapping ribs echoed and Karrak coughed, blood spewing from his snout.

Bennik pulled himself to a sitting position and clutched at his own ribs. He closed his eyes in desperation and prayed. "Mitra, please. I have called upon you many times this day and you have not failed me yet. We cannot face this goddess alone. Help me!"

The knife, a childlike voice said in Bennik's mind. *The knife . . . and the eyes.*

"I've already tried the eyes!" Bennik said. "I couldn't—!"

Then the jeweled hilt of the priestess's kris blade caught the gleam of the torchlight. The dwarf skittered across the floor, snatched the blade up, and looked upon it with wonder. Such a thing of beauty . . .

No time. He looked back to the statue where Karrak rolled his eyes towards Bennik, pleading.

One of the minotaur's arms was free.

"Karrak!" Bennik cried and tossed the dagger to his friend.

Understanding registered in the minotaur's eyes; he was used to fighting for his life. This was just another arena for him. He reached out and caught the dagger by the hilt.

"The eyes!" Bennik cried and Karrak looked at the leering face. The rubies gleamed, reflecting the candle and torchlight in a spectrum of stars.

"Got . . . you," Karrak coughed and drove the dagger into the statue's left eye. An explosion sang out and the construct fell towards the altar. Karrak flew several feet the other direction. Still, he held tight to the dagger. As the Kali-thing stood once again, Karrak noted the black void where its one eye used to be. "So that's your weakness," he said, and a flip of his wrist sent the knife soaring across the room, into the statue's remaining eye.

The Kali-thing stood tall and froze, arms wide. It stood for an eternity of seconds, until a rumbling began deep inside. Cracks spider-webbed up the statue's legs, to its torso, then out through each of its arms to the tips of its fingers and back, finally over its chest, throat, and ravaged face. Another moment of silence and the monster exploded in a shower of rock shards. Karrak and Bennik hit the floor and rolled up to protect themselves.

It was over. A film of dust settled over the devastation. The two friends groaned and dug their way out of the rubble. The horror, loss, and victories of the day were too much to bear, and both of them burst into laughter and tears.

"I suppose," Karrak said, "We should find our way out of here."

"Aye," Bennik agreed. "And bury our dead."

"Well," a bright, feminine voice said between coughs, "This certainly was a show!"

Bennik and Karrak turned their faces to the doorway, where stood a young, dark-skinned girl with tightly braided black hair. She wore a neatly tailored tunic and shining bronze breastplate. A sword bounced at her side, but she seemed far too young to be an adventurer. Though little more than a child, an aura of sheer power radiated from her.

"Okay," Bennik said, "I've had about enough. Who are you?"

"Look into my eyes," she said, "and know."

Bennik glared into the girl's dark eyes for an instant, an embarrassed fear washed over him. He took a knee and said, "Prithee forgive me, M'lord!"

"My lord?" Karrak said, awed. "You mean this is…?"

The girl smiled. "Most know me as Mitra."

"I thought Mitra was male!" Karrak said.

"I am whatever I wish to be." She turned to Bennik. "And you, my servant, have done well."

"Excuse me, lord, but how have I done well? I've lost three dear companions this day!"

"No," Mitra said. "You've sacrificed three rather than betray me. Such conviction brings hope that one day the forces of darkness may yet be defeated. Rise."

Bennik stood, trembling. "Still, I wish there were another way."

"Be at peace. I do not allow my warriors to suffer needlessly. Their deaths were not preordained, and for your service today, I grant you this one boon. Awaken and remember."

* * *

Bennik sat bolt upright, covered in sweat, and reached madly for his sword. He hit the cold, stone floor with a thud and stood, rubbing his rump through his nightshirt. He . . .

Wait, his nightshirt? The dwarf looked around feverishly. The room was dark, but it was clearly his own. He was at the inn, and the sun rose over the peaks in the distance. What in Mitra's name was going on?

* * *

"Helluva dream," Carlos said, sitting with Xavier, Squeaks, and Karrak. He dug at his plate of eggs and mutton, pouring back gulps of mulled wine and talking with his mouth well full. "I mean, I'm still hungry. I've never been this hungry before. I dreamt that I was . . ."

". . . a zombie?" Squeaks finished.

"I told you to stay out of my head."

"No, I dreamt the same thing. I was a zombie after you died."

"Wait," Karrak said. "I did as well! There was a mausoleum. We got separated—"

"And I was consumed by fire from a priestess of Kali," Xavier put in. "What forces cause us to share this dream?"

Bennik joined the group. "It wasn't a dream."

"Of course it was," Carlos said. "It had to be a dream. We're all alive."

"By the grace of Mitra. You owe him your lives."

"We've been over this before," Xavier said. "Do not proselytize to me, dwarf!"

Bennik tossed a jeweled, kris-bladed dagger, and two large rubies upon the table. They skittered to a halt directly in the center. The group stared, awestruck.

"We have a mission, now," Bennik said.

The rest of the meal passed in silence.

Introduction

Everyone engages in fantasy, especially gamers. The typical gamer takes great pleasure in the escapism involved in creating a fictional character—be it one based upon a pre-existing figure from his favorite film, TV show, or book; or one purely of his own creation—and engaging in imaginary stories in which that character plays a central role. In its most basic sense, that's what fantasy is. It's just pretend. Anything that isn't real qualifies as fantasy.

But that's obviously not the "style" of fantasy to be found here. No, this book is concerned with dark labyrinths and mystical temples; warriors with sinewy arms straining as they twirl their bloodied blades and wade into hordes of enemies; or warrior women who hack their way through dank dungeons to rescue the hapless prince of a small kingdom, because honor or the promise of wealth demands it. This book is dedicated to what is popularly known as Heroic Fantasy, or Swords and Sorcery. And since this is *All Flesh Must Be Eaten*, there are hordes of undead in the mix, just for good measure.

The Heroic Fantasy tradition has been around ever since the early days of humankind. It began with the ancient myths and legends primitive humans created to explain where their sun came from, and why the leaves turned red and yellow during the autumn. Tales told around fires late at night and scrawled in pictures on cave walls depicted the deeds of great heroes prevailing against immeasurable foes. Through these tales ran the constant theme of hope that we could rise above the trials and tribulations laid upon us by nature and the gods above. The characters became iconic: warriors, witches, wizards, gods, and monsters. From these tales arose the great heroes of legend: Hercules, Perseus, Gilgamesh, Thor, Beowulf, and hundreds of others.

Eventually, Western society evolved and no longer gave much credence to these myths and legends, and the old gods died. Humans as a race, however, never lost or forgot the need for heroes, and for escapism into magical and wondrous worlds, and so fantasy continued. In the 1970s the genre leap into the realm of pen-and-paper roleplaying games. These games gave birth in turn to a new resurgence of Heroic Fantasy literature, and the science fiction sections in local book stores became "Sci-Fi/Fantasy" sections. It has been that way ever since, and Heroic Fantasy literature and games show no sign of going away.

So what happens when this classic genre is turned upside down and crossed with zombie survival horror? Welcome to *Dungeons and Zombies*. This ain't your grandma's fantasy.

Chapter Summary

Chapter One: Delving Down includes these opening remarks.

Chapter Two: Swords, Sorcery, and Shambling details character creation for Heroic Fantasy Cast Members, new Qualities and Drawbacks, and Metaphysics, as well as some new rules and tips on fantasy Deadworld design.

Chapter Three: Dead Gods and Demon Lands presents the first of four Deadworlds, this one based upon the gritty pulp fantasy tradition of Robert E. Howard and Fritz Lieber. Evil, ancient, and forgotten gods overrun a world with demons and undead as the heroes stand alone against an overwhelming darkness.

Chapter Four: Dawn of a Dead Age is modeled after literary fantasy in the tradition of J.R.R. Tolkien. It tells the tale of an ancient evil rising in the South and sending his armies of undead to conquer the peaceful lands of the North.

Chapter Five: Death of the Round Table gives a new spin on the beloved legend of King Arthur. In this reality, Arthur's knights never found the Grail; Mordred and Morgana beat them to it and corrupted the sacred relic. Together they have raised a massive army of the dead to sweep over Britain and lay siege to Camelot. If they aren't stopped, the tides of darkness will cover the entire world.

Chapter Six: The Eastern Dead is oriental in style, and perhaps best suited for crossover play with another *AFMBE* sourcebook, *Enter the Zombie*. It concerns an incursion of the dead from Jigoku, an Asian conception of Hell.

Chapter Seven: The Tomb of Doom presents the kind of dungeon universal to fantasy roleplaying games and computer games. Venture down the hall, open door, kill monster, take stuff. After all, you can't have a book called *Dungeons & Zombies* without including a dungeon.

How to Use Dungeons and Zombies

Dungeons and Zombies is structured like most *All Flesh Must Be Eaten* supplements. Chapters One and Two are for both players and Zombie Masters, and include rules for using the game in a fantasy context.

Chapters Three through Six detail different fantasy Deadworlds and are intended for the Zombie Master. Chapter Eight is something a bit different. It's a ready-to-run dungeon adventure, complete with bad guys, plotline, and detailed rooms. Think of it as plug-and-play material.

While we obviously can't stop nosy players from taking a peep at the later chapters, they run the risk of ruin the fun for all players if they look too deeply. Then again, there may be some info in those chapters that a Zombie Master wants his players to have. Players should check with the ZM before peeking at these last five chapters.

Conventions

As with every *All Flesh Must Be Eaten* sourcebook, *Dungeons and Zombies* uses the following conventions.

Text Conventions

This book uses different graphic features to identify the type of information presented. This text is "standard text," and it is used for general explanations.

Certain text is set off from the standard text in this manner. This is sidebar text and it contains additional, but tangential information, or supplemental charts and tables.

Other text is set apart in this way. It details Supporting Cast or Adversaries that may be used in Stories at the Zombie Master's discretion.

Dice Notations

This book uses several different dice notations. D10, D8, D6, and D4 mean a ten-sided die, an eight-sided die, a six-sided die, and a four-sided die, respectively. A number in parentheses after, or in the middle of, the notation is the average roll. This number is provided for those who want to avoid dice rolling and just use the result. So the notation D6 x 4(12) means that players who want to skip rolling just use the value 12. Some notations cannot provide a set number because their result depends on a variable factor. For example, D8(4) x Strength is used because the Strength value to be plugged into this notation varies depending on who is acting.

Gender

Every roleplaying game faces a decision about third person pronouns and possessives. While the male reference (he, him, his) is customarily used for both male and female, there is no question it is not entirely inclusive. On the other hand, the "he or she" structure is clumsy and unattractive. In an effort to "split the difference," this book uses male designations for even chapters, and female designations for odd chapters.

Measurements

This book primarily uses U.S. measurements (feet, yards, miles, pounds, etc.). For those using metric scales, rough conversions can be done by multiplying miles by 1.5 to get kilometers (instead of multiplying by 1.609), equating meters to yards (instead of 1.094 yards), halving pounds to get kilograms (instead of multiplying by 0.4536), and so on. If a Zombie Master feels she needs more precision, she should take the U.S. measurements provided and apply more exact formulas.

Inspirational Material

A comprehensive list of fantasy literature, films, and television would take up an entire library. Jet down to a video or bookstore in your area, and check out the "Sci-Fi, Fantasy, and Horror" section to see for yourself. Listed below are just a few books, films, and TV shows that you might enjoy.

Books

The Annotated Dragonlance Chronicles, by Margaret Weis and Tracy Hickman, published by Wizards of the Coast, Inc., October 2002

The Coming of Conan the Cimmerian, by Robert E. Howard, published by Ballantine Books, 2003

The Icewind Dale Trilogy Collector's Edition, by R.A. Salvatore, published by Wizards of the Coast, Inc., 2001

Lankhmar: Tales of Fafhrd and the Grey Mouser, by Fritz Lieber, published by White Wolf Publishing, Inc., 2000

The Lord of the Rings, by J.R.R. Tolkien, published by Houghton Mifflin, 2003

Dhampir, *Thief of Lives*, and *Sister of the Dead* by Barb and J.C. Hendee, published by Roc Books, 2003-2005

Sabriel, Lirael and *Abhorsen*, by Garth Nix, published by Eos, 1997-2004

Silverthorn, by Raymond E. Feist, published by Bantam, 1993

Movies

Conan the Barbarian (1982)

Conan the Destroyer (1984)

Lord of the Rings Trilogy (2001-2003)

Red Sonja (1985)

Willow (1988)

Television Series

Hercules: the Legendary Journeys (1995-1999)

Xena: Warrior Princess (1995-2001)

Roar (1997)

About the Author

Jason Vey has been writing as long as he can remember, and playing roleplaying games since the age of five (he rolled dice when told to, and had no idea what was going on). He never did take to the "literary" prose of Eddings or Tolkien; he was drawn more to the gritty works of Howard and Saberhagen, and to the down-to-earth feel of Margaret Weis, Tracy Hickman, and R.A. Salvatore, and it was these authors he sought to emulate in his own storytelling. He continued writing throughout high school and moved on to pursue a degree in fiction writing from the University of Pittsburgh. His first wide-circulation publication came from Palladium Books, an article followed by a sourcebook. This is his first work for Eden Studios and he is thrilled to be contributing to the **Unisystem** line. Jason is 29 years of age and lives in Pittsburgh, PA with his girlfriend Julie and a psychopathic cat. He hopes to continue to leave his mark on games and fiction in the years to come.

Chapter Two

Aedhan's crystal blue eyes flashed, his square-cut, raven-black mane rippled in the foul breeze. He was in a cavernous pit, and several zombies surrounded him. He cried out to the Goddess and divine energy coursed through his limbs, boosting his combat prowess. He gave into the battle rage growing within him. The zombies were targets, enemies to be torn limb from limb.

"Abominations!" he cried, "I shall send you screaming back to the pits of Tartarus!"

The zombies didn't respond. The creatures closed slowly, mindlessly, their only expression one of primal hunger. They were starved and Aedhan was dinner. They weren't going to like just how tough this meal would be. Aedhan didn't wait for the zombies to crowd him in; he charged the wretch directly before him as he bellowed a thunderous battle cry.

The zombie was small and gaunt; Aedhan bowled it over like a sapling. The creature flailed, trying to latch its teeth onto him, but Aedhan tore its jaw off, then drove his stone-hard fist into its face three times, shattering its skull. One down.

A dead hand grabbed at Aedhan's shoulder. He kicked back, shattering a rotted knee. The corpse dropped to the ground. The barbarian twirled his greataxe above his head and brought the heavy blade down on its neck.

Then there were five.

Consumed with rage, Aedhan became a force of nature, his bloodlust setting even these simple creatures on their heels. They paused before moving in again. "So, you sons-of-whores have some spark of mind after all," Aedhan hissed, and charged, pressing the advantage while he could. A leap, a slash, and a third head smacked the floor, sliced neatly from undead shoulders.

Four left. Aedhan threw an overhand slash at the next corpse and took its arm off. He recovered to follow through with a backhanded swipe across the throat, but was a split-second too late. The remaining zombies were working in tandem now. Two grabbed him from behind while a third leaned in and bit down hard. Fortunately, Aedhan's hide armor absorbed the blow and shattered the zombie's teeth. Aedhan fell backwards, toppling the zombies holding him, kicking and punching wildly as he went down. The creatures clawed at his face and he had to thrash about to avoid their bony claws.

He frothed at the mouth, hissed, and called again on the divine energy of his god. "Halt!" he cried, and two of the four froze, agony and confusion etched upon their faces. A twist and kick freed Aedhan, and he dashed across the pit, away from the enemy. The two unfrozen zombies rose.

"So be it," Aedhan said, "No quarter given." He launched himself again into the air, and with a single swipe decapitated the two frozen zombies. Now he spun and drove the greataxe down, cleaving the skull of the third neatly in two. The axe sang out with a resounding clang as it struck

a stone wall behind the creature and stuck fast. He pulled at it but was unable to free it. He dove away just in time to avoid a lunge from his remaining foe. Snarling, he rolled to his feet, hurled the zombie into the wall, then pounced and tore into it with his bare hands.

Silence. Aedhan stood, panting, covered with ichor, amidst the stinking corpses. It took seconds for the rage to wear off, before the sounds of battle registered above. The groans of zombies mixed with the villagers' screams, the sickening crack of breaking bones, and the slurping sound of tearing flesh tell the tale of the scene above. He tore free his greataxe with a last mighty heave and scrambled out of the pit. If the Goddess was good, he might still get out of this alive.

Swords, Sorcery, and Shambling

Introduction

Rules, rules, and more rules. That's what this chapter is about. Here we cover all the alterations and additions required for a fantasy game. For those of you hungry for new tweaks, this is where you'll find the crunchy bits.

New Character Types

In order to better represent the kinds of characters seen in fantasy stories (and the kinds gamers expect), the rules include two new Character Types—the Adept and the Talented Hero. Otherwise, fantasy characters should be created using the Survivor Character Type; they have enough "oomph" to stand up to the typical fantasy campaign. Similarly, Inspired Cast Members make good "cleric" types in a fantasy game. Norms serve mostly as peasants, townsfolk, and other background characters populating a fantasy world.

The Adept Hero

Adepts are mages, sorcerers, and wizards; men and women with a gift for power that comes not from a divine force, but within them and from the world around. They devote their lives to acquiring power and knowledge, and can perform incredible feats of magic. Unfortunately, strange occurrences seem drawn to Adepts like moths to the flame, and they are often swept up against their will in the currents of destiny and fate.

Adept Cast Members get 15 points for Attributes, 15 for Qualities (and up to 10 from Drawbacks), 20 for skills, and 20 for Metaphysics. All Adepts must purchase The Gift with Quality or Metaphysics points. Adepts may use Invocations or Necromancy (see pp. 35-48), but may not purchase Inspired powers, unless they opt for the Inspired Invoker Quality (see p. 23).

The Talented Hero

Talented Heroes are natural-born athletes and heroes. They tend to be stronger, smarter, tougher, and just plain luckier than average men and women. Such characters have higher Attributes and more Qualities than average. Players looking to adopt one of the Profession Qualities presented later in this chapter should opt for this Character Type, as it provides the additional Quality points needed to create such specialized heroes.

Talented Heroes have 20 points for Attributes, 20 for Qualities (and up to 10 from Drawbacks), and 30 for skills. They can purchase the Gifted Quality (granting them access to certain profession Qualities).

Toughening Things Up

The basic Unisystem rules for damage are pretty lethal, designed to simulate the effects of being shot or stabbed more realistically. In a fantasy setting, combat is a far more common occurrence than in the average survival horror game, so at the ZM's option human Cast Members can begin with two levels of Hard to Kill at no cost, and can buy up to five more. The normal human limit for attributes can also be raised to seven, rather than six, with certain notable exceptions like paladin (see p. 25).

Removing damage type multipliers from weapons is also possible, making slashing/stabbing damage equivalent to bashing. This makes Cast Members more hardy when combat is more prevalent, but reduces the horror impact. If damage type multipliers are removed, multipliers for actions like targeting specific body parts should remain, as these maneuvers are designed to kill or disable instantly.

New Qualities and Drawbacks

Humans make up the vast majority of people in many fantasy settings and the rules assume humans will be the default race for any *AFMBE* game. Playing a human costs no additional character points. Human beings, however, are not the only choice available in may fantasy settings. Dwarves, elves, gnomes, and so on populate the landscape as well. If a player wishes to portray a race other than human, he must purchase the appropriate racial

Quality with Quality, Drawback, or Metaphysics points. Racial Qualities grant abilities, bonuses, and Drawbacks specific to the race. Note that Drawbacks packaged with racial Qualities may be bought off normally with experience points (*AFMBE*, p. 35), or even may be neutralized by spending additional Quality points at character generation.

Also standard to most fantasy settings, characters conform to certain archetypal professions, such as paladin, ranger, thief, and so on. Choosing a Profession Quality allows players to quickly generate these typical fantasy "character classes."

Cast Members are not required to take a Profession Quality. Players can create their own professions or classes simply by choosing Qualities, Drawbacks, and skills, just as they do with any other *AFMBE* sourcebook. In all cases, unless a Profession Quality specifies an Attribute can be raised higher, Cast Members are still bound by racial limitations.

Monsters as Good Guys

Minotaurs, goblins, and orcs are generally "the bad guys" in fantasy and it might seem inappropriate for players to use these creatures as Cast Members. These races are presented as possibilities for playing grittier characters, like in a "pulp fantasy" Deadworld (see Chapter Three: Dead Gods and Demon Lands). Just because most orcs and goblins are unsavory doesn't mean exceptional individuals who become champions of good do not exist. Such creatures present an interesting challenge, for they have bigotry and hostility to overcome while they pursue their goals.

On a practical note, certain combinations like orc and paladin can create incredibly powerful characters. While the rules don't specifically forbid this, ZMs should think carefully before permitting such combinations. Also, the player and ZM should work out where such a character received his highly specialized training, and how he came to be accepted by those who normally view his kind as evil.

Age
5-points/level Physical Quality

Some races live for hundreds of years, gaining the experience and knowledge shorter-lived races cannot. Each level adds 100 years to the character's current age, and provides bonus skill points equal to the character's Intelligence. Each level also adds Metaphysics points equal to the character's highest mental Attribute, and one extra point to their Essence Pool per Willpower level. Characters may have Age levels to a maximum of three or the character's highest mental Attribute, whichever is lower. Also, for each level taken, the character must take one level of either Adversary or Secret, but gains no points for the Drawback.

Ambidextrous
3-point Physical Quality

Ambidextrous Cast Members have a natural advantage in combat situations. This Quality provides one extra action at no penalty each Turn, if fighting with a weapon in each hand. The extra action can be used for attack or defense, but not both.

Danger Sense
1-point/level Supernatural Quality

Some people have a knack for knowing when something isn't right. Any time a Cast Member with Danger Sense is unaware of potential danger, he may make a Simple Perception Test to notice the danger, adding levels of Danger Sense as a bonus to the Test.

Dwarf
5-point Racial Quality

Dwarves are hardy subterranean folk with broad shoulders and long beards. They stand four to five feet tall and live up to five hundred years. Dwarves generally dislike the kind of magic that comes in spells and sorcery, though they love magic items and revere Inspired characters. Usually dwarves and elves don't get along well, since dwarves dislike the open sky and the wind in the trees. They are hard workers whose sense of humor is dry and cynical. They like their ale and are renowned brewers. Dwarves can raise Strength and Constitution scores to a maximum of eight, and gain +1 to Strength and Constitution, two levels of Hard to Kill (may have up to eight maximum), one level of Resistance (Magic), Infravision, +1 level in any Craft skill Type and the Rune Carving Specialty in that Type (see p. 28).

On the down side, dwarves are gruff, stubborn and hardheaded, and famous for their honorable natures. Dwarf characters suffer a one-point Drawback (choose one): Addiction (Heavy Drinker), Humorless, or Negative Buoyancy; a two-point Honorable Drawback; and a two-point Socially Inept Drawback. The dwarf gains no points for these Drawbacks. Dwarves usually may not take Invocations or Necromancy, but may be Inspired. The Inspired Invoker Quality (see p. 23) grants access to both Invocations and Miracles.

Elf
5-point Racial Quality

Elves are a near-immortal race marked by sharp features, almond-shaped eyes, and pointed ears. They average six to six and a half feet in height and live for a thousand years or longer if not killed. There are no historical records of elves dying of old age; some say once an elf reaches a certain age, they receive a mystical calling to journey to a land beyond the reaches of non-elvish peoples. Elves often have a great affinity for nature and woodlands, perhaps appreciating its fragility more than humans or dwarves. Elves can raise Dexterity and Perception to a maximum of eight. They gain +2 to Dexterity and Perception, Acute Senses (Vision), one level of Attractiveness, and +1 level in the Science (Animals) and Survival (Forest) skills.

On the downside, elves tend to be haughty by nature, believing they have the wisdom of the ages behind them. They suffer two levels of Socially Inept when dealing with non-elvish peoples, and a two-point Delusion (Delusions of Grandeur). The elf gains no points for these Drawbacks.

Essence Channeling
Variable Supernatural Quality

Essence Channeling is bought in levels. A character can draw one point of Essence from his Essence Pool per Turn for each level of Essence Channeling, and recovers Essence equal to his Essence Channeling levels every minute. Essence Channeling costs two points per level up to level five, and five points per level thereafter. Essence may never be drawn below zero; even drawing it down to zero is dangerous (see *AFMBE*, p. 114).

Gnome

5-point Racial Quality

Gnomes are found both in underground areas and forests. They are miners, tinkers, gadgeteers, and magicians. Some say they comprise the best of elves and dwarves, and at a height of three to four feet and sporting long beards, almond eyes, and pointed ears, they resemble a cross between the two. Gnomes are notorious pranksters and this can get their companions into trouble.

Gnomes can raise Constitution and Intelligence to eight and gain +1 to Intelligence and Constitution, Nerves of Steel, one level in the Dodge, Lock Picking, and Stealth skills, and the Nightvision Power. Gnomes aren't very strong, are notorious practical jokers, and tend to rush into trouble. They are fiercely loyal to friends and family, and when far from home they often identify with their companions a little too closely. Gnomes suffer –1 to initial Strength scores (this cannot reduce Strength below one), the Clown and Reckless Drawbacks, and a one-point Obligation to the chosen "family." The gnome gains no points for these Drawbacks.

Gadgeteering

Those who own Pulp Zombies may wish to use the gadget-making rules found therein. Gnomish characters should excel at gadgeteering. It is also possible to extend these rules to goblin characters, creating the "tinker goblin," which adds an interesting twist to these little green meanies. As always, including such material is at the option of the ZM.

Goblin

5-point Racial Quality

Goblins resemble greenish-brown chimpanzees with sparse, wiry black hair, large ears, and watery yellow eyes. Their limbs are long and gangly, and they are quite agile. They aren't especially intelligent, and tend to border on feral in temperament. They also aren't known for bravery. Luxuries like fine clothing and cooked food are lost on goblins, though they do love anything shiny, including gems and coin. Goblins can raise Dexterity and Perception to eight, and gain +2 to initial Dexterity and Perception, +1 rank each in the Climbing, Dodge, Notice, and Stealth skills, Acute Senses (Hearing), Situational Awareness, and Brachiation.

Unfortunately, goblins are sniveling, weak, ugly creatures looked down upon by others and often hated by most of society. They suffer –1 to initial Strength and Intelligence (penalties cannot reduce attributes below one), a two-point Attractiveness Drawback, one-point Cowardly Drawback, and a three-point Minority Drawback. Goblins gain no points for these Drawbacks. Goblins may not become Gifted.

Holy Order of Light Priest

5-point Profession Quality

Prerequisite: The Gift

The Holy Order of Light is a society dedicated to the study of supernatural evils to learn their names and how to best combat them. Often, members seek out paladin to serve together, helping wipe out the forces spreading across the land like an unholy fire and threatening to engulf everyone in their dark flame. Priests of the Holy Order of Light gain +1 to any physical Attribute, one level in Hand Weapon (choose one), two levels in Occult Knowledge, two levels in Myth and Legend related to the priest's religion, and Inspired Invoker, but suffer from a three-point Obligation (Find and destroy supernatural evil) and a three-point Adversary (Demons and Undead). The priest gains no points for these Drawbacks.

Inspired Invoker

3-point Supernatural Quality

Prerequisite: The Gift

Gifted Cast Members with this Quality can somehow reconcile the mystical differences between Miracles and Invocations. They are not bound by the restriction against combining Miracles and Invocations (see p. 34), and may learn both (but not Necromancy or other types of Metaphysics). Use of Invocations is still bound by Essence Channeling (see p. 22), and the Inspired Quality is still required to gain Miracles.

Minotaur

7-point Racial Quality

Minotaurs are very large, between seven and eight feet tall, with the body of a human and the face of a cow or bull, massive horns and all. They live approximately 60 years. They are bred for war, and are coveted trackers, mercenaries, and gladiators. Loyal and honorable, they willingly fight to the death for a cause. Minotaurs can raise Strength and Constitution to eight. The Minotaur Quality provides +2 to initial Strength and Constitution scores, two levels of Hard to Kill (may have a maximum of 10), one level of the Brawling skill, Acute Senses (Smell/Taste), Fast Reaction Time, Infravision, and a natural weapon—horns (D8(4) x Strength slashing/stabbing damage).

On the downside, minotaurs are defined by their honor and sense of purpose. Minotaur characters suffer a two-point Honorable Drawback, the Humorless Drawback, and three-point Minority Drawback (most people are terrified of minotaurs). Minotaurs gain no points for these Drawbacks. Minotaurs may never learn Invocations or become Inspired, but may learn and use Necromancy, and may be paladin.

Obligation (Type)

Variable Social Drawback

Some rights are accompanied by duties. An Obligation must be followed to various degrees, and grants a number of points depending on the strictness of its dictates. Normal obligations to friends and family are worth no points.

Important: The character is expected to routinely risk himself for the cause, and go above-and-beyond the normal call of duty. An Important Obligation is worth one point.

Major: The character is expected to put the welfare of the group or cause above their own. He is always on call, and does not have time to pursue such activities as a normal job, or have much of a personal life. The penalties for disobedience or selfishness are severe, and may include death. This is worth two points.

Total: The character is expected to die for the group or cause, if need be. Missions are generally extremely hazardous, and the character is constantly in danger of imprisonment, torture, or execution. This is worth three points.

Orc

5-point Racial Quality

Orcs are human-sized brutes with piglike faces and mottled brown and dark green skin. Some believe orcs are distant relatives of goblins, but orcs are bolder and deadlier. They take few prisoners, preferring to slaughter their enemies wholesale. Orcs can raise Strength and Constitution to eight. The Orc Racial Quality adds +1 to initial Strength and Constitution scores, one level each in the Brawling, Intimidation, and Running (Marathon) skills, one level of Hard to Kill, a two-point Resistance (Fatigue) Quality, and the Nightvision Power.

On the downside, orcs are brutal, ugly, barbaric, and not well liked by the goodly races of the world. They suffer a two-point Attractiveness Drawback or two-point Cruelty Drawback (or may take one point in each), and a three-point Minority Drawback. Orcs gain no points for these Drawbacks.

Paladin

5-point Profession Quality

Prerequisite: The Gift

paladin are born with a spark of divinity that erupts into full power sometime during their adolescence. Nobody knows why some are chosen to become paladin and others are not; the Revelation is different for each paladin. Some have a vision of a radiant being who reveals their power and purpose. Others are approached by a monastic order that journeys the world seeking those who can stand against darkness. Whatever their reason, paladin boldly set forth looking for evil to destroy and innocents to protect. paladin gain +1 to Strength, Constitution, and Willpower, one level of Danger Sense, three levels of Hard to Kill (and can have up to 10 total), Nerves of Steel, and one level in the Hand Weapon (choose type) skill.

On the other hand, they suffer a four-point Adversary (Demons and Undead), a three-point Obligation Drawback (hunt and destroy supernatural evil), and a three-point Honorable Drawback. paladin gain no points for these Drawbacks. paladin cannot purchase any other profession Quality.

Paladin Metaphysics

paladin may not purchase any Metaphysics or be Inspired, but are Gifted and possess all the abilities below. paladin who act dishonorably (ZM's discretion) immediately lose the metaphysics below, and must undertake a quest to purify themselves before they can again be paladin. paladin can channel as much Essence at one time as they wish without Essence Channeling, but are still subject to effects from Essence Loss.

HEALING: paladin heal one Life Point to themselves or others per Essence spent.

SENSE SUPERNATURAL CREATURES: Sense ghosts, demons, and undead within 100 feet by concentrating for one Turn and making a Simple Perception Test. This ability costs one Essence to use and gives a vague impression of presence and direction, not exact location or the ability to see invisible beings.

Psychic Invoker

3-point Supernatural Quality

Prerequisite: The Gift

Some Gifted have such an affinity for Invocations they do not require the formulae other wizards do. Gifted who possess this quality do not suffer penalties for casting Invocations without incantations, gestures, and rituals (see p. 35). Psychic Invokers still need Essence Channeling, and the Quality has no effect on the Inspired or necromancers.

Ranger

5-point Profession Quality

Rangers prefer the company of the plants and beasts of nature to civilized beings. They are hunters, trackers, and guides, and their services are in great demand whenever an expedition into the unknown wilds is undertaken. They are dark and shadowy figures, never fully trusted in civilized society. This Quality provides Situational Awareness, one level in the Hand Weapon (select one), Notice, Stealth, Survival (choose a type), and Tracking skills.

Alas, rangers don't deal well with civilized folk and suffer from a two-point Socially Inept Drawback. The character gains no points for this Drawback (the social ineptitude of dwarves and elves is not cumulative with that for rangers).

Swashbuckler

5-point Profession Quality

The swashbuckler is the renegade in black—the masked rogue who battles his opponents with rapier in hand and a tongue as sharp as his blade. The swashbuckler abhors armor, a tool of cowards who rely on heavy weapons because they lack the dexterity to wield anything requiring finesse. He doesn't need two-handed swords or plate mail to be effective in battle; his speed and wit are his greatest weapons. This package provides +1 to Dexterity, one level in Hand Weapon (Rapier, Cutlass, or Saber) (choose one), one point of Danger Sense, Fast Reaction Time, Nerves of Steel, one level in Smooth Talk and that skill's Specialty Taunt (see p. 29).

On the other hand, Swashbucklers are daredevils and brave to a fault. They suffer from the Reckless, Showoff, and one-point Honorable Drawbacks, for which they gain no points. Swashbucklers cannot purchase Metaphysics.

Creating Package Qualities

The racial and profession Qualities described herein are not extensive, and may not fit some players' ideas for their game. Fear not—creating your own package Quality is a matter of balancing numbers. Drawbacks and penalties cancel out Qualities and bonuses, and what's left is the final cost or bonus of the Quality or Drawback. Generally, the ZM should create package Qualities.

Remember, if it can be done without a Quality, don't make a Quality for it. Generic thieves, for example, should just be built off of the Survivor or Talented Hero Character Types as standard. Only races and unique professions should be modeled with Qualities. Also, keep the total package cost to five points or lower. More than that and the Quality begins to replace, rather than supplement character generation.

Here's an example to work with—the mystic entertainer.

START WITH BENEFITS: Traveling entertainers need to have performance-related benefits, a level of Acting, Play Instrument (one of choice), or Singing. Smooth Talking should also be a must, so a rank of that goes in. Since the character is mystical, we'll package The Gift Quality, and one level in Affect the Psyche (see p. 37). Since this character is an entertainer, his Invocations should be boosted by using his talents. By making a skill Task before casting an Invocation, he adds his Success Levels as a bonus to the next Invocation he casts. Here we have to make a judgment call, since there's no set value for this ability, a nice benefit, but not incredibly unbalancing. We'll make it worth two points. So far that's 11 points of benefits (two to Attributes, two to skills, five for Qualities, two for a level of an Invocation, and two for the boosting).

ON TO DOWNFALLS: Entertainers enjoy attention, so Showoff (−2) and Clown (−1) are appropriate. Since entertainers tend to be passionate and impulsive, Reckless (−2) also works. While we're at it, there are certain Invocations that aren't appropriate, so let's say that this character can't take Soulfire or Elemental Invocations. Since this is minor and doesn't have a set point value, we'll call it −1 points. That's a total of six points of Drawbacks and downfalls to this Character Type.

Adding these together, we end up with a five-point Mystic Entertainer profession Quality. Note that the six points of downfalls packaged in don't count against the 10 points allowed for Drawbacks during character creation. Using this method, you should be able to work out any archetype you wish for your games.

Racial Qualities work on the same principles.

Powers

A Power or Vulnerability is a character element available to both zombies, in the form of Aspects, and certain Cast Members, by spending Quality or Metaphysics Points. They are in all other respects the same as Qualities and Drawbacks. All of the Powers below have a prerequisite of "Nonhuman." Players should check with the Zombie Master before purchasing these abilities, to be sure they are appropriate for the game and the Cast Member's race.

Other Aspects

The following Aspects from AFMBE and Enter the Zombie are available to nonhuman races as Powers, at the ZM's discretion. Aspects linked to Attributes cost living characters three points to purchase. These abilities may be purchased with Quality Points. Those marked (M) are supernatural Qualities that can be purchased with Metaphysics Points. We suggest that Spitter, Spew Flame, and X-Ray Vision, if allowed, require spending three Essence per use.

AFMBE Aspects: Leaping, Damage Resistant, Flame Resistant, Infravision, Life Sense (M), Regeneration (M), Scent Tracking, Spitter (M), Spew Flame (M), X-Ray Vision (M).

ENTER THE ZOMBIE Aspects: Iron Shirt Body, Just a Flesh Wound, Wall Crawling (M).

Smart Monkey Powers

Two of the Powers listed were nipped from Terra Primate, another Eden game that includes tons of ideas, Qualities, and Drawbacks that could be used with this book to create customized races, extensive psionics rules, even a fantasy Apeworld that needs a few zombies to round out the mix. It also has ogre, troll, and wyvern stats, among others.

Brachiation

1-point Physical Power

Characters with Brachiation move through the trees like apes. Swinging from branch to branch is nothing for them, and unlike most characters, they can do so with such ease that they can move through trees, or even go from building to building, at their full base speed. Those without Brachiation move at the speed of their Climbing skill level divided by two.

Mystic Targeting

3-point Supernatural Power

Characters with this Quality are so adept at the art of ranged combat they develop a mystical bond with distance weapons. Cast Members with Mystic Targeting add a bonus equal to their Willpower to ranged attacks.

Negative Buoyancy

1-point Physical Vulnerability

If this character falls off the boat, he'll sink like a stone. His bodily mass doesn't provide buoyancy to stay afloat. Any Cast Member with this Drawback who ends up underwater drowns in a number of Turns equal to his Constitution (unless rescued). Most Cast Members with Negative Buoyancy also have Delusions (Phobia of Drowning).

Nightvision

2-point Physical Power

Characters with Nightvision can see perfectly in areas of dim light, be it moonlight, starlight, or candlelight, where humans normally would have difficulty. However, in areas of total darkness, the character is just as blind as any normal human.

Underground Direction Sense

2-point Mental Power

When underground, this character may intuit his approximate depth below the surface and the direction in which he is traveling, simply by concentrating for one Turn. By making a Perception and Notice roll while underground, the Cast Member can always find his way to a place he has been before (assuming tunnels connect the two locations), without the need for a map.

Walk In Shadows

4-point Supernatural Power

These characters are so stealthy that in areas of long shadow or darkness, they become almost invisible and nearly silent. Those who Walk In Shadows may add a bonus equal to their Willpower to all normal Dexterity and Stealth tests.

> **Powers and Nonhuman Zombies**
>
> In a fantasy setting not all zombies will be human. Whatever the cause of the Rise, it could affect elves, dwarves, even dragons (at the Zombie Master's discretion, of course). Nonhuman zombies are tougher and more threatening than their human brethren, due to the special abilities possessed by nonhuman races. A nonhuman zombie keeps all Powers it had in life, added to the basic zombie template for the Deadworld. Only Powers are added, not standard Qualities, Skills, or Metaphysics (unless otherwise noted). ZMs are encouraged to use this against players to add mystery and horror to their games.

Skills

This section includes new and modified skills for use in fantasy campaigns. Some represent new or altered uses for the skill as listed in the *AFMBE* corebook; others are new additions.

Craft (Type Rune Carving)

Rune Carving is a skill Specialty used in the creation of magic items. This is a specialization because every type of item has a different, signature means by which runes must be carved upon it. Thus, a skill in Craft (Jewelry Rune Carving) Specialty means the character is expert in creating jewelry and preparing it for enchantments using runes. For details, see Creating Magic Items, p. 48.

Language

All Cast Members are fluent in the merchant tongue of humans, and in their own racial (or regional) language, as appropriate to the setting at hand, without spending points for this skill.

Magic Bolt

This is the skill for targeted Metaphysical attacks, used in place of an Invocation or other power, but only for targeted effects. A Magician could use Magic Bolt instead of Elemental Air to cast a lightning bolt, for example, but not for causing a gust of wind (ZM's discretion). Because Magic Bolt is easier to learn than most Metaphysics, characters can become quite adept at tossing around supernatural attacks fairly quickly, at the expense of lowered levels with other effects (which use the Invocation level for Tasks). Use Dexterity and Magic Bolt to strike, Perception and Magic Bolt for aiming (see *AFMBE*, p. 102).

Science (Alchemy)

Gifted Cast Members who possess Invocations or Miracles can combine their magic with this skill to create magic potions by gaining four Success Levels in an Intelligence and Science (Alchemy) Task, while casting the spell into the mixture (requiring a normal Invocation Task). If successful, the potion works. If not, the potion fails in some obvious way (becomes black and putrid, bursts into flame, and so on). For example, an Inspired Alchemist who creates a potion of Heal Wounds spends 10 Essence on the spell; his potion, with a successful Task, heals 10 Life Points when consumed. Brewing a potion requires 30 minutes per Essence point spent in its creation.

Science (Animals)

The Science (Animals) skill covers everything from identifying species, tracks, and signs to training, handling, calming, and otherwise dealing with domestic and wild animals, diagnosing injury and illness in animal species (though Veterinary Medicine is needed to treat maladies). Zombie Masters should choose an appropriate attribute and skill combination, depending upon the circumstances. For example, identifying a creature would require an Intelligence and Science (Animals) Task, while calming an agitated beast would require a Willpower and Science (Animals) Task.

Shield (Type)

This skill is for all aspects of shield use, from parrying blows to shield bashing. Each type of shield (target, small, medium, or large) is a separate Type (–2 penalty is applied when using the wrong type shield). It functions similarly to the Hand Weapon skill, but unskilled shield users cannot default to Hand Weapon to improvise shield use (see *AFMBE*, p. 101).

Smooth Talk (Taunt)

Taunt is a skill Specialty of Smooth Talk. Using Taunt, a Cast Member can use jibes and insults against an opponent. With a resisted Willpower and Smooth Talk (Taunt) Task, the character inflicts a penalty on all of his opponent's Tasks the next Turn, equal to the Success Levels modified by his opponent's Success Levels on a Simple Willpower Test. For example, if a Swashbuckler gains three Success Levels and his opponent gains one, the opponent suffers –2 (3 – 1 = 2) on all Tasks the following Turn, due to being flustered. As with all Specialties, anyone with Smooth Talk can take this ability, but those who have specialized gain a +2 to attempts to do so. Using this ability requires an attack or defense action.

Restricted Skills

Most modern skills are off limits to fantasy characters, such as Computers, Computer Hacking, Computer Programming, and Electronic Surveillance. Other skills receive slight alterations. Driving, for example, can be used to drive any kind of animal-drawn cart.

New Combat Rules

The fantasy milieu requires certain additional rules to the normal **Unisystem** rules set. These include the inclusion of shields, some tweaks to armor, and a few notes about combat.

Shields

Medieval shields were typically made of wood with a central iron disk (the "boss"), often with a metal rim on the edge. Other cultures have used wicker, leather, plywood and even more esoteric materials.

Shield Table

Shield Type&	Armor Value*	Damage Capacity*#	Barrier Value#	Encumbrance Value
Chair	6	20	12	1
Target	20	30	15	1
Small	15	80	15	4
Medium	15	100	20	10
Large	15	150	30	20
Table	12	100	15	25

& All values assume the shield is made principally of wood. For wicker, leather or softer material shields, reduce BV and AV by five and the DC by 20%. For bone, metal or harder material shields, double EV, increase BV and AV by 10 and DC by 50%.

* AV and DC apply to the shield only.

Halved against bullets.

Occasionally, all-metal shields are constructed but they are usually too heavy for most people. Shields typically got hacked into a lot during combat, and rarely survived a battle intact.

Shield sizes vary from Target (a tiny all-metal shield, usually strapped to the forearm), Small Shield/Buckler, Medium Shield (typically round), and Large Shield (kite shields, cavalry shields, Roman Scutum, Tower Shields). Combatants may also improvise shields by using such items as light furniture, barrel lids, or jury-rigged shop signs. Such items suffer the normal improvised weapon penalties (see p. 101).

Shields, whether specifically constructed or improvised, have a Barrier Value, Damage Capacity, and Armor Value (in keeping with their treatment as inanimate objects like doors and walls, shields are given a flat rather than variable AV). These are summarized in the Shield Table.

A shield's Damage Capacity and Armor Value determine how much damage the shield can take before being rendered useless.

Bracers are treated as part of armor in the Unisystem. They are treated with the AV of leather or metal helmets but only if the arms are struck (via random strike or through targeting a specific body part).

Shields can be used in three different ways: to block incoming attacks (a defense action), to provide cover (a defense action used against missile attacks), or strike as a secondary weapon (an attack action).

Shield Blocks: This is a parry defense action using a Dexterity and Shield Task. The task gains a bonus depending on the size of the shield.

Shield Size	Bonus
Target	None
Small, Chair	+1
Medium	+2
Table	+3
Large	+4

If the block Task total is equal to or greater than the attack Task total before the shield bonus is factored in, the attack is deflected cleanly and no damage is suffered by the combatant or by the shield. This is just like parrying with a weapon.

If the block Task total is equal to or greater than the attack Task total only because of the shield's bonus, the shield itself is hit. The shield's Damage Capacity is decreased by an amount equal to the attack damage minus the shield's Armor Value. Once Armor Value is subtracted, any remaining damage is modified by damage type before being applied to the Damage Capacity.

If the shield is hit, it acts like cover for its wielder, but some damage may carry through. If the attack damage is greater than the shield's Barrier Value, the defender takes Life Point damage equal to the difference in those numbers. For example, if 20 points of damage are inflicted against a Target shield, five points carry through. Carry-through damage must then contend with any personal armor that the defender wears. Damage type modifiers (slashing/stabbing, bullet) are applied only to damage that overcomes both the shield's Barrier Value and any armor's Armor Value.

If the block Task including bonus is less than the attack Task roll, the shield has no effect on the strike. Full damage goes on to the combatant and his body armor (if any).

For those wishing a simpler system, ignore the rules regarding damage carrying through a shield. If the block Task total is equal to or greater than the attack Task total, the attack is deflected, just like parrying with a weapon. The shield's AV, DC, and Barrier Value never come into play, unless an opponent actively tries to break or blast through the shield.

Shield Cover: By hiding behind a shield, a character can "duck for cover" against missile attacks without actually losing other actions. On a successful Dexterity and Dodge Task with bonuses for shield size (as above), the attack hits the shield and must overcome its Barrier Value before having a chance to damage the character. Piercing attacks (arrows, bullets, etc.) do little actual damage to the shield itself. Even if they succeed in overcoming the shield's Armor Value, Damage Capacity is decreased by only one point per attack.

Shield Attack: As a weapon, a shield inflicts D6 (3) x Strength blunt damage. Shields equipped with spikes convert that to slashing/stabbing damage.

Long Swords, Sabers, and Cutlasses

Long swords, sabers, and cutlasses aren't included in the main weapons table (see *AFMBE*, p. 132) because game mechanic differences between these and existing weapon descriptions are flavor-based. In game terms, there is no difference between long swords and broadswords. Sabers are curved, single-edged rapiers, and cutlasses are curved short swords, often with basket hilts. While not the most realistic interpretation, it's close enough for play.

Armor

In a fantasy medieval setting, it's more common to find people swathed in leather, padded quilt, or chainmail shirts than in your typical contemporary setting, and no self-respecting adventurer would explore a tomb of horrors without armor (see *AFMBE*, p. 138). Zombie Masters are encouraged to enforce penalties for armor EV (see *AFMBE*, p. 126). In addition, wrapping oneself in metal inhibits the flow of Essence. Invocations and Necromancy suffer a –2 penalty when cast while wearing metal armor. If the ZM feels this complicates the game too much, however, ignore it. It simply serves to add a bit of game balance to your setting.

Pole Arms and Mounted Combat

In mounted combat, riders get a +3 bonus to any attacks against ground troops, and a +1 bonus to Strength for determining damage. Ground troops suffer a –3 penalty to hit the mounted warrior. However, infantry using spears or pole arms negate the rider's bonus, and don't suffer a penalty. Worse, a successful hit with a pole arm or spear requires the rider to make a Dexterity and Riding Task to avoid being unhorsed, applying Success Levels on the attack roll as a penalty to Riding Task.

Alternately, the rider can urge his horse to attack, but this requires a Dexterity and Riding Task, or else he is thrown clear. Stats for horses are in the *AFMBE* corebook (see p. 141).

For those wishing a more detailed system for mounted combat, including rules for mass combat, we encourage you to check out the *Army of Darkness* roleplaying game, also published by Eden Studios. If using the rules in the *AoD* game, they should replace these guidelines.

> **Limits on Multiple Actions**
>
> In Dungeons and Zombies, highly skilled characters may be common, and even the −2 cumulative penalty for multiple actions may not deter them from making an inordinate amount of attacks each Turn. If desired, the ZM may impose a maximum of three attack actions per Turn. No limit should be placed on defense actions, however.

Economy

In the Middle Ages, dollars and cents weren't the standard means of exchange. Barter was the most common method of payment—two sheep for one blanket, for example, or 12 cows for a parcel of land. This included exchanging services, such as trading four horseshoes for a visit by the local doctor (if there was one). Before this, the Romans used a monetary system, and in the later Middle Ages, European kingdoms returned to a system of coin for goods. Thus, barter and coin are the types of economy to consider when playing a fantasy game.

Barter

In a barter economy, a person trades one thing for something he wants, with the relative value of the objects being agreed upon by the two parties. This last bit is the important part, for both sides must agree that the trade is fair. In other words, if someone wanted to trade a blanket to get a sword, both sides have to agree; maybe the blacksmith doesn't need a blanket; maybe he thinks his sword is worth three blankets. Whatever the particulars, barter economies are inefficient, in that each participant has to figure out the relative value of the goods and services being exchanged. And, it's not easy to arrange for payment (unless you always carry around blankets). In a medieval society horses are commodities and those with horses to trade may find themselves in a seller's market. Because a horse is so useful, the seller can drive a hard bargain. That blanket, on the other hand, just isn't on par with a horse. In other words, you'd have to trade a lot of blankets to get one horse. Similarly, produce in a famine-stricken area is a valuable commodity, while water in a lakeside community would be practically worthless. Values fluctuate in a barter economy, which in many ways is the beauty of it.

A barter economy could make for an interesting twist on the traditional fantasy game. Rather than being paid for their services in coin, the king might offer a few horses, some bolts of silk, and a visit to his chirurgeon. This brings up another wrinkle in a barter economy—both sides have to have something the other wants. If the Cast comes back to town with precious artwork, and what everyone wants are sacks of rice, then they have a problem. Certain "trade goods" become more desirable for the adventuring party. What makes barter interesting is that the Cast ends up looking for bolts of silk, sacks of spice, and artwork rather than the ubiquitous chest of gold coins. Yet barter opens up a whole set of logistical problems for both the Cast Members and the ZM—namely, the ZM and players have to play out haggling for trade items, and a "wealthy" party has to transport all that stuff.

A quick method for barter is simply to compare the dollar values of items in the *AFMBE* corebook. Items roughly equivalent in dollar value could be equivalent as trade items in a fantasy world. For those desiring more realism, the Zombie Master should consider the item's importance, as discussed above.

Coin

What makes coin so appealing is its intrinsic value. The moment the Cast finds a chest of gold at the bottom of a dungeon, the usefulness of a barter economy goes out the window—because lots of folks value precious metals and gems. Bartering two nuggets of gold for a sword is essentially *paying* two gold. Coin is also easier to deal with. In a coin economy, the seller establishes a value for his work, and the buyer either elects to pay the price, or tries to haggle the seller down. Either way, no one has to stand around trying to figure out how many blankets are worth one sword. In addition to this abstracting of value, coin is a lot easier to carry and generally everybody wants it.

Coins are commonly minted out of copper, silver, and gold. To convert the dollar values in *AFMBE* to coin, divide by ten. The resulting figure is the equivalent cost in whatever the ZM defines as a medium-value coin. Generally, assume one gold coin equals ten silver coins, and one silver coin equals ten copper coins. Thus, an item costing $200 in the core book would cost 20 silver pieces, or two gold in a fantasy setting. An item costing $15 in the *AFMBE* corebook would cost one silver and five copper, or 15 copper (15 divided by 10 is 1.5). Armor is the only exception to this rule. For armor, dividing the value by 10 determines the cost in whatever the ZM defines as the high value coin (usually gold). For reference, some average prices for common goods and services are listed in the Common Goods and Services Price Chart. Zombie Masters can use these prices as a guide for assigning value to other items.

Common Goods and Services Price Chart

Armor, Chain: 50 gold

Armor, Leather: 20 gold

Armor, Padded: 5 silver

Armor, Plate: 100 gold

Armor, Plate and Mail: 75 gold

Back Pack: 5 silver

Flagon (ale or mead): 2 copper

Glass of Good Wine: 10 copper or 1 silver

Glass of Milk: 1 copper

Helmet, Leather: 5 silver

Helmet, Metal: 10 gold

Horse, Riding: 50 gold

Horse, War: 100 gold

Lantern, Hooded: 15 silver

Meal with Drink (ale or mead): 3 copper

Night in an Inn, no meals: 5 copper

Oil, per pint: 1 silver

Room and board (all meals included): 10 copper or 1 silver/night

Rope, 50 feet of hemp: 2 silver

Tinderbox: 1 silver

Torch: 5 copper

Starting Equipment

While in a modern setting, you can assume characters have a certain amount of equipment with them (or ready access to what they need). In a typical medieval setting, it's important to define a Cast Member's starting equipment. Many games give characters a starting pool of coin with which to purchase any goods they might need. Since most players buy the same equipment for their characters anyway, this can be a waste of time. To keep things simple, all Cast Members begin play with the starting package of equipment listed in the Starting Package List. They may use the money included on the list if players wish to upgrade or purchase additional equipment before play begins. Also, each level of the Resources Quality adds an additional 100 gold coins to a Cast Member's starting total.

Starting Package List

Backpack

Bedroll

Belt

Boots

Cloak

Leather Armor
(exception: paladin begin with chainmail)

Rope, 50 feet

2 sacks

2 suits of clothes

Tinderbox

5 torches

1 weapon of choice

Traveling rations (1 Week)

Water skin

D8 x 10(40) gold pieces

Metaphysics

A common element of fantasy literature and games is the inclusion of magic. The word "fantasy" brings to mind Merlin or Gandalf casting their spells, and Conan battling against an evil sorcerer. To work magic, the Gifted channel Essence, the fathomless energy of the Cosmos, to affect the world. The magician (or sorcerer, or wizard) uses Invocations, ritual actions and words that help focus his will and imagination, to produce release energy, cause wounds to heal, and alter matter. Mages must purchase the Gift and Essence Channeling Qualities with either Quality or Metaphysics points in order to use Invocations or Necromancy.

It is important to note that normally, Inspired character types cannot learn any other type of Metaphysics, such as Invocations or Necromancy. Inspired characters who purchase the Inspired Invoker Quality (p. 23) can cast Invocations, but not Necromancy.

Inspired and Miracles

Inspired characters should be required to choose a god; Miracles work based upon the tenets of the deity, rather than by purity of intent (*AFMBE*, p. 62). An Inspired of an evil deity can and will call down Holy Fire against a good character, while a "good" Inspired might still be bound by purity of intent.

Magic and Metaphysics

The magic system included herein has been excerpted from the Armageddon roleplaying game. Those readers who desire a more detailed system that includes ritual and group magic, and the effect of crowds, places of power, times of power, and so on, should consult Armageddon or WitchCraft, both of which contain expanded magic rules and additional Invocations and effects.

In addition, psionics have not been included in these rules. Zombie Masters wishing to include psychic powers in their games should look to either of the games above, or to Pulp Zombies, which includes rules for "mentalism," a streamlined system for high-action AFMBE games.

Invocations: Spell Magic

Invocations are tools employed to weave Essence into a desired effect. Magicians acquire an innate understanding of how Essence is used to create specific effects. Each Invocation helps the Magician understand one specific pattern or matrix, which can be used for any of the specific effects listed under the Invocation or any other effect of a similar vein (assuming the ZM approves of it).

Learning Invocations

During character creation, spell-casters learn each Invocation as a separate skill, which costs two points per level up to level five, and five points per level thereafter. Learning a new Invocation after character creation costs 10 experience points for the first level; improving existing Invocations with experience costs five points per level to level five, and eight points thereafter.

Casting Invocations

Using an Invocation requires three steps—Summoning, Focus, and Dismissal. First, the spell-caster visualizes the desired effect while gathering Essence. Next, once all the needed energy has been summoned, the caster releases it, using the Invocation to give it shape. Finally, these energies must be Dismissed, lest they harm the spell-caster. Generally the second two steps are combined into one Task.

The Summoning: The spell-caster visualizes the effect while gathering needed Essence. The Summoning takes as many Turns as required to accumulate the Essence needed. If the Magician summons it all in one Turn from his Essence Pool, he may perform the Focus Task immediately. Characters without Essence Channeling can ready one Essence from their pool every 10 minutes, and must use complicated rituals to cast their spells. Summoning requires no Task rolls, and may be done each Turn for those effects requiring steady Essence feeding (assuming the Magician's channeling level is greater than the per-Turn Essence requirements).

While the Summoning takes place, other Gifted may notice the "glow" of Essence around the magician. This requires a Simple Perception Test at +1 bonus for each five Essence points gathered around the caster. A successful Test also tells the observer roughly (within five) how much Essence is present. Summoning a lot of Essence may be detected by other Gifted with a Difficult Perception Test at a range of a half-mile per 20 Essence Summoned. The Gifted do not know exactly where the power is being summoned, only the general direction and how much power is present. The Shielding Invocation (see p. 42) can be used to avoid detection.

It is possible to Summon and "hold" energy until needed, though the longer a character holds Essence, the more it affects his senses and stability. Like drinking shots of hard liquor, the longer the caster holds Essence, the more drunk he gets. Characters can hold Summoned Essence for Willpower plus 10 minutes. Every five minutes after that, the drunk feeling temporarily lowers a mental Attribute by one (ZM's choice). When any mental Attribute reaches zero, the magician passes out, and the Essence is released randomly (see p. 36).

Focus and Dismissal: Once the needed energy has been Summoned, the magician casts the spell, then dismisses the energy. This is the Invocation Task. A successful Invocation means Essence is given form and harmlessly dismissed. The Focus and Dismissal are generally resolved as a single Task, usually Willpower and Invocation, plus situational modifiers. The process takes one Turn.

Invocations require spoken words and gestures to help the magician focus the power. If the magician is restrained so that words and gestures are impossible, casting takes an additional Turn and suffers a –2 penalty. If blinded, Invocations with targets other than the caster aren't possible, unless the Magician can somehow sense the target.

Preventative Dismissal: When an Invocation fails, the energies do not fade away. Essence is still spent and may turn against the magician, or produce unpredictable and dangerous effects. A magician who has failed an Invocation Task must Dismiss the Essence as soon as possible; random effects can happen at any time. Such Dismissals are a separate Willpower and Invocation Task, suffering a penalty of –1 per each five Essence to be Dismissed (rounded up). If the Dismissal succeeds, all is well. If unsuccessful, a Random Essence Effect (see p. 36) results.

Invocations and Intent

Magic may be colored by the spell-caster's intent. Those who have evil in their hearts end up casting magic that reflect their inner desires, and the ZM is encouraged to take this into account. At the ZM's option, any Invocation cast in anger or with malicious intent (self-defense or to destroy an abomination is not malicious) requires a mandatory Dismissal Task at a penalty of –1 to –5, depending on the severity of the situation.

Random Essence Effects

Essence not Dismissed produces a random effect within 24 hours, in the vicinity of the Magician who summoned it. The ZM picks one of the entries on the Random Essence Effects Table, or rolls D6 for a result.

Invocations and Range

Most Invocations have a range of line-of-sight. If the magician cannot clearly see the target, a –3 penalty is applied to all Tasks. Casting an Invocation through a remote viewing device only works if the magician intimately knows the location the device is showing. Even when possible, Invocations through such a device suffer a –4 penalty.

Attacking Invocations

Some effects can injure targets. The Focus result in casting is the "attack" Task, unless the magician knows the Magic Bolt skill (see p. 28). If the victim can detect a magical attack, a standard defense Task can be used to escape it.

Lesser Invocations

Some of the more common Lesser Invocations can be found on the following pages, covering most aspects of magic from commanding the elements to power over emotions and senses. These descriptions include several effects and their related Essence costs. The effects described cover basic examples, and players are encouraged to come up with additional effects. ZMs should use the examples provided to determine Essence costs. Most sorcerers never advance past this level.

Random Essence Effects Table

Roll	Effect
1 or 6	**Reiteration:** The original Invocation effect manifests itself somewhere around the magician.
2	**Activation:** An Invocation the magician knows activates, fueled by un-dismissed Essence, suddenly and without apparent cause.
3	**Burn:** The magician becomes feverish, but with a cold sweat. He loses one Endurance point per un-dismissed Essence point. If reduced below zero Endurance, he collapses into unconsciousness.
4	**Grounding:** The Essence "grounds" itself on the magician, who convulses and goes rigid. After a few seconds, the seizure passes but may return. One convulsion occurs for every five points of un-dismissed Essence (round up). Each one costs the magician D6(3) Life Points and D10(5) Endurance Points. The magician is helpless for the duration of the seizures (usually a Turn).
5	**Hallucination:** Hallucinatory lights and sounds, lasting one minute per 10 un-Dismissed Essence (round up), plagues the Magician. During this time all Perception and Intelligence-based Tasks suffer a –5 penalty. Mundanes cannot see the lights, but other Gifted can sense the Essence flaring up around him.

> **Other Invocations**
>
> Some Invocations have been removed due to redundancy with Miracles or Necromantic abilities. Also, all of the Invocations presented here are Lesser Invocations, and some players and ZMs may wish to include more powerful magic. Greater Invocations and additional Lesser Invocations like Blessing, Healing, and Spirit Mastery can be found in Armageddon or WitchCraft.

Affect the Psyche

This Invocation can change a person's feelings or thoughts, and can impress, charm, or scare the target. The ZM decides whether the Invocation changes behavior in the way the sorcerer intended—a scared would-be attacker might flee, surrender, or attack like a cornered animal, for example.

Beguile

This effect allows the caster to charm a subject, and is resolved as a Resisted Task between the sorcerer's Willpower and Invocation against the victim's Simple Willpower Test. If successful, the victim believes the sorcerer is a trusted friend or even someone beloved. The caster may make any request one would make of a loved one, and the victim will do his best to grant it, whether it is "would you grab me that glass of water?" or "you need to get us out of this jail cell before they kill us," or even "by the gods, don't let them harm me!" This effect costs one Essence if the target is friendly (love or infatuation results), two if the victim is indifferent towards the caster, or five if hostile. The effect lasts one minute per Success Level on the caster's Willpower and Invocation task. An additional two Essence spent doubles the duration.

Induce Sleep

This effect instills a feeling of weariness in the target, making him exhausted and ready to sleep. Under the right conditions, targets fall unconscious. Cost is one Essence if the person is already tired and ready to sleep, two Essence for an awake or alert person, and five Essence if there is some sort of external inhibitor, like pain, insomnia, or drugs. A Difficult Willpower Test is required to resist this effect (though the target can voluntarily fail this Test). The sleep induced is normal and not magically maintained, so any situation that would normally rouse a sleeping person rouses the target of this effect.

Cleansing

Essence colored by bad emotions or evil intent can "pollute" places, things, and people. Areas where violence and other ugliness occurred often retain the taint of the Essence released during those events. This can make people uncomfortable, especially the Gifted, who can sense the great evil; people often complain of nightmares in these places. The Cleansing Invocation is used to remove this taint, but can also help against harmful magics lingering around a victim.

All Cleansing Invocations require separate dismissal Tasks. Failure to dismiss a Cleansing Invocation means the negative Essence follows the spell-caster around instead. A new Cleansing Invocation is needed to remove these effects.

Remove Curse

This effect neutralizes a curse or other harmful effect that has been temporarily attached to the target. It works against curses of all types, metaphysical and supernatural. This effect does not work on those with the Accursed Drawback (see *AFMBE*, p. 47). Removing harmful magic costs Essence equal to the original effect, and is resisted by the Task of whoever inflicted the curse. Failure to dismiss means the cleanser is afflicted by the original curse.

Remove Emotional Debris

When people suffer strong emotions, Essence is inadvertently "spilled" onto objects and areas. This can affect the well being of people, making them short-tempered, prone to nightmares, even unlucky. Cleansing a room or an object of such negative "vibes" costs three Essence. Cleansing an entire manor costs six Essence. Failure to dismiss this effect causes the cleanser to suffer a mental Drawback equal to half the amount of Essence spent in the cleansing, rounded down, until another Cleansing is performed.

Communion

Through this Invocation, the magician achieves a powerful connection with the land, and is aware of everything in it, from the plight of insects to the intentions of powerful spirits. Such a connection is full of dangers, however. When achieved in a place of evil or negative emotions, the backlash can harm the magician's body and sanity.

Communion Invocations are usually conducted in forests, gardens, or other places of Nature, where the majority of the spiritual forces are benevolent and friendly. Using the Invocation in a city fills the spell-caster with the cries of dying trees, the cold calculation of rats and vermin, and the maliciousness, bitterness, and anguish of humans living there. Spell-casters who make this mistake often find their sanity permanently impaired as a result.

One With the Land

Becoming one with the land costs two Essence per minute. The spell-caster enters a trance state in which he is aware of everything occurring in the surrounding area. This Invocation has a radius of 10 yards per Willpower level of the caster. The radius can be increased by five yards, or the duration by one minute, per additional Essence spent.

Once Communion is established, the caster can sense the whereabouts and emotions of every living thing in the area, including spirits and supernatural beings. The spell-caster can pinpoint the location of anybody entering the area, even if Shielded or hidden by illusions. Attempts to communicate, invoke, or awaken spirits in the area gain a +5 during the Communion. The caster can also cast any Invocation on anyone or anything in the area as if he were in direct contact or line of sight of them during the effect.

Unfortunately, this exposes the spell-caster to any pain, suffering, anger, or other negative feelings of every living thing in the area, and risks a psychic backlash. When performing Communion in an area plagued by suffering or anger, the caster must pass a Difficult Willpower Test to avoid harm from the experience. Note that the entire area must be permeated with negative emotions to pose a danger. If a group of men with murder in their hearts entered an otherwise tranquil forest, the spell-caster would know of them, but would not be affected. If the spell-caster uses this Invocation in the middle of a burning forest, a slum, or a prison camp, the misery and agony in such places would sear him. Penalties to the Willpower Test are determined by the ZM. Places of some misery and pain (a dirty park, a lightly polluted forest) have no penalty to the Test. A city slum suffers a –2 penalty (more for really bad areas where everybody is suffering). A burning forest or a prison camp suffers –4 to –6. A zombie lord's torture dungeon would incur –8 or worse. If the Willpower Test is failed, the caster loses D4 x 10(20) Essence. If brought below zero, he may suffer physical or mental harm (see *AFMBE*, p. 114).

One With the Beasts

This effect allows the spell-caster to merge his consciousness with an animal at a cost of three Essence per minute, though the caster can cancel it early with a Simple Willpower Test. He must make a Willpower and Perception Test to locate an animal within the effect's range of one square mile. Range can be increased; each Essence spent increases the range by a half mile. Once an animal is located, the spell-caster temporarily joins his consciousness with it. The animal resists the Invocation Task with a Simple Willpower Test. If the caster succeeds, his mind joins with the beast's and he can control the animal's actions.

While joined with the animal, the spell-caster sees, hears, and experiences everything the creature does, making the animal an ideal spy. He can also draw upon the animal's Essence to use Invocations or other Metaphysics on any creature or object the animal

Cleansing and Communion as Miracles

Cleansing and Communion, at the ZM's discretion, can be used as Miracles in addition to or instead of Invocations. Miracles work exactly the same as the Invocations, except Inspired characters do not rely on Essence Channeling, and do not require Tasks or Dismissals. Resisted Tests should be resolved with the Inspired character's simple Willpower Test replacing the Invocation Task.

sees, as though the caster had direct line of sight. However, should the animal's life become endangered in any way, he must pass a Difficult Willpower Test at –1 for every five Essence points below 10 the animal has remaining in order to sever the tie. Should the animal die while joined to the caster, he must make a Survival Test or see his own Life Points and Essence Pool reduced to –5 each.

Elemental Air

Elemental Air grants control over the forces associated with it, from changing wind direction and speed, to the creation of air where none existed before, to control over electricity. Creating and maintaining such effects for long periods of time has severe effects on the weather, however. Even a relatively small wind, if not Dismissed, can trigger storms, tornadoes, and worse, hundreds of miles away. All weather effects require a separate Dismissal Task, or cause both Random Essence Effects (see p. 36) and random weather patterns.

Alter Wind Speed

The spell-caster can cause mighty winds to blow, or stop them in their tracks. Calming a steady wind costs one Essence for every one mph of speed, plus one Essence for every minute the calm lasts, and one Essence for every 10 yards of width of the wind. The effect creates an area of relative calmness around the character. For example, stopping a hurricane-level wind (100 mph) over a 10-yard radius for five minutes would cost a total of 106 Essence! This effect can also create a continual wind at the same cost as calming the wind. For example, creating a steady wind with a speed of 10 mph lasting 15 minutes and affecting an area 100 yards wide would cost 35 Essence (10 for the wind speed, 15 for the duration, and 10 for the area).

Lightning Bolt

The magician can ionize the air and channel a powerful electrical discharge capable of shocking people and starting fires. The bolt inflicts D6(3) points of damage per Essence spent. Divide the Armor Value of metal armor by five before applying it to these attacks. The base range of the effect is 20 yards times the Willpower of the spell-caster. This can be extended at the cost of one Essence per extra 10 yards of range.

Sheet Lightning

The spell-caster creates a powerful electrical field that blankets an area with white-hot lightning. The sheet lightning inflicts damage equal to D4(2) times the caster's Willpower to every creature in range, and can ignite flammable objects. Divide the AV of metal armor by five before applying it to these attacks. The base range of the effect equals five square yards and costs three Essence. Each additional Essence point spent extends the range by five square yards, or adds one to the damage multiplier (caster's choice).

Elemental Earth

This Invocation gives the spell-caster control over earth. Given enough Essence, a spell-caster can cause avalanches and earthquakes.

Mold Stone

The caster can reshape stone for two Essence per five pounds, up to a maximum of 100 pounds. Afterwards, it costs one point per 100 pounds. The shape can be anything the caster envisions, though without the Craft (Sculpture) skill the spell-caster has difficulty creating works of art. Creating a rough shape like a cube, sphere, pillar, or wall requires a Willpower and Invocation Task. Creating more complicated shapes, with some amount of detail (say, a humanoid form with little more than rough features) suffers a –2 penalty, while creating finely detailed shapes (a sculpture of the king) incurs a –5 penalty. Magicians with Craft (Sculpture) may substitute their skill ranks for their Invocation level and do not suffer penalties.

Stone Attack

The caster can cause any stone within 10 yards to fly out and strike a target. Loose stones must be available. Damage is D4(2) times Willpower, and range equals 10 yards per level of the caster's Willpower, at the cost of five Essence. The character can raise the damage multiplier, or the range of the attack, by one for each additional point spent. Multiple targets can be hit by spending one point per additional target (each target is hit with full damage).

Elemental Fire

The element of fire makes for a powerful weapon. It is a two-edged sword, however, for it just as happily consumes the caster and his allies as it does his enemies. Failure to Dismiss a Fire Invocation almost always ends up with the caster feeling the agonies he inflicts on others. Many "fire sorcerers" have nasty scars on their hands, bodies, and (sometimes) faces as a result of their dangerous games.

Blast Furnace

The spell-caster can superheat the air in an area, causing flammable objects to burst into flame, and damage to any people. The effect is instantaneous, a flash of heat costing two Essence per square yard, dealing damage equal to D8(4) times the caster's Willpower to all objects and creatures within the area of effect. Any combustibles, such as hair, cloth, and paper, burst into flame. In addition, the effects of the heat may manifest in particularly gruesome ways, like blistered and even melting skin, and physical defects (intense heat could blind victims, though a Simple Constitution Task spares them this agony). Every two Essence spent adds one to the multiplier. Because of the severity of the effect, this power may require a separate Dismissal Task with appropriate penalties (see Invocations and Intent, p. 36).

Heat Metal

The caster raises the temperature of any metal object targeted. Heating cold metal to comfortable costs one Essence. Heating warm metal to an uncomfortable, but not harmful, temperature also costs one Essence. Heating uncomfortably hot metal to the point where it scalds and burns inflicts D4(2) points of damage per Essence point spent (not counting any Essence needed to get the metal to the uncomfortable stage). Anyone touching heated metal must succeed at a Difficult Willpower Test or drop the scalding item. Heating non-magical metal until it loses its shape costs five Essence per pound of metal, and requires a separate Dismissal Task with a –2 penalty. Metal held or worn by anyone when it is melted inflicts D10(5) points of damage for D4(2) Turns until it cools and hardens again. The misshapen object is no longer useful for its original purpose.

Striking Flames

The spell-caster can summon flames to strike his foes, which manifest either as a blast originating from his hands, or as a rolling wave starting at his feet (more expensive to maintain and more difficult to avoid). This is an extremely destructive Invocation—the flames readily ignite flammable substances and may spark deadly conflagrations.

It costs one Essence to create a jet or bolt, inflicting D6 x 2(6) points of damage with a range of 10 yards per Willpower level of the character. Each additional Essence spent increases the damage multiplier by one, or the range by 10 yards. For example, a jet of flame inflicting D6 x 10(30) points of damage would cost nine Essence (one for the base, and an additional eight for the extra damage). A wave of flame is one yard wide for every four additional Essence spent on it. Dodging a wave of flame incurs a penalty equal to the width of the wave in yards.

Elemental Water

Elemental Water allows the spell-caster to control water in all its forms—liquid, gas, and solid. This Invocation is often used to increase the chance of rain, although careless use of this powerful effect produces droughts in other areas.

Create Fog

One Essence per cubic yard creates a thin mist that imposes a –1 penalty on Perception-based Tests or Tasks. Tripling the cost creates a thick fog capable of blocking visibility beyond two yards and makes most Perception Tests or Tasks based on vision nearly impossible. The fog rises during the time it takes to cast the Invocation. The duration of the effect depends on local weather conditions (as judged by the ZM).

Drown

With this effect, the victim's lungs fill with water, causing them to immediately begin to suffer the effects of drowning. The effect is resisted by the target's Constitution and Willpower Test. Victims who fail to resist cannot breathe, suffer a –4 penalty to all actions, take D6(3) points of damage to both Life and Endurance Points each Turn, and must make survival checks each Turn with a cumulative –1 penalty for each Turn after the first. All effects last until the victim receives first aid or the effect passes. Duration is equal to the Success Levels of the Task in Turns, after which the water secretes from the victim's pores, inflicting an additional D4(2) points of damage. If the victim survives this long, no further ill effects are suffered. This devastating effect costs five Essence, and always requires a separate Dismissal Task, with a penalty equal to the Success Levels on the Invocation Task to conjure the effect. Failure indicates the caster also suffers the effects.

Farsight

Farsight grants the magician the power to see into other places and search areas by projecting a fraction of his Essence beyond his body. Failed Dismissals often cause inconvenient visions and flashbacks that bother the spell-caster for D4(2) hours.

Farsee

Five Essence points allow the spell-caster to look into any area within range, if aware of the general location of the area. The caster decides the viewpoint, limited by range (he can select a bird's eye view, look in a specific direction, and so on), but cannot change this unless he re-casts the Invocation. Base range is 100 yards per level of Perception. This can be raised to one mile times Perception for another five Essence, and an additional one mile per Essence spent thereafter. The vision lasts for up to one minute.

Find Person

This effect searches for a person in the area covered by the Invocation. The spell-caster must know the target personally or by contact with his Essence signature (left by all Gifted when they use powers). The more powerful the target, the easier it is. The cost equals 10 points to search for a non-Gifted character, five points for a Gifted character with less than 30 Essence, and two points for those with more than 30 Essence. If the target has used magic or other supernatural abilities during the past few hours, all Focus Tasks gain a +1 bonus per five Essence points used by the target. If target is Shielded (see p. 42), his Essence is hidden and he must be sought out like a Mundane. This Task uses Perception and not Willpower. Base area equals a one-mile radius per level of Perception. Each additional mile costs one extra Essence.

Insight

All the Gifted are sensitive to the supernatural in its many forms. Insight allows the spell-caster to go even further and understand another being's true nature, even its deepest secrets.

Perceive True Nature

With this Invocation, the spell-caster gains a degree of understanding about the person's wants, fears, and flaws, revealing all of the target's mental Qualities and Drawbacks, as well as main goals. Victims of this effect resist with their Intelligence and Willpower. On supernatural creatures, this effect reveals the being's general nature (Demon, Ethereal, Nature Spirit, and so on), goals, and personality. Cost is six Essence. An Essence Shield (see p. 42) blocks this power, showing the presence and strength of the Shield, but nothing else. This power comes as an instant flash of knowledge, and must be cast on each person the caster wishes to "scan."

See Mind

This effect allows the caster to peer into the mind of another person, gleaning his intents, secrets, and even his innermost fears and desires. Victims resist with a Simple Willpower Test. The cost of the effect depends on what information the caster is trying to glean. Simple, surface thoughts or the detection of lies costs one Essence point. Deeper secrets, or hidden agendas or motives, cost two Essence, while childhood fears, nightmares, passions, and similar secrets cost three Essence per piece of information. Discerning buried and repressed memories even the subject has forgotten requires the expenditure of five Essence, and the victim gains a +2 bonus to resist the Invocation. Further, when trying to uncover hidden or repressed memories, the victim cannot voluntarily forego resisting the effect.

Lesser Curse

By surrounding a person with negative Essence, a sorcerer may inflict all manner of misfortunes on a victim. Unwarranted use of this power often turns back on the caster, however. Even on a successful Dismissal, spell-casters who curse others for petty reasons may be visited with the same maladies they inflict, and then only the Cleansing Invocation can remove them.

Ill Luck

This gives the character a bad luck "pool"—each point of Bad Luck costs three Essence and functions like the Bad Luck Quality (see *AFMBE*, p. 48), controlled by the ZM. Worse, spending a point of Bad Luck when a character attempts a Task or Test causes immediate application of the Rule of 1. In a roleplaying situation, things take a turn for the worse—people take what the victim says the wrong way, some unforeseen circumstance turns success to ashes, and so on. This lasts until the Bad Luck is spent, the spell-caster who cursed him removes the spell (separate Dismissal Task), or he receives a Cleansing Invocation (Resisted Task using the casters' Willpower and Invocation levels).

Minor Illness

By spending two Essence, the caster inflicts the victim with nausea, vertigo, and fever not unlike food poisoning, which lasts for one hour per Success Level on the Invocation Task. This curse causes the affected victim to suffer a –2 penalty to all actions for the duration of the effect, until the wave of nausea and illness passes. The effect is resisted by the victim's Willpower and Constitution Test.

Lesser Illusion

Essence can be used to fool the senses, creating a simulacrum that may appear, sound, and even smell like the real thing. Such illusions are not solid, however, nor do they cast a shadow (although the illusion of a shadow can be created to get around this). Sometimes, illusions do not look quite right, allowing people to realize their true nature. Most illusions work as a Resisted Task, pitting the caster's Focus result against the Perception and Intelligence of those who see the illusion. Illusions are not selective—the effect can be perceived by everyone. Illusions with an extended duration must remain in the spell-caster's line of sight or other senses, or they disappear.

Full Illusion

This effect creates a realistic illusion capable of fooling all senses except touch. This costs five Essence per cubic foot of the illusion, and lasts one minute.

Visual Illusion

This illusion can look like anything the character can picture, but is soundless. This costs one Essence per cubic foot of the illusion. The illusion lasts for five minutes.

Shielding

Shielding weaves pure Essence around the sorcerer, protecting him from harm. Some Shields work only against Essence effects, and some protect against physical harm. A powerful sorcerer may be virtually invulnerable thanks to Shielding. Essence and Physical Shields can be combined; the spell-caster must pay the Essence cost for both. A Shield need not be woven around its caster.

Shields may be seen by the Gifted with a Simple Perception Test. Their actual appearance is up to the caster. Some appear as spheres of light, others like suits of armor, crystalline structures, or exoskeletons.

The main drawback of a Shield is its requirement of a continuous stream of Essence, which must come from within the caster; it cannot come from ambient Essence or Essence stored in objects. Essence used on a Shield is lost until the Shield is dispelled. The character can keep the Shield around himself indefinitely until an outside force destroys it, or until he dispels it with a second Focus Task.

Essence Shield

The simplest Shield available, this blocks Essence-based attacks (like other Invocations). For three Essence, the Shield has a Protection Level of 10 plus the Success Levels of the Focus Task. Each additional point of Essence spent adds one to this Protection Level. Any hostile magic or other supernatural power aimed at the character must have a Focus result higher than the Shield's Protection Level or the Metaphysical effect does not work. The Shield only resists powers and effects directly affecting the target.

Example: Lisa has a Shield with a Protection Level 19, at a cost of 11 Essence (one Success Level in the Focus Task). An enemy spell-caster tries to inflict a hostile attack on her. His Focus roll is six, and his combined Willpower and Invocation levels are eight, for a total result of 14. This is less than the Protection Level, so the Invocation fails.

Attacks that drain Essence can damage the Shield. These attacks reduce the Shield's Protection Level by one per three points of Essence damage inflicted.

Essence Shields also block attempts to sense anything about the spell-caster (other than the fact that he is surrounded by a Shield).

Invisible Shield

Any type of Shield can be made invisible at the cost of 15 Essence, thus hiding its very existence. With such a Shield, a powerful sorcerer could appear as a simple Mundane, even fooling other Gifted. Nobody can see or sense the Shield until it flares up to stop an attack. The Invisible Shield even resists detection Invocations and abilities, though insistent mental probing may finally pierce the invisibility. This is a Resisted Task, pitting the Willpower and Shielding Task against the opponent's abilities or Invocations.

Physical Shield

Physical Shields deflect any attack that might damage the subject directly. It works against swords, punches, and energy blasts, somewhat like armor does, and has an Armor Value and/or a Damage Capacity. Each Essence spent gives the character either one point of Armor Value or five points of Damage Capacity. Any damaging attack hitting the Shield must exceed Armor Value, then exhaust the Damage Capacity. Remaining damage is applied normally. The maximum Armor Value possible is equal to the character's Invocation level times 10. There is no limit to the Damage Capacity of the Shield.

Example: Jana has Shielding 3. She is about to rush through a gauntlet of powerful zombies, so she decides to put 45 Essence into protecting herself. She can have a maximum AV 30 (her Invocation level x 10) so she spends 30 points to that purpose. The remaining 15 points she puts into Damage Capacity, for a total of 75 points. When she ventures out, the zombies attack. She is hit 17 times by claws and teeth. Fourteen of the attacks inflict less than 30 points of damage, and fail to penetrate the Shield's Armor Value. Three other attacks inflict 34, 42, and 41 points of damage, respectively. Subtracting 30 points from each produces 4, 12, and 11 points of damage, for a total of 27; these 27 points of damage reduce the Shield's Damage Capacity from 75 to 48 (75 - 27). Jana is unharmed—for now.

Shields do not stop movement or actions taken by the spell-caster, who can walk without bouncing off walls or people, and can attack without interference from the Shield. However, he could also run into a spike and impale himself, and the Shield would offer no protection. Shields are of no use against falling damage.

Soulfire

Essence can be used as a weapon. This Invocation allows the caster to fire bolts of pure Essence. To the mundane, the bolts are invisible; the Gifted see them as swirling streams of blue-white energy. Soulfire is extremely lethal when used against supernatural beings. Against humans, it causes Essence loss, which may be dangerous (see *AFMBE*, p. 114).

Soulfire Blast

Soulfire inflicts damage equal to D6(3) x Essence spent. Corporeal supernatural entities (like zombies, for example) take Life (or Dead) Point and Essence damage at the same time (if 10 points of damage are inflicted, the target loses 10 Life Points and 10 Essence). Soulfire is less effective against human beings; they lose one Essence for every three points of damage inflicted by the attack. Soulfire can strike any target within line of sight. Non-Gifted cannot Dodge the attack, because the Soulfire is invisible; Gifted and supernatural beings can see Soulfire, and may Dodge normally.

Soulfire Burst

Similar to Soulfire Blast, and subject to the same restrictions regarding the effect on humans and supernatural creatures, this effect targets an area rather than a single target. Soulfire Bursts cost three Essence, inflict D6(3) x the caster's Willpower, and affect three targets. Each target may resist the burst with a Difficult Constitution Test. Additional Essence can be spent to increase the number of targets, or the damage multiplier. Each point adds one target, or increases the multiplier by one.

Example: Xavier, Willpower 3, wishes to hit a group of six zombies simultaneously with Soulfire. He spends six Essence to hit all six zombies, who resist with Difficult Constitution Tests. Every zombie that fails suffers D6 x 3(9) points of damage to both their Essence and Dead Points.

Warding

This Invocation creates a field of Essence that blocks magical senses and the passage of supernatural beings. Most Wards are drawn, painted, or sketched on the ground. The Warding acts as an invisible barrier against most otherworldly beings, spirits, astral characters, and similar creatures.

Once created, a Ward remains in place until Dismissed by its creator, or until the drawing on the ground is destroyed. Spirit entities cannot affect the Ward in any way, although a human could. As long as the Ward is in place, the spell-caster must keep it fueled by temporarily reducing his Essence Pool by five points, which cannot be regained until the Ward has been Dismissed or destroyed.

Create Ward

This effect creates a Ward with a Strength Rating, which represents its power and the amount of Essence spent on it. Spirits or supernatural beings trying to cross the Ward (either to leave or enter it) must win a Resisted Task, using their Strength and Willpower against the Strength of the Ward, doubled. If the supernatural being loses the contest, it is barred from crossing, suffers D4(2) points of Essence (Vital Essence in the case of spirits) damage and is wracked by pain (–4 on all Tasks/Tests for the next Turn or two).

The Ward also interferes with any location or sensory power trying to peer into it, but does not affect other Metaphysical powers and abilities. The base Strength of a Ward is five, costs 10 Essence, and includes the five points that cannot be regained as above. Strength can be increased by one per additional four Essence spent.

The Ward covers a radius equal to the Magician's Willpower in yards but can be made smaller as desired. Larger Wards (to protect buildings or houses) cost one additional Essence per extra yard of radius.

Necromancy

Necromancy is a form of divination, communicating with the spirits of the dead. It is mostly used for information gathering, though more powerful Mediums can control, harm, and destroy spirits, and tap into their power. In *AFMBE*, Necromancy also has darker elements; it is the Art used to raise and control zombies, generally for less-than-genteel reasons. Despite these dark overtones, Necromancy is not entirely evil. Like all Gifted powers, it can be used for good or evil.

This Art has several specialties, each purchased as a separate power, and a Necromancy skill that applies to the use of all the powers. The four elements are Death Lordship, Death Mastery, Death Speech, and Death Raising.

> **Death Raising**
>
> Those familiar with other Unisystem games may not recognize all the powers listed. In AFMBE those dark mages who raise and control armies of the dead are a necessity. Thus, we introduce Death Raising, an Art that involves the creation and control of zombies. We have removed Death Vessel, whereby spirits inhabit the body of the medium. Those wishing to insert this power are encouraged to look at either WitchCraft or Armageddon.

Purchasing Necromantic Powers

The Necromancy skill is a special skill purchased with Metaphysics points, costing two points per level until level five, and five points per level thereafter. Each Necromantic element is purchased as a separate power, costing three points per level. This price must be paid for each power; it is possible to have one power at level five and another at level two, for example. After character creation, new powers cost 10 points for the first level and improve thereafter as standard special skills. The power level of each Art determines what a Cast Member can do—the higher the level, the more abilities available. Most Necromantic Tasks use the Necromancy skill plus a mental Attribute.

Death Lordship

Death Lordship is the power to manipulate the Essence of spirits. Early on, the spell-caster can force spirits to depart an area, or perform simple actions. In

AFMBE, this power is also useful in controlling zombies, both those raised through the sorcerer's Death Raising skill, and those not already controlled by another necromancer. Higher power levels allow for greater control, as well as the ability to harm or destroy spirits. Death Lordship Tasks use Willpower and Necromancy, and cost Essence. Spirits or zombies can resist with a Simple Willpower Test. If another necromancer controls a zombie, the resisted task is made against the necromancer's Willpower and not the zombie's.

Level 1—Expel Spirit

The spell-caster can try to force a spirit or zombie to leave an area. This ability costs two Essence points per attempt. Non-human spirits (like elementals or Fiends) may also be commanded, but the spirit gains a +2 bonus to resist and the attempt costs four Essence.

Level 2—Enforced Obedience

The necromancer can command a spirit or zombie to perform one specific action or task. This activity may not last more than a few minutes. Note that powerful spirits or zombies are able to resist Death Lordship Powers and do not take kindly to attempts to control them. This costs five Essence points per task.

Level 3—Rule the Dead

The spell-caster's control can be maintained over the spirit or zombie for one hour. During this time, the being does whatever the necromancer tells it to do, except facilitate its own destruction (resisting such orders with a +6 bonus). Forcing the being to perform Tasks it does not wish to do may beget a grudge or a feud, however. This costs 10 Essence points per hour.

Level 4—Dominion

As in level 3 above, but the control lasts for an entire day and night, at the cost of 20 Essence.

Level 5—Necromantic Bolts

The necromancer can weaken spirits and zombies, inflicting damage equal to D4(2) x Death Lordship level directly to the spirit's Vital Essence. This power affects any incorporeal spirit (including elementals) and undead at full strength. Each bolt costs three Essence points; the multiplier level can be increased by one per additional Essence point spent.

Corporeal beings, including zombies, can also be damaged, but at half strength—every two points of damage inflicts one point of Essence loss. Zombies reduced to –10 Essence are destroyed. The power manifests itself as bright bolts of fiery red energy invisible to the Mundane but visible to Gifted. This power can be resisted by any power that restricts the flow of Essence.

Death Mastery

Death Mastery is perhaps the most powerful ability available to necromancers. With it, power over the very forces of Life and Death can be brought to bear, to heal and to destroy both spirits and living beings.

Level 1—Delay/Accelerate the Departing

The necromancer can "pull" or "push" the soul of a person near death, either to snuff his life out, or to keep him alive a while longer. Use Willpower and Necromancy; each Success Level keeps the subject alive for one extra minute, or reduces his life expectancy by the same (causing immediate Survival and Consciousness Tests with the proper modifiers). In the latter case, the Task is resisted by the victim's Willpower and Constitution. This costs five Essence.

Level 2—Death Sight

This power is as much a curse as a blessing, as the necromancer becomes acutely aware of the futile race against the inevitable coming of Death. The spell-caster can sense if somebody is in imminent danger of dying by noticing the shadow of a spiritual avatar of Death approaching the person or animal. Death Sight also allows the caster to readily identify killers and predators, for their auras glow darkly while the power is active. This vision may allow the caster to do something to cheat the Reaper and save a person's life (that person, of course, could be the necromancer himself).

While this power is activated, the caster sees everything through Death's eyes—all living things seem to be decaying too rapidly. Every man and woman appears like a corpse in the beginning stages of decomposition. In some cases, the necromancer sees the future causes of their death—cancer bursting through the stomach, a pulsing brain tumor on the head, the bloodied lungs of a consumptive hideously displayed on the chest. The caster may need to pass a Fear Test to avoid being shocked and depressed by these revelations—and he should avoid looking in a mirror if he has not been living right. Activating this power uses Perception and Necromancy, costs four Essence points, and lasts for one minute.

Level 3—A Taste of Death

The necromancer can briefly push a being's Essence out of his body, causing a momentary out-of-body experience, and some damage. This Task uses Willpower and Necromancy, resisted by the target's Willpower and Constitution, and costs six Essence. If the caster wins, the victim "dies" for one second. This experience inflicts D4(2) Life/Dead Points damage, D6(3) points of Endurance and Essence loss, and shocks the victim for one to four Turns, imposing a –3 penalty to all Tasks. Gifted and supernatural beings may resist this attack with any power or Invocation that counters psychic intrusions or mind control.

Level 4—Death Projection

The necromancer gains the power to send his soul forth as a ghostly astral force, connected to his body by a psychic link. The power uses Intelligence and Necromancy, and lasts for one hour per Success Level. The character must leave a minimum of five Essence behind as an anchor to his body, and astral travel drains one Essence per hour. While in spirit form, the necromancer can travel through walls and fly at speeds of up to 100 mph per Willpower level. He can use powers while incorporeal, but those other than detection and sensory powers do not affect the material world.

Level 5—Wishkill

The necromancer can harm and kill enemies with a thought. This power is dangerous, for it attracts the attention of the dead, a beacon to all zombies within a mile of the user. This power calls for a Resisted Task using the caster's Willpower and Necromancy Task and the victim's Constitution and Willpower Test. If the necromancer wins, the victim takes D6(3) Life Points of damage per Success Level in the Task. This base damage costs no Essence to use. Spending extra Essence can inflict additional damage—increase the multiplier by one for every Essence point spent. Further, the victim suffers terrible agony, incurring a –2 penalty to all actions per Success Level in the Task, for one Turn.

Death Raising

Death Raising is the ability to raise, manipulate, and control zombies. At lower levels, this power simply allows the necromancer to pass unnoticed among the hungry dead, or command one or two zombies. At higher levels, zombies can be created and imprinted by the necromancer; these creatures become loyal pets. In all cases, powers use a Willpower and Necromancy task, and where the undead resists with a Simple Willpower Test. Trying to wrest control of a zombie from another necromancer requires a resisted Task between the two necromancers.

Level 1—Aura of Undeath

The necromancer infuses himself or an ally with an aura of undeath, making him appear to zombies and other Gifted as an undead. In this fashion, he can move unmolested among zombies, who recognize him as just another of their kind. This ability lasts for a number of minutes equal to the necromancer's Willpower per Essence point spent. This ability can be used on others, but costs double the Essence cost.

Level 2—Command Simple Zombies

At this level, the necromancer can issue basic, one-sentence commands (such as "Stop," "Attack the orcs," or "Defend me") to zombies with Intelligence 2 or less. Zombies resist with a Simple Willpower Test, or the Willpower of their controller, whichever is greater. Attempting to command zombies under the control of another necromancer always results in both necromancers becoming aware of the opposing influence.

Level 3—Raise Zombies

Necromancers using this power can raise undead corpses to do their bidding. All zombies raised with this ability consist of the basic zombie common to the Deadworld. Use of this power costs 10 Essence per zombie raised.

Level 4—Enhance Zombies

Necromancers with this ability can actually empower their zombie minions by adding Aspects to already risen dead. Aspects can be added to any zombie, costing Essence equal to the power level of the Aspect added. However, would-be zombie lords using this power lose half of the Essence points spent, so long as the zombie in question remains animated.

Example: Bert wants to allow a zombie servant to comprehend greater commands. He wishes to grant the creature Long-Term Memory (five points) and Language (one point). He channels the Essence necessary (six points total), and rolls Necromancy and Willpower to give the creature the abilities. The zombie can now comprehend language and remember complex commands. Still, Bert only recovers three of the expended Essence point normally; the other three (half of the six he expended for the Aspects) is lost until his zombie is destroyed, after which he regains the Essence normally.

Level 5—Raise the Dead

The necromancer gains the ability to return the soul of a deceased person to his body, and raise it as an intelligent zombie! Such a person comes back much as he was before (except for the decay and stench), but isn't as sharp as he used to be. Raised Cast Members retain all of the skills they possessed in life at –1 level (if this reduces a skill to zero, the skill is forgotten) and have the following Aspects added to their Deadworld's basic zombie template: Long Term Memory, Problem Solving, Tool Use (3), Language—senses and movement are Life Like and Like the Living, respectively. Weak Point is All and Dead Points are calculated as normal. Cast Member zombies retain Qualities, Drawbacks, Aspects, or Powers they had in life, and gain 10 points which they may use to purchase new Aspects. A dwarf zombie could still possess Underground Direction Sense, for example. However, they lose any Metaphysics they may have had in life in favor of the zombie Aspects that give them a new semblance of life. All other elements from the basic zombie are unchanged; they even rot and smell like other zombies. A Cast Member can only be raised using this power once; further raisings are impossible due to the extensive damage required to kill them a second time. This power costs 100 Essence points to use.

> **Zombie Cast Members**
>
> Zombie Masters who own Enter the Zombie may choose to substitute the zombie Cast Member creation rules for the Raise the Dead zombie Cast Member described under the power. This is reasonable and shouldn't affect game play in any way; however, given that zombie Cast Members in that book are inherently more powerful than the one described here, the cost of this power should be 130 Essence points. Zombie Cast Members from that book should require a new level of power called Death Raising 6 (Basically giving necromancers two options for creating intelligent zombies).

Death Speech

Death Speech allows a necromancer to communicate with and perceive the spirits of the dead, and to summon specific spirits to Earth to answer questions and provide knowledge it had in life. Note, this power applies only to spirits of the dead and not to zombies; speaking with corporeal undead is covered under Death Raising.

Level 1—Glimpse the Dead

By spending one Essence point and using a Perception and Necromancy Task, the necromancer can see a spirit within the range of the power, and mentally "hear" what the spirit says to him. The range is five yards per level of Willpower. The Glimpse lasts for one minute per Success Level of the Task.

Although the Gifted Quality itself allows a Cast Member to sense the presence of a supernatural being like a spirit, Death Speech pinpoints the appearance and location of the spirit.

Level 2—See the Dead

The necromancer can see spirits of the dead without needing to spend Essence or make Perception Tasks, unless the spirit is trying to make itself invisible, in which case a Resisted Task (using the caster's Perception and Necromancy versus the spirit's Willpower and Intelligence) is necessary.

Level 3—Recall the Dead

The necromancer can try to summon and communicate with the spirit of a recently dead person (no more than three days gone). This costs three Essence points. Many spirits linger near their bodies after death, so attempts made in the presence of the body have a +3 bonus. The Task uses Willpower and Necromancy. The spirit may resist with a Simple Willpower Test. Once summoned, the spirit can be asked questions; those who refuse to answer may be forced, but only at higher levels (see Command the Dead).

Level 4—Command the Dead

The necromancer can summon the spirit of anybody who died within the previous month, at the cost of five Essence points. Unwilling spirits may be compelled to come as in Recall the Dead. Also, the necromancer can compel answers to questions. This uses the caster's Willpower and Death Speech against the spirit's Willpower and Intelligence, and costs six Essence. If the necromancer wins, each Success Level guarantees an answer to one question. The spirit only answers with either "Yes," "No," or "I don't know." Only simple questions can be answered; asking an improper question (at the ZM's discretion) still counts.

Level 5—Summon the Dead

The caster can call upon any spirit of the dead dwelling on Earth in incorporeal form, or any spirit who has died within the past year. This process costs eight Essence points, which is "fed" to the spirit to keep it talking, or 10 Essence if the spirit must be forced to speak. More detailed answers can be made forthcoming; spirits answers in the form of one sentence.

Magic Items

Magic items are a fixture in fantasy roleplaying games—they are the objects Cast Members want most, because of the incredible powers they confer. In *Dungeons and Zombies*, Cast Members can create magic items, but the process is expensive and draining. Most Cast Members who create magic items will do so for themselves, and not as a career or hobby.

The magic item creation system described here is geared towards a swords-and-sorcery feel. For those wishing higher-powered and legendary items, and a detailed system, we direct you to *Armageddon*, which contains rules for Atlantean Immortals and specialized magic items, as well as magic items created by Old Gods.

Creating Magic Items

Magic items are created through Blessing, as per the Inspired ability (see *AFMBE*, p. 64). While some Deadworlds will have specific guidelines on the effects of Blessing, at the ZM's option it is possible to imbue a weapon with incredible abilities, if the Inspired works closely with a mage or necromancer. Inspired Invokers are the most likely Cast Members to create magic items, due to their ability to mix Miracles with Invocations.

Basic Magic Items

To create a magic item, an appropriately crafted item is needed, with a minimum of three Success Levels on a Dexterity and Craft Task for the item to hold Essence. Such items are inscribed with runic symbols that hold the Essence in the item. Items must be created with a standard Craft check, and inscribed with runes, using a Dexterity and the appropriate Craft (Rune Carving) skill. Inscription of runes costs five Essence points, which are replenished normally. Zombie Masters should consider that forging weapons, armor, or any high-quality item takes days or even weeks; this can serve as a limiting factor to how quickly the Cast creates magic items.

Rune Carving

Not all runes are magical, and those characters with a skill specialty in Rune Carving can inscribe "decorative" runes on items without spending Essence, though this has no effect on the carved item.

Next, an Inspired must perform the Blessing (see *AFMBE*, p. 64). The Essence cost is permanent; the Inspired never gets it back, though he may purchase Increased Essence Pool with experience to make up for the loss. Once Blessed, the item's Armor Value increases by one die type (up to D12, or by +1 if already D12). If a weapon, the item gains a +1 bonus to hit and to base damage inflicted. Items without a normal Armor Value gain an AV of D6(3), making them harder to damage or break. The item is now ready to receive magical effects.

Any Blessed weapon that has no effects already attached to it can be granted powers. This means if the Cast comes upon a sword in an ancient tomb that has been Blessed, but not endowed with magic qualities, their mage may attempt to do so. A mage or necromancer can, through permanent expenditure of Essence, imbue an item with any Invocation or Necromantic power they possess. Each time the mage or necromancer casts a spell on the item, that power functions once per day, to a maximum of three. Only one spell or necromantic power may be imbued into an item, and all Essence expended to cast the spell is permanently lost. Imbuing weapons with Metaphysical powers requires a separate Dismissal Task each time a spell or a Necromantic power is cast; failure means the item is ruined and can never again be Blessed. Powers used from an item never require a roll to activate, always function exactly at the Success Levels of the power when imbued into the item, and work as an action or part of an action. Dismissal Tasks are never necessary when using powers from magic items.

Imbuing items with power takes 30 minutes per Essence spent in casting, including the initial Blessing. The character creating the item may only stop to rest between the Blessing and the imbuing of power. No breaks may be taken during the Blessing, or during the empowerment stage, or the item is forever ruined.

Multiple Powers

The ZM may wish to allow characters to create weapons, armor, and items that hold multiple powers. If so, an Inspired must prepare the item for multiple powers. For each 10 Essence points he spends beyond the initial 10 (see Blessing, *AFMBE*, p. 64), the item gains an additional Blessing, with all bonuses attached (see above), and may hold an additional Metaphysical power. This additional Essence is permanently sacrificed, just like the initial 10.

Charged Items

Charged items revert to mundane objects when the power imbued in them is expended, making them temporary use items. After the item is Blessed, a mage or necromancer casts a spell or power into the item. Once the spell has been successfully cast (and Dismissed), it may be used once for every additional point of Essence the caster commits to charging the item. However, he only regains the Essence spent in the spell casting. The rest is lost until the item is used up, at which time he regains it normally. Once all charges are used, the item becomes mundane (no longer Blessed) and can never again be imbued with Metaphysics. In addition, when an item reverts to mundane, the Inspired who blessed the item recovers Essence used in the blessing as normal. Charging an item takes 30 minutes per point of total Essence spent, as normal.

Example: Argo, an Inspired Invoker, wishes to create a ring that can cast Heal Wounds, but eventually wants his Essence back. He spends 10 Essence points to bless the item, and 10 more to cast a 10-point Heal Wounds Invocation. He successfully completes him Dismissal Task. The item is now ready to be charged. He decides on 20 charges, so spends another 20 Essence points on charging the item, for a grand total of 40 Essence points spent. The creation of the item has taken 20 hours of work (30 minutes per point of Essence spent). He may take a break after the first five hours (the Blessing), but will most likely be exhausted after the next 15 hours of casting. He gets 10 Essence points for his Invocation back normally; the rest is lost until the ring's charges are spent, at which point the ring becomes a mundane item and he regains the other 30 Essence points normally. In the meantime, he has a ring that can cast 20 Heal Wounds Invocations, each of which automatically succeeds and heals 10 Life Points of damage.

Creating Worlds

Every story has to take place *somewhere*. In a typical game of *AFMBE,* the campaign is typically set in the modern world (or a reasonable approximation)—everyone knows where New York City is located, how much a cup of coffee costs, and when major holidays occur. In a fantasy game, players expect a suitably fantastic world—a world of the Zombie Master's creation.

You might be surprised to discover that designing an entire world is not nearly as difficult or complex as it may at first seem. Most readers are familiar with setting books for games that run into the hundreds of pages. But stop and think a moment—is all of that material really necessary to begin play in a setting? *All Flesh Must Be Eaten* sourcebooks provide players with campaign settings in the space of a relatively few pages. As the Cast adventures in the setting, it naturally grows bigger and more detailed, but all of those places, names, figures, and locations are not necessarily part and parcel of the initial setting detail. The Zombie Master adds a building here, a town there, and Supporting Cast characters everywhere, and these become part of the overall landscape. What the Zombie Master really needs are some basic elements upon which to build. While this section will probably be of most use to Zombie Masters looking to create their own fantasy setting, players might find some inspiration to spur on their own creativity and add to the world as it grows.

Where to Begin?

The process of creating an entire milieu may seem daunting to those who have never made the effort. A ZM seeking to create a unique setting for his fantasy game has far more to accomplish than one who is working with an historical or modern-day setting. When we talk about fantasy roleplaying, we are generally referring to something specific—medieval fantasy. That is to say, there are often kings and queens, peasants and farms, feudalism, and all the other trappings of the Middle Ages. Onto this, people usually graft an assortment of other elements, common to European fairy tales and mythology—dwarves, elves, orcs, goblins, dragons . . . Then, there's a dash of the really strange, to make the fantasy seem more fantastic, such as floating castles, vast underground empires, and magic. All of these elements have to be created from whole cloth by the Zombie Master, who must decide whether a king or a council of sorcerers rules the land, where the dragons live, and the relationship between the dwarves and elves. Certainly, one can draw from sources like books, films, and TV, and undoubtedly part of the creation will. Still, the ZM has to fill in many details for fantasy games.

Where does one start? There are generally two ways to go about setting design; we'll call them Bottom Up and Top Down.

The Bottom Up Method

The Bottom Up method is the simplest and quickest way to create a world, because there's not a lot to create right off. In this method, the Cast begins in a town, village, or city. Maybe they all grew up there, and are just coming of age to venture out into the world. Maybe they come from somewhere nearby, and have all managed to congregate at the same town (in which case, the ZM can ask the players to do a bit of work designing where they came from and what it's like). As they explore, the world grows, expands, and develops, often in exciting and surprising ways. After an adventure in the town (killing zombies, of course), they go out to the ruins nearby. The Zombie Master didn't plan for ruins so close by, but he figures, "what the heck?" Now he has to figure out the origin of the ruins—a bit of history. Maybe there's an evil cleric hiding there, and he's behind the zombie attacks . . . who is this person? What is the evil religion he practices? Why is he interested in controlling zombies? This can be a great deal of fun for players and ZM's alike, for no one knows what's next.

This method, while easy to start with, can become difficult to maintain as the Zombie Master and players add more and more on to the setting. The Cast and ZM run into issues like, "why is the desert next to a forest?" or, "why hasn't the oriental culture become intermixed with the European one?" The ZM should keep a watchful eye on how things develop; keep notes about new places added and new historical tidbits uncovered. Still, if the group is willing to suspend disbelief enough, the Bottom Up Method is an exciting and easy way to create a world in which to adventure that works well in episodic-style campaigns.

The Top Down Method

The Top Down method is the way to go if the game is big on concept, large stories, and major conflict (as many fantasy settings are). It requires more up-front work and initial thought, but creates a cohesive and epic setting. Top Down world building starts with the creation myth, works out the cosmology and conflicts between the deities, moves down to the roles each divinity played in Creation, and how they affect the lower inhabitants of the world. Sketch each of these elements out as briefly as possible to get a general idea of where your world is headed and what it will be like. As an example, we present Dawn of a Dead Age (see p. 74) broken down into its basic elements.

Historical Elements

Creation: A deific figure named Danna created the heavens and the Earth. Danna is a mother-goddess type who seeks to nurture and guide her followers. She named the world Domhain and saw that the world needed inhabitants to appreciate its beauty.

Coming of the Races: Danna employed servitor beings known as Tuatha de Dannan. She set these beings to work creating all manner of creatures to inhabit the world. The first race created were the Sidhe, an immortal and near-perfect race. The Sidhe were beautiful but slow to change, and Danna feared this would doom the world to entropy. So she set the Tuatha de Dannan to create other, less perfected races, resulting in dwarves and gnomes. Powerful dimensional travelers known as dragons arrived in Domhain, attracted by the world's peace and serenity; they exist outside of the plans of Danna or the Tuatha de Dannan.

The Fall: Unfortunately, some of the Tuatha de Dannan grew tired of an eternity of constant servitude and turned away from Danna. Their fall from the heavens tainted them, made them dark and evil, and they dabbled in new creations—the orcs and goblins and other vile creatures. Thus did evil enter the world. These fallen Tuatha de Dannan are known as Shedim.

The Rise of the Enemy: One of the Shedim, Adramalech, embraced his tainted nature and worked to develop it. In secret, he had his servants forge an Apocalypse Blade into which he poured his life essence. With this sword Adramalech became invincible, and sent his orcish servants out to conquer the world. During the war, the sidhe managed to strip the Shedim of their physical bodies, but fifty of the greatest sidhe magi were captured in a daring orcish assault and brought back to Adramalech's dark fortress. There, they were tortured, twisted, and forced to become new hosts for disembodied

Shedim. Desperate, the sidhe and dwarves created a race of their own to aid them in the war, and humans came into being. Outraged over the sidhe's presumption, Danna stripped them of much of their power.

Defeat of the Enemy: Adramalech's forces spread, overrunning the free peoples of Domhain. A grand alliance of all the goodly races, led by a great man named Albrecht, finally defeated him. Albrecht wielded a sword constructed by all the races of Domhain, with which he was able to destroy the Apocalypse Blade of Adramalech and strip the Shedim of their power and bodies.

These are the basic elements of Domhain's cosmology laid out. All that remains is to flesh out the elements with details and color, as in Chapter Four of this book, and the cosmology is as complete as it has to be to get started.

Detailing the World

What happens following the major events in the creation of the world and society? Periods like this are important in fantasy worlds, because they give an option for adventuring that isn't tied to some grand historic event or epic quest. No overarching struggle is present but numerous minor but still important missions can be undertaken.

Finally, we move to the final stage, when the world comes full circle with an epic quest and a climactic battle for the future. In Domhain this is the reawakening of Adramalech after thousands of years in slumber. His power is such that he begins to search for the pieces of his sword to take physical form again. The Cast must find and destroy the sword before Adramalech can awaken, and find the lost sword of Albrecht, the only thing that can stop Adramalech should they fail.

Once the cosmology and major elements are written, it's time to narrow focus and concentrate on practicalities. The ZM still has a great deal of work to do to flesh out the setting. There is a world to detail.

The World: Some Zombie Masters may want a map of their world, to establish the location of major towns and cities, important geographic features (such as mountains and rivers), and the borders of the major nations. Space does not permit a full discussion of the geologic and historical processes that go into shaping a fantasy landscape, and there are a lot of other books that do a much more thorough job. But the ZM should think about the cosmology he's created, and think about the impact on the world. For example, in Dawn of a Dead Age, we have sidhe, dwarves, gnomes, orcs, humans, dragons . . . where do these peoples live? Where are they in relation to each other? Where are the major sidhe, dwarf, and human cities? The sidhe and dwarves live mostly in the east, and various human kingdoms lie in the west. The south is an area of high volcanic and tectonic activity, where the Black Citadel, home of Adramalech, stands. That is enough to begin adventuring. The rest can be filled in as time goes on and the Cast adventures in the realm.

Politics: The political landscape can be as important as the physical one. Why? Because this tells you how the various races get along, and how they organize themselves. What political systems do the people of your world support—Monarchy? Democracy? Meritocracy? Maybe the sidhe of Domhain practice enlightened Democracy, with everyone over the age of 200 getting a vote. The humans might be more fractious—a barbarian king here, landed nobility there, the odd council of elders. How do the various peoples of the world interact? In Dawn of a Dead Age, following the defeat of Adramalech, the sidhe and dwarves withdrew, their contact with humans limited mostly to gnome emissaries, for example.

History: These are all the lesser elements that may or may not fit in with the overall cosmology—the wars, famines, disasters, and great achievements that fill the pages of human history, and chronicle the events of the fantasy world. In short, they are the "random events" that took place (much like those in real life). These can be important to the ZM to either explain the reason why things are the way they are, or provide a bit of backstory to the current situation.

Religion and Magic: These two powerful forces often play an important role in a fantasy setting. The ZM should consider the role of religion in the world, and some of its basic tenets. This links back to the setting's cosmology, but also gives the ZM a powerful tool. Who are the gods in your setting? What do they want? How do they interact with their creation (or do they)? In Domhain, the Tuatha de Dannan may not engage shedim or Adramalech in direct confrontation, though they may take physical form and guide the lesser beings in their quest; Danna wants the people of Domhain to fight for themselves. Similarly, the role of magic is important. How prevalent is magic? Does everyone know about it? Are sorcerers a common sight? What can magic do? Defining this early on can save the ZM headaches later on.

Inspiration

Where does the inspiration for all this creating come from? For this, the easiest and often best answer is to turn to existing stories. Try a local library and world mythology books. It may seem trite to base a fantasy world on Roman or Norse mythology, as this has been done time and again. However, if the familiarity of these stories appeals to the group, by all means run with it.

Still, there are thousands of faiths and philosophies out there. Try pulling elements from several different mythologies and twist, fit, and force them together like a jigsaw puzzle. With the exception of Death of the Round Table, this was how all of the mythologies of this book's Deadworlds were built. Dead Gods and Demon Lands draws from Zoroastrian and Hindu mythology; Dawn of a Dead Age is derived from Kabalistic lore and Celtic mythology; The Eastern Dead is a melting pot of elements from various Asian and Western myths. If carefully done, the ZM can create cohesive, original mythologies by adapting existing ideas.

Elements of Mythology

Several elements seem to be shared by mythologies across the board. Mythology exists to explain the inexplicable. Every myth and legend story begins with creation. What, if anything, was there before the world came into being? What made the god or gods desire to make a new world? How and why did they go about creating people? Divine beings in an imagined cosmology must serve this purpose to the people of their world. This is the place where a cohesive cosmic order must begin.

Every mythology shares a story of terrible disaster. The people commit a terrible sin that angers the gods, or become so evil as to become unredeemable. Sometimes, a great and evil power arises, which upsets the balance of light and dark, and disaster results. Only a final stand and dear price can set things right. Often, this disaster destroys the majority of life, so that things may start over. Sometimes it affects only a city or nation. Always it plays a major role in the evolution of society.

The fall from grace is another common theme in mythology, the tale of some great being or group who for various reasons—pride is a popular one—fall out of favor with the gods. These beings become evil deities, who seek to destroy everything good and beautiful out of spite or jealousy, and seize power for themselves. This element is essential; without a line between good and evil, people have nothing to strive for, no promised reward for staying on the path of righteousness. Somewhere in the early stages, a cosmology must include the rise of evil for the people to struggle against.

Where every mythology begins with a creation story, many also have an Armageddon prophecy. If an item is not destroyed, the world will end; if an evil power is allowed to rise it will bring war, famine, pestilence, and death. Sometimes, this can be avoided through the efforts of a great hero, who rises up to unite the people and usher in an age of peace. Other times not. Such tales give people a reason to hope and believe.

Finally, every mythology includes heroes who perform great deeds, and villains who behave very badly. Both serve as examples to followers—heroic virtues to emulate, and evil deeds to avoid. Much has been written about The Hero's Journey, much of it better than can be found in a roleplaying sourcebook. For those Zombie Masters looking for an epic feel to their fantasy worlds, it is important to understand the role of the hero. The Cast should leave their safe environs and journey far and wide in a quest to combat some great evil, confronting many challenges along the way. And in *All Flesh Must Be Eaten*, their enemies will likely be terrible zombie lords, and their hordes of slavering, brain-eating undead.

Archetypes

The following pages include Archetypes for any fantasy setting. They may be used as-is, modified to make them more unique, or as templates for your own creations.

Gnome Loveable Rogue

Talented Hero

Str 2* **Dex** 5 **Con** 4*
Int 4* **Per** 3 **Wil** 3
LPs 43
EPs 32
Spd 18
Essence 21

Qualities/Drawbacks

Acute Senses (Smell/Taste) (2)
Adversary (Law Enforcement) (–2)
Clown*
Covetous (Greedy) (–2)
Fast Reaction Time (2)
Gnome (5)
Good Luck (3)
Hard to Kill (3)
Nerves of Steel*
Obligation (Friends) 1*
Reckless*
Situational Awareness (2)
Socially Inept (Annoying) (–1)

Skills

Climbing 3
Dodge 4*
Escapism 4
Hand Weapon (Knife) 4
Lock Picking 4*
Notice 3
Pick Pocket 4
Stealth 4*
Traps 4

Powers/Metaphysics

Mystic Targeting (3)
Nightvision (2)*
Walk in Shadows (4)

* Modified or granted by Gnome Quality

Gear

Backpack, Bedroll, Leather Armor, Lock Picks, 50-foot Rope, 2 Sacks, 6 Knives, Tinder Box, 5 Torches, 1 Week of Traveling Rations, Water Skin, 20 Gold Pieces

Personality

They grumble and complain a lot, don't they? Always upset because I pulled the wrong lever or snuck off to see what was down a hallway. I can't help it if I like to see new things. They're just too careful, sometimes. Anyway, I know they love me. If they didn't, they wouldn't have saved me from the town watch all those times. Look, I didn't mean to wind up with the duke's purse. Sometimes things just sort of fall into my hands, you know? I'm like a magnet for shiny things, especially shiny things that belong to other people.

Anyway, sometimes they're really mean to me, when I get in trouble. But I think I'll stick with them. I mean, without me where would they be when all the zombies come? Speaking of zombies, I remember the time when I first met them. I was surrounded by zombies and they showed up and I had to rescue all of them. The zombies must've been six—no, ten—feet tall, and there were at least a dozen of them. Maybe two. Every time I think about it I realize there were more than last time I thought about it. Regardless, I was surrounded and they showed up and let me rescue them, and now we're together. I'm pretty sure they need me. After all, who else can pick a lock and spy on the bad guys like I can?

Quote

"What does this lever do?"

Human Psychic Tagalong

Adept Hero

Str 2 **Dex** 3 **Con** 2
Int 3 **Per** 3 **Wil** 2
LPs 32
EPs 23
Spd 10
Essence 30

Qualities/Drawbacks

Danger Sense (1)
Emotional Problems (Emotional Dependency) (–1)
Essence Channeling 3 (6)
The Gift (5)
Hard to Kill (2)
Honorable 2 (–2)
Increased Essence Pool (3)
Psychic Invoker (3)
Recurring Nightmares (–1)
Socially Inept (–1)

Skills

Brawling 1
Dancing (Folk) 3
Dodge 4
First Aid 3
Hand Weapon (Knife) 2
Notice 4
Occult Knowledge 1
Streetwise 1

Powers/Metaphysics

Affect the Psyche 3
Elemental Fire 2
Farsight 2
Insight 3

Gear

Backpack, Bedroll, Leather Armor, Knife, Tinder Box, 5 Torches, 1 Week of Traveling Rations, Water Skin, 40 Gold Pieces

Personality

Things work out funny, you ever notice that? I mean, there I was on the streets like usual, just a fifteen-year-old girl begging for a meal, maybe using one of my "special talents" to convince a merchant to throw me a few extra coins. Then next thing I know, I was being fingered as an accomplice to a gnome who'd just lifted someone's purse. Thank the gods his friends were nice enough to help me out of that predicament. They had a few words with the town guard, told them I didn't have anything to do with it, and gave the purse back. They probably would've just sent me on my way after that, except that just then all the dead bodies in the town graveyard sat up and started attacking people!

Well, I'm not dumb. These guys were adventuring types; I could tell by the swords and armor. So I hid behind the orc and used another of my special talents to torch a couple zombies. Well, the group must've thought my talents were useful (or maybe I'm just persuasive—wink, wink) 'cause they asked me to tag along with them. Hey, it's a better life than begging for scraps on the streets. Even with all the zombies.

Quote

"I've got a bad feeling about this."

Human Woodland Scout

Talented Hero

Str 4 **Dex** 4 **Con** 4
Int 2 **Per** 4 **Wil** 2
LPs 54
EPs 35
Spd 16
Essence 20

Qualities/Drawbacks

Ambidexterity (3)
Charisma +2 (2)
Fast Reaction Time (2)
Good Luck (2)
Hard to Kill (4)
Honorable (–2)
Nerves of Steel (3)
Obligation (Defend those in her charge) (–2)
Ranger (5)
Situational Awareness*
Socially Inept*

Skills

Dodge 4
First Aid 2
Hand Weapon (Long Sword) 4*
Hand Weapon (Short Bow) 3
Hand Weapon (Short Sword) 2
Language (Elven) 2
Notice 2*
Riding (Horse) 3
Science (Animals) 2
Science (Herbalism) 2
Stealth 3*
Survival (Forest) 3*
Tracking 3*

* Modified or granted by Ranger Quality

Gear

Backpack, Bedroll, Leather Armor, 50-foot Rope, 2 Sacks, Long Sword, Short Sword, Short Bow, Tinder Box, 5 Torches, 1 Week of Traveling Rations, Water Skin, 10 Gold Pieces

Personality

My life has been turned completely on its ear. If you'd have told me that I'd be traveling with an orc a year ago, I probably would've either laughed at you, or challenged you to draw your sword. And yet, here I am. I've got an orc with me who is not only my traveling companion, but a trusted friend and ally. As if that weren't bad enough, I seem to have picked up a gnome and a teenage girl (and I think she's got a crush on me). There are nights when I sit and wonder why I just don't walk away from them all.

So why don't I walk away? Simple, really. They need me. I'm their protector and their guardian. And something tells me we've all got a part to play in the dark times ahead. I have an obligation to protect them, and honor dictates I heed my obligations. That, and all the zombies walking the land. I've saved each of my friends from those stinking corpses at one time or another, and the fact is—it's just not safe to be alone in the wilds anymore.

It's best to have some company these days, someone to cut off my head and put my undead body back in the ground. I'm sure I can count on my companions to do that.

Quote

"These are dark times, and we must stick together if we're to come through them alive."

Orc Tribal Outcast

Adept Hero

Str 4* **Dex** 2 **Con** 4*
Int 2 **Per** 2 **Wil** 3
LPs 51
EPs 38
Spd 16
Essence 27

Qualities/Drawbacks

Attractiveness –1*
Cruel –1*
Emotional Problems (Fear of Rejection) (–1)
Essence Channeling 2 (4)
Gift (5)
Hard to Kill 3 (2)*
Honorable (–1)
Increased Essence Pool (2)
Minority*
Obligation (Other Cast Members) (–2)
Orc (5)
Reckless (–2)
Resistance (Fatigue) 2*
Socially Inept (–3)

Skills

Brawling 4*
Dodge 3
Hand Weapon (Battle Axe) 4
Intimidation 3*
Occult Knowledge 2
Running (Marathon) 3*
Survival (Forest) 2

Powers/Metaphysics

Death Mastery 2
Death Raising 2
Death Speech 2
Necromancy 4
Nightvision (2)*

* Modified or granted by Orc Quality

Gear

Backpack, Bedroll, 4 Candles, Leather Armor, 50-foot Rope, Two-handed Battle Axe, Tinderbox, 3 Torches, 1 Week of Traveling Rations, Water Skin, 10 Gold Pieces

Personality

Everything change for me when meet others. They takes me prisoner after orcs raid small village, but no kill me. Wanted information. I no give information, tell them kill me. They refuse. Finally, let me go, says they don't know why, something tell them not kill me. But I have nowhere to go now. Tribe won't take back me. Orcs no take prisoners, kill everyone, so not like orcs who get taken. So me follow others for while, they treat me well. Throw me scraps from dinner. One day bunch of dead-'uns come. They stand to fight, and me help. Use power of Gruugash to make dead'uns fight each other. Others impressed.

People no like orcs. When in village I keep hood up and face down so no cause trouble for others. Others friend, treat me good. I pledge life to them, and learn about things like honor and friendship. Together we kill many dead'uns.

Quote

"You want kill him? You go through me, first!"

Chapter Three

I could tell you that things have always been as they are. Indeed, that's what we're expected to say and to think. And for many in our world, such a statement is truth. But there are those of us still alive who remember the times before, when there were no forces of corporeal evil walking the world. Not in the sense that there are now, in any case. There was a time when the sun rose in the morning over lush green fields in the spring, with dandelion seeds wisping through the air on a quiet breeze. There was a time in the dead of winter when the blinding white of unmarked, virgin snow was as breathtaking as it was deadly for the unprepared. In those days, humankind lived in peace with the elves and dwarves, even the minotaurs held trade agreements with many of the kingdoms by the sea.

There was a time, my child, when the dead stayed dead.

Alas, that golden age is long gone, before the gods took notice of us. In those times we were a simple and animistic world. The only deities we held to were the Earth, the Sun, and the Stars in the sky. It was like that universally. When we passed on to the next world, our spirits cycled back through the grand wheel, returning to nourish the world or to be reborn into a new life. Things were as they should be.

Three thousand years ago the gods of darkness came and changed everything. Banished from their world of origin by dying faiths, they came together, the remnants of several devastated pantheons, to seek new worshippers and new powers. To make certain they acquired those worshippers, they made their presence known with a vengeance. Had it been Ishtar, or Mitra, or even Tiamat who arrived first, things may have turned out differently. Instead, it was Ahriman and Kali who brought their legions of demons and death to our world. By the time the gods of light made their presence known, those of darkness had established a firm hold on our world. Now the snow runs red in the winter, and the Zombie Lords of Kali and Ahriman rule vast portions of our world.

But perhaps the worst travesty to come out of the deific invasion is this: No longer do the dead return to the cycle of things. They arise again, their souls trapped within their decaying bodies, to feast upon the living and create more soldiers in the ever-growing army of the Dark Ones. Once destroyed, their souls remain trapped within hidden receptacles from which the Zombie Lords draw their power. Alas, the most successful legion to do battle against the forces of Kali and Ahriman has been that of the reptilian empire

of Tiamat, who seeks only to spread war and chaos. The elves and dwarves and other races have gone into hiding, hunted to the point of extinction, and it is only the rare exception to their breed that still mingles among mankind.

And yet, there is still hope. The gods of light, Ahura Mazda and Ishtar, Mitra, Indra and Hanumaan, have arrived, and it is whispered that even among the nonhumans there are champions of these forces of light. Our world is forever altered, but not yet lost, so long as we keep the hope alive, that someday the Godswar will end and the dead may rest once more.

DEAD GODS AND DEMON LANDS

Introduction

Dead Gods and Demon Lands is based on the grim pulp fantasy of writers like Fritz Lieber and Robert Howard. What characterizes pulp, or adventure, fantasy, is its notion of adventure for its own sake. The heroes in pulp fantasy stories seek adventures, large and small, to have a good time. They are directed by their own internal desires, rather than the epic struggle between good and evil, often making them appear amoral and almost as dark as the villains. They often hold no lofty goals, no high ideals. They want money, or fame, or a quiet place where they can have a drink in peace. They do not fight for king or country, nor do they risk their lives to save the world (though sometimes they end up doing just that). While they may possess great skill with a sword, they have no epic quest to follow. Often, they stumble into adventure by being in the wrong place at the wrong time, or by accepting a job that turns out to be far more than they bargained for. Their enemies are often powerful (and strange) gods, power-mad sorcerers, and *unnameable things*, which they must defeat as much with guile as with their swords. These heroes make their way through the world with strong arms, dark magics, and heavy blades.

In Dead Gods and Demon Lands, the once-peaceful land of Iurth has been invaded by the cast off gods of other dimensions. These beings crave worship and power, and new playthings to toy with. They fancy Iurth for its unspoiled people. Unfortunately, the arrival of these gods has upset the cosmic balance, and now the dead of Iurth cannot pass on to the afterlife. They remain, undead flesh-eaters plaguing the land.

The Coming of the Gods

Dead Gods and Demon Lands takes place in a world dominated by gods, who frequently meddle in the affairs of men (and elves, dwarves, and anyone else, really).

The First Age

The world of Iurth was once a lush, green realm where faeries and elves frolicked under the moon, and dwarven smiths crafted elegant objects in the forges deep within their mountains. Long ago, the earth and nature spirits of Iurth had brought peace and bounty to the people of the land. The people worshiped Earth, Sun, and the many Stars, and did not know of evil. Occasionally, dark forces peeked out from their caves and pits, the first signs there were forces other than the spirits of nature, but these creatures were always driven back. This was the way for three thousand years, the First Age of Iurth.

The Second Age

This peace and beauty did not escape notice. Ahriman, a fell god banished from another dimension, wandered the Otherworlds in search of a home. Everywhere he looked, he found powerful forces arrayed against him, for these other worlds had gods of their own. But on Iurth, he found a green and pleasant land, ripe for the taking. He stole into the world quietly, and whispered in ears and marshaled his forces. Uncorrupted and naïve, some dwarves and elves listened, and drew strength from Ahriman. They turned away from the veneration of Father Earth and Mother Forest, and worshiped Ahriman. They became the goblins and orcs, twisted by the corruption of Ahriman. Thus began the Second Age of Iurth.

Evil takes root easily within the mortal heart, especially when promises of power and glory are attached, and Ahriman delivered. Those who took up his mantle gained power over spirit and shadow, and the ability to raise and control armies of the dead. These became the Zombie Lords, and were placed first among all of Ahriman's other servants. An army of goblins and orcs poured down from the mountains, and attacked dwarf, elf, and human lands. Few among the uncorrupted people knew about war, a disadvantage Ahriman seized upon. His armies crushed all who stood in their way, and the twin cities of elf and man were overwhelmed. It looked as though Ahriman would claim Iurth as his and command the worship of a world once again.

Then, a new power arrived in Iurth. This god, calling itself Ahura Mazda, claimed to be the god of light who had created the world. None could be sure if he spoke the truth. The priests proclaimed Ahura Mazda as the means to defeat Ahriman and his legions of darkness. Ahura Mazda taught the free peoples how to fight. The dwarves made weapons and armor of steel. The elves learned to harness the power of nature to cast spells. And the humans took to war easily

The Afterlife

With the coming of Ahriman, Ahura Mazda and the other gods, something in the cosmic balance shifted. Rather than returning to the Wheel of Life upon which all souls could find reincarnation, the souls of the departed found they were trapped in the world, unable to move on. Many rose again as zombies, hungry for flesh and vulnerable to the machination of Ahriman. This was the Rise.

enough. Over time, the free people pushed back Ahriman's Zombie Lords and his armies of goblins and orcs and reclaimed their lands, though they could not drive this alien god from their world.

Then came the vampiric goddess Kali, the Black Earth Mother, perhaps drawn through the cosmos by the clash of metal and the stench of blood. With her came a host of demonic beings, called Asuras—fresh reinforcements for Ahriman. She became consort to Ahriman, and together the battle was joined anew. She too granted power over the dead, and her own Zombie Lords joined Ahriman's war councils.

Soon, other gods appeared on Iurth. The dwarves took to the teachings of Mitra and Indra, while humans worshiped Hanumaan. Many elves turned to Ishtar, goddess of love and fertility, and withdrew from the conflict with Ahriman to wait the day when they could once again emerge. And with these gods came more war, more dissent, more division, until the world appeared as it does today.

Yet one more god was still to trod upon the stage—this was Tiamat, the five-headed, draconic goddess of chaos and destruction. Unlike the others, she remained hidden and worked towards her own ends. She cared nothing for good or evil, nor did she wish to see the ultimate domination of any race. Domination brought order, and in order there can be no chaos. Tiamat dabbled in creation, and spawned the saurians on a remote tropical island. When the time was right, Tiamat unleashed them upon the world. She neither fought on the side of Ahriman nor Ahura Mazda, surprising both. To this day, Tiamat's forces represent a third faction in what has come to be known as the Godswar.

The Third Age

Now the battle is joined anew, not only between the forces of light and dark, but between Order and Chaos as well. Alliances between the gods come and go at their whim, both forged and broken out of convenience. With the afterlife closed to mortals, the lost souls of the departed remain trapped in the world. Many remain within their bodies, shambling across the countryside until killed a second time. Others remain trapped in hellish prisons of nothingness, feeding and powering the gods and their minions. This is the world in which the Cast walks.

Cosmology

Given that as with most fantasy worlds, a history of the world is rarely concise and often convoluted, this section aims to present the various deific beings and their angelic and demonic servants, so players and ZMs can better follow the machination of the deities on Iurth.

The Gods

Since the beginning of the Second Age of Iurth, numerous gods have entered the land. Some of them fight for good, others evil. Some value stability, others chaos. And still other gods, perhaps yet to reveal themselves, have nothing to do with the Godswar and pursue their own ends (that's a hint to you ZMs out there).

Ahriman

Ahriman is the central evil deity, one of the four major deities, and the current ruling power in the world. Two thousand years ago, he began his insurrection, bringing with him an army of demons known as Daevas and granting power over the dead to his minions. His incursion came as a surprise to a complacent world, and thus he managed to spread his forces quickly. Ahriman embodies anger, betrayal, rage, domination, and death, and his final goal is to turn Iurth into a mirror of himself. His consort is Kali, and he lavishes affection upon her, allowing her sole dominion over a number of kingdoms throughout Iurth. However, the day will come when he tires of her, and on that day he will betray her, for she stands in the way of his sole domination of the world.

Ahura Mazda

The self-proclaimed brother of Ahriman and the second major deity in the pantheon, Ahura Mazda is Ahriman's eternal enemy and the Lord of Wisdom. Ahura Mazda is the chief of the pantheon of Gods of Light and is prophesied to defeat Ahriman in the final battle at the end of the Third Age, a time known as the Reckoning. No one knows when the Reckoning will come, and many suspect it never will. Ahura Mazda leads an army of angelic beings known as the Spentas, who deliver messages from Ahura Mazda to his servants, and who grant power to his Inspired.

Hanumaan

A god worshiped solely by humans, Hanumaan represents victory in battle and valor on the field—concepts easily understood by mankind. He is a minor god in the pantheon, though he is honorable and just. Warriors and generals alike can be found praying before idols of this simian-looking god before battle. He often allies with Mitra and Indra, the gods most associated with dwarves.

Indra

Indra is the god of war and bringer of storms, the defender of mortals against the gods of darkness. He is the third of the four major deities and represents conquest and order. Indra is attended by the Maruts, his own army of angelic beings who are said to grant power to those Inspired by him, and to create paladin through a process known as the Chemical Wedding. Indra is second only to Ahura Mazda in the pantheon of the gods of light, for it is he who preserves the order to whatever Ahura Mazda sets in motion. Indra stands against Kali and is regarded as her opposite, the god of the pure sky opposing a goddess of the black earth.

Ishtar

Ishtar is the goddess of love and fertility, favored among many elves. It is she who taught the elves to harness the power of creation to produce magic, and encouraged them to await the Reckoning in their forest strongholds. She is anything but a goddess of war and perhaps the most incorruptible and pure god in the pantheon of Iurth. Unfortunately, some human-dominated cults who worship in her name have corrupted her message into one of decadence and lust. Ishtar's Inspired concentrate on healing and life, rather than war. Among the elves is a belief that it is actually she who will defeat Ahriman at the Reckoning by healing his wounded heart.

Kali

Kali is the final of the four major deities, the four-armed Black Earth Mother, a vampiric goddess of death and rebirth. Kali is more of a neutral goddess than an evil one, and generally fulfills her promises of power and riches to their fullest potential. She is the sister of Indra and stands opposed to him in most conflicts, which combined with her attraction to Ahriman has led her to side with darkness in this conflict. An army of Asuras, demons who grant power to her followers, attend Kali. In return for her support and loyalty, Ahriman allows Kali sole dominion over several kingdoms; however, on the day he finally betrays her, she plans to turn against him and side with the forces of light.

Mitra

Mitra, like Indra, is a warrior god and guardian of the cosmic order. Mitra generally appeals to dwarves because they value order and stability. He often acts as a general for Indra, and stands in the defense of mortals against the darkness. As a minor deity, he is more accessible to mortals; he often leads Indra's Maruts in celestial campaigns, but has no attendants of his own. He grants his powers and delivers his messages in person, and this direct approach has lead a great many dwarves to Mitra.

Tiamat

Tiamat is a wild card in the battle for Iurth, though it is safe to say she is just as dangerous to the world as Ahriman. Tiamat is a five-headed dragon goddess of chaos and destruction. She breeds her own species of reptilian followers, the saurians, and stands against most of the other gods, as it suits her will. She is inclined to change sides on a whim and owes allegiance to none. Tiamat, however, doesn't appear to have any interest in conquering the world. Though her hordes spread, she is more concerned with fostering dissension in the ranks of the other factions than with conquest, territory, or followers. It is quite possible she is insane.

Saurian Lizard Men

Strength 3 **Constitution** 3
Dexterity 4 **Intelligence** 2
Perception 2 **Willpower** 2
Life Points 34 **Speed** 14
Endurance Points 29 **Essence Pool** 16
Skills: Brawling 2, Hand Weapon (Sword) 2

Attacks: Two short swords D6 x 3(9), tail D6 x 3(9), bite D4 x 3(6)

Qualities/Drawbacks: Ambidexterity, Infravision, Minority, Zealot

Celestials and Infernals

Each of the four major gods of the Iurth Pantheon has their own attendants, who carry messages for them, convey the power of their god to the faithful, and serve as their god's eyes and ears.

The Chemical Wedding is the joining of a divine or infernal spirit with a physical being, such as a Zombie Lord, a paladin, or an Inspired Character Type. The spirit literally merges with the character's soul, altering it in subtle and fundamental ways, and imparting powers beyond those of normal beings. This celestial or infernal entity serves as a conduit through which the power of the gods flows. This link is immutable and unbreakable, and no power wrought by mortal or elf can sever it. Gods, however, may be another story, but this is left to the ZM to decide.

The experiences and methods of the Chemical Wedding are far too numerous and personal to detail here. A character might venture out into the wilds for fasting and meditation, and return carrying a celestial spirit dedicated to Ahura Mazda inside him, while a willing servant of Kali might participate in an elaborate ritual intended to summon one of her Asuras and bond with it. Zombie Masters are encouraged to be creative with regards to the nature of the Chemical Wedding.

In most cases, the Chemical Wedding serves as flavor information for those characters with a connection to a higher power. Just as Inspired Character Types derive their abilities through their faith in the divine, characters in Dead Gods and Demon Lands gain their Miracles through their belief in the likes of Ahriman and Ahura Mazda; they just do it through spirits as intermediaries. For ZMs who want a bit more detail, a necromancer with Death Lordship 1 or higher can attempt to sever the bond between character and patron spirit, temporarily interfering with his abilities. Resolve this with a Willpower and Necromancy Task opposed by the spirit's Simple Willpower Test. In most cases, spirits powerful enough to engage in the Chemical Wedding have a Willpower score of at least five or six (if not higher). Inspired characters who are the victim of such a necromantic attack can use Denial (see *AFMBE*, p. 62) to counter the assault. If the necromancer succeeds, the link is severed for one hour per Success Level on the Necromancy Task.

A necromancer could attempt to bind or dismiss a Marut, Spentas, or similar entity, once he has severed the bond between it and its vessel. Zombie Masters are encouraged to devise severe consequences for those who fail such attempts.

Unlike this limited use of Necromancy, Invocations and Miracles have little effect on celestials and infernals; the magic of lesser beings cannot challenge that of a god, and gods are loathe to interfere in the Chemical Weddings of other gods.

Asuras: These infernal spirits serve Kali, and confer powers of darkness upon her mortal servants. Necromancers who use the Death Raising ability run the risk of attracting Kali's notice and becoming Wed to an Asura demon. Kali zombies result when an Asura demon inhabits the body of a dead mortal.

Daevas: Demonic beings under the command of Ahriman, Daevas confer their master's power to characters dedicated to his service. Ahriman particularly likes the martial spirit of paladin, and those who distinguish themselves in battle may find themselves Wedded to a Daeva (even those dedicated to another god, which can present problems for the character). Ahriman zombies result when a Daeva inhabits the body of a dead mortal.

Maruts: These are the angelic attendants and messengers for Indra, and it is from Maruts that Inspired characters derive their Miracles. Characters who become Wedded to Maruts often become paladin, having attracted their attention through battle prowess. Many magi revere Maruts directly, rather than Indra, for they believe these celestial beings bring Essence into the world.

Spentas: The servants of Ahura Mazda, Spentas act as his messengers and servants. Inspired characters dedicated to Ahura Mazda achieve their status through the Chemical Wedding, and often gain the power to wield both Invocations and Miracles (take the Inspired Invoker Quality). Clerics and priests who frequently use either the Blessing or Holy Fire Miracles have a good chance of attracting the attention of Ahura Mazda and becoming Wed to a Spenta.

Celestial/Infernal Reference

Name	Type	God
Asuras	Infernal	Kali
Daevas	Infernal	Ahriman
Maruts	Celestial	Indra
Spentas	Celestial	Ahura Mazda

The Zombies

There are no less than three kinds of zombie inhabiting the world of Iurth. Two are raised by the dark machination of Ahriman and Kali, and can often be found in the service of a Zombie Lord or trusted Inspired character. The final type of zombie, the restless dead, is by far the most common, and in some ways the most dangerous.

Ahriman Zombies

Zombies of Ahriman serve as the physical shell for a Daevas, the demonic beings under Ahriman's command. In this way, these disembodied demons gain the ability to affect the physical world. As the servants of the god of destruction and death, Ahriman zombies delight in causing as much devastation as possible before their mortal shell rots away. Zombie Lords and necromancers under Ahriman's sway often send these zombies to raze entire villages. With their monstrous strength and claws, they can tear through almost any substance. What makes them terrible foes for adventurers to confront, however, has to do with their ability to climb and swing. Many a group of adventurers has fallen under the sudden onslaught of undead dropping down from a forest canopy, or from the shadowy eaves of an abandoned temple.

Ahriman zombies must kill a victim by consuming their heart, and then bury the body for the victim to rise as a new Ahriman zombie (often as the host for another Daevas demon). For this reason, most Ahriman zombies are created by his Zombie Lords rather than through infection.

Ahriman Zombies

Strength 4	**Constitution** 2
Dexterity 3	**Intelligence** 1
Perception 2	**Willpower** 2
Dead Points 34	**Speed** 14
Endurance Points n/a	**Essence Pool** 14

Skills: Brawling 2

Attack: Claws D6 x 4(12) (armor-piercing)

Weak Spot: All [0], Blessed Objects (clerics of Ahura Mazda or Indra) [–3]

Getting Around: The Quick Dead [+10], Climbing [+2], Brachiation [+1]

Strength: Strong Like Bull [+5], Claws [+8]

Senses: Like the Living [+1], Life Sense [+4]

Sustenance: Occasionally [+2], Sweet Bread (Heart) [–3]

Intelligence: Tool Use 1 [+3]

Spreading the Love: Only the Dead [–2] and Bury the Body [–2]

Power: 32

Kali Zombies

Strength 2 **Constitution** 2
Dexterity 3 **Intelligence** 1
Perception 2 **Willpower** 2
Dead Points 15 **Speed** 18
Endurance Points n/a **Essence Pool** 12
Skills: Brawling 2, Stealth 3 [+3]
Attack: Bite D4 x 2(4) or by weapon
Weak Spot: Heart [+7], Blessed Objects (clerics of Ahura Mazda or Indra) [–3]
Getting Around: The Quick Dead [+10], Leaping [+3], Walk in the Shadows [+4]
Strength: Dead Joe Average [0], Damage Resistant [+5]
Senses: Like the Living [+1]
Sustenance: Occasionally [+2], Blood [-2]
Intelligence: Teamwork [+4], Tool Use 1 [+3]
Spreading the Love: Only the Dead [-2] and Bury the Body [–2]
Power: 38

Kali Zombies

Kali zombies result when an Asura demon inhabits the body of a dead mortal. In this way, they gain a material body and can affect the physical world. Once embodied, they try to cause as much pain and suffering as possible before the body rots away. As servants of the dark goddess, oftentimes their activities run to the more lascivious and more than one adventurer has found themselves the target of macabre propositions. Make no mistake, however, Kali zombies are extremely deadly, and they kill without warning. Their quick speed, stealth, and ability to hunt in packs make them dangerous to encounter, and typically a servant of Kali dispatches a group to assassinate a hated foe.

Kali zombies must completely drain a victim of blood and then bury the body in order for the victim to rise as another Kali zombie (often as the host for another Asura demon). For this reason, most Kali zombies are created by her Zombie Lords rather than through infection.

The Restless Dead

There is no rest for the dead on Iurth. The Godswar has sealed off the heavens, locking mortals away from their final rest. Instead of moving on, the souls of mortal beings who die on Iurth are condemned to walk the planet as disembodied spirits. Aware of the passage of time and their separation from the world, but unable to do anything other than lament, these lost souls long for something real.

Some of these unfortunates haunt the world of the living, often inhabiting the place where they died, or latching on to a friend or relative (this makes a good justification for the Bad Luck Quality). Those with the Death Lordship power find themselves with no shortage of spirits to command; those possessing the Death Speech power may discover an army of ghosts demanding an opportunity for a little conversation. Full spirit creation rules can be found in *WitchCraft* (see p. 266).

Many disembodied souls find new bodies to occupy—those of the recently deceased. Those who escape often find a more painful existence in the world when they rise as zombies. If not captured and

Restless Dead

Strength 2 **Constitution** 2
Dexterity 1 **Intelligence** 1
Perception 2 **Willpower** 2
Dead Points 15 **Speed** 2
Endurance Points n/a **Essence Pool** 10
Skills: Brawling 2, appropriate weapon skill 2 [+2]
Attack: By weapon
Weak Spot: Brain [+6]
Getting Around: Slow and Steady [0]
Strength: Dead Joe Average [0]
Senses: Like the Living [+1]
Sustenance: Who Needs Food? [+8], All Flesh Must Be Eaten [0]
Intelligence: Tool Use 1 [+3]
Spreading the Love: Special
Power: 25

enslaved by necromancers, Zombie Lords, or evil Inspired, these pitiful creatures, without a master, mind, or will of their own, are driven by the desperate need to feed upon warm flesh.

Anyone on Iurth who dies by any means at all rises as a zombie in D6(3) days, unless the body is cremated or the brain destroyed.

> **Zombie Lords**
>
> This Deadworld borrows the concept of Zombie Lords from the AFMBE corebook. In addition to the powers listed in that book, all Zombie Lords are considered to have Necromancy 5 and Death Raising 5. This power raises Kali or Ahriman zombies as appropriate, but never common zombies. Keep in mind that as "elite" high priests of the faith, Zombie Lords almost always are attended by a contingent of lesser initiates, most of whom are necromancers or Inspired (not to mention all those pesky zombies). Zombie Lords are discussed in detail in the Rise of the Zombie Lords Deadworld (see AFMBE, p. 206).

Nonhuman Races

Finally, we come to the mortals living on Iurth, in the shadow of gods, demons, and zombies. Humans, dwarves, elves, and minotaurs make their home on this world. Players should use the Racial Qualities presented in **Chapter Two: Swords, Sorcery, and Shambling** for their Cast Members. Goblins and orcs also live on Iurth, though as servants of Ahriman and Kali they may make inappropriate Cast Members. Consult with your ZM before playing an orc or goblin.

Saurian Cast Members

Lizard men could certainly make an appropriate nonhuman race for players in a fantasy-style *AFMBE* game. To use the race as a Cast Member, the ZM can make the following Quality available to players. Note this produces a lizard man considerably more powerful than the sample Supporting Cast Member (see p. 63), but most Cast Members are a step above the norm, anyway.

Saurian
5-point Racial Quality

This race gains +2 to Dexterity, +1 to Strength and Constitution, the Ambidexterity Quality, and the Infravision Power. They may use two natural weapons—their tail does D6 x Strength bashing damage, their bite D4 x Strength slashing damage. On the downside, they suffer from a three-point Minority Drawback and a three-point Zealot Drawback. Lizard men gain no points for these Drawbacks, but may "buy them off" where appropriate.

Story Ideas

The kinds of stories the Zombie Master can tell using this setting range far and wide, from simple "seek and destroy" missions, to epic raids on some sorcerer's tower, to digging through ancient tombs to find artifacts of power.

The Cast Members are unlikely to confront an actual god. When the major villains are deities, it's not as likely the protagonists would be able to stand against them directly. The gods exist mostly in the background, as a motivation for lesser powers. The enemies they face should be more along the lines of a serpent-obsessed priest of Tiamat or a horde of zombies led by a necromancer.

Most adventures should be episodic in nature. That is to say, there is no grand, epic quest on which the Cast Members journey. They seek no magic ring that must be destroyed to save the world. Instead they should often stumble into adventure, like a certain muscle-bound barbarian. One day, they come upon a witch's shack, and they must kill her before she turns them all into zombies. Another day, it's stealing a gem from the temple of some insane god. The Cast might pursue the sorts of missions they expect from other fantasy games, a mysterious stranger tells a tale of treasure in a forbidding-looking hole, but there should often be something more going on (he didn't tell you it was a powerful artifact that could help Ahriman, and that he's a priest of Ahriman, did he?). Money is a driving force in pulp fantasy, and the acquisition of wealth and power almost always a goal.

The Cast can still play a smaller but no less important role in the annals of history. Given an opportunity, they can influence the course of events through a well-cast spell and accurately timed sword blow. As they kill marauding Zombie Lords and raid sacred temples, they earn a name for themselves (and attract the attention of ever more powerful foes). Keep the tales moving at breakneck pace, with a quick setup, the introduction of a villain or goal, and loads of grief heaped upon Cast Members' heads.

The Package

In this adventure, someone of importance sends the Cast on an assignment. This person should be someone trusted and familiar to the Cast Members. On the one hand, this could be someone with whom the Cast has interacted before—a regular Supporting Cast character. On the other hand, the ZM can build a bit of backstory quickly, especially if this is the group's first adventure in Iurth, by simply explaining the relationship of this person to the Cast Members. This might be the captain of the guard, a priest of Ahura Mazda, or a sorcerer. Whoever they are, this person should be in a position of authority, capable of bestowing a great reward (or, at least, the promise of one) upon the Cast Members.

Their confidant wants the Cast Members to take something—a trinket really—to a friend several days journey away, in a nearby city. It's a scroll, a message to a dear old friend. The scroll tube has been affixed with his lead seal, so they Cast can't immediately figure out that what they're really carrying is a powerful Invocation. (What this Invocation does is left entirely up to the Zombie Master). Nefarious Cast Members may try to get a look inside the tube once out of sight of their powerful patron, but this requires a Dexterity and Craft Task with a –6 penalty in order to duplicate the seal.

Throughout their travels, minions of Ahriman attack the Cast. Start off with a simple roadside mugging involving a few orcs or goblins. Next, ratchet up the difficulty and danger by introducing an attack by the Restless Dead. As they get closer to their destination, the attacks become more blatant and persistent, and involve Ahriman zombies. It should be apparent that someone wants the scroll they carry.

And someone does. A Zombie Lord dedicated to Ahriman wants the Invocation the Cast carries with them. He does not want this scroll to fall into the wrong hands—those of the scroll's recipient. This person might be a secret agent working for the forces of Ahura Mazda, or one of his high priests, or a sorcerer of some renown.

Of course, it's not at all certain the person to whom they're supposed to deliver the package is still alive . . .

The Nameless Village

In this scenario, the Cast Members stumble upon a village that has fallen under the sway of a High priestess of Kali. Located in a remote area, this town is isolated from the rest of the world by rugged mountain passes. Primarily populated by humans, with a few dwarf craftsmen and minotaur laborers, this village appears from the outside to base its existence on sheep herding. In other words, it's a sleepy, one-horse town, good enough perhaps for lodging for the night.

Zombie Lord of Ahriman

Strength 4 | **Constitution** 3
Dexterity 3 | **Intelligence** 4
Perception 4 | **Willpower** 4
Life Points 253 | **Speed** 12
Endurance Points 38 | **Essence Pool** 47

Qualities/Drawbacks: Charisma +2, Cruel 3, Delusions (Delusions of Grandeur), The Gift, Hard to Kill 5, Increased Essence Pool 5, Zealot

Skills: Brawling 2, Dodge 4, First Aid 2, Hand Weapon (Sword) 4, Intimidation 3, Myth and Legend 5, Notice 2, Occult Knowledge 3, Smooth Talking 4

Powers/Metaphysics

Might of the Dead: Adds 200 Life Points.

Seal of the Dead: Imprint Ahriman zombies or humans with an identifying mark (the Mark of Ahriman) at a cost of one Essence point. Humans may resist by beating the Zombie Lord in a Simple Willpower Test. Marked humans rise as marked zombies. Zombies do not attack those with the mark of Ahriman. The seal may be removed by the Zombie Lord who placed it.

Rule the Dead: Zombie Lords and any sealed humans may command any sealed Ahriman zombie within earshot. Simple commands cost one Essence point. Detailed commands or large groups of zombies cost two Essence points.

Create Zombies: Ahriman's Zombie Lords can create zombies as per the Death Raising 3 power. This ability automatically functions (no Necromancy roll is necessary) and always results in an Ahriman Zombie.

Necromancy 5, Death Lordship 5, Death Mastery 5, Death Raising 5, Death Speech 5. Some of the more powerful possess Invocations or Miracles as well (due to Ahrman's influence, Zombie Lords are not subject to the restrictions regarding Miracles and other Metaphysics).

Gear: Long sword D8 x 4(16), chain mail armor AV D6 + 6(9)

For her own reasons, the priestess of Kali has chosen this place as the site from which to build her own empire. From among these simple shepherds and stable hands will arise a mighty kingdom dedicated to Kali and led by her. During the day, she poses as a simple shepherdess, though the Cast may notice the frightened glances the townspeople shoot her way (with a successful Perception and Notice Task).

When the Cast Members arrive, likely from some other adventure that takes them through the area, they find nothing amiss. People in the wilderness aren't known for their hospitality, anyway, so any strange glances and furtive movements can be explained. No one is particularly talkative, though they're not unfriendly either. Play them as ambivalent. The Cast can find a public house easily enough, where the local shopkeepers and townspeople get together for some refreshment around a warm fire. As the Cast eats and drinks, let them interact with several Supporting Cast characters. They might even get chummy, perhaps with one person in particular.

When night comes on and it becomes apparent the Cast Members plan to stay the night, things should turn unfriendly fast. The innkeeper doesn't have any room available right now, or he doesn't rent out space on his floor overnight. If the Cast insists, a few of the locals step in to encourage them to leave. Keep in mind, they don't want to hurt the Cast; in fact, they're trying to save them. Have their new-found friend try to smooth things over, but he too wants them to leave town. Have him make dire, cryptic warnings ("you should leave this place, while you can.").

During the night, Kali zombies make their appearance. Commanded by the priestess, they rouse the occupants of the town to get to work on a temple to Kali. This includes the Cast Members. It's up to them at this point whether to go for a straight up fight or to blend in with the crowd until they can get close enough to kill the priestess of Kali. Alternatively, they may even try to convince the priestess to let them join her, before they kill her once they've gained her trust.

High Priestess of Kali

Strength 3 **Constitution** 4
Dexterity 4 **Intelligence** 4
Perception 2 **Willpower** 4
Life Points 253 **Speed** 16
Endurance Points 38 **Essence Pool** 46

Qualities and Drawbacks: Attractiveness +2, Charisma +2, Cruel 2, Delusions (Delusions of Grandeur), The Gift, Hard to Kill 5, Increased Essence Pool 5, Inspiration, Zealot

Skills: Brawling 2, Dodge 4, First Aid 2, Hand Weapon (Knife) 4, Intimidation 3, Myth and Legend (Kali) 5, Notice 2, Occult Knowledge 3, Smooth Talking 4

Powers/Metaphysics

Might of the Dead: Adds 200 Life Points.

Seal of the Dead: Imprint Kali zombies or humans with an identifying mark (the Mark of Kali) at a cost of one Essence point. Humans may resist by beating the priestess in a Simple Willpower Test. Marked humans rise as marked zombies. Zombies will not attack those with the mark of Kali. The seal may be removed by the Zombie Lord who placed it.

Rule the Dead: Priestesses and any sealed humans may command any sealed Kali zombie within earshot. Simple commands cost one Essence point. Detailed commands or large groups of zombies cost two Essence points.

Create Zombies: Kali's priestesses can create zombies as per the Death Raising 3 Necromancy power. This ability automatically functions and always results in a Kali Zombie.

Miracles: The Binding, Holy Fire, Strength of Ten, Visions

Necromancy: Necromancy 5, Death Raising 5, Death Lordship 4

Gear: Knife D4 x 3(6), chain mail armor AV D6 + 6(9)

When Darkness Falls

In this Story, the Cast stumbles upon a ruined small town during their travels. Naturally, they stop to investigate. A preliminary search of the ruins turns up no immediate danger, though the ZM should periodically call for Perception and Notice checks to keep the Cast on their toes. While they investigate, call for an Intelligence and Tracking Task to try and determine what happened. If they gain two Success Levels, they can determine that a small army of saurians attacked the town (by the telltale three-toed footprints they left behind).

Then, they find a young, human girl. She's hiding in a root cellar under her house. The Cast might come upon her while they explore the ruins, with a successful Perception and Notice Task. Otherwise, as dusk approaches the Cast spots her running across a deserted street on her way back to her hiding spot. Have them make Tests to try and catch up to her. However they locate the girl, they get no information out of her before the fun starts; she's either too hungry or too scared to tell them what happened. Although many of the buildings appear to have been burned, the Cast can find a suitable place to stay (if they want to) for the night at the edge of town.

Once the sun goes down and night's dark blanket covers the sky, zombies attack. Specifically, they're zombie saurians (see Restless Dead, p. 65), and the Cast may think they've solved the mystery of the town's devastation. In fact, they are the remains of saurians who originally attacked the town. The attack is fairly predictable—a slow and steady shamble to the food. The next day, when the sun rises, the Cast can leave the abandoned town, taking their young charge with them (maybe they offer to take her to relatives, or perhaps they intend to sell her in the slave bazaar).

After a day of marching, it comes time to make camp. By this time, the girl has become pretty chatty, telling the Cast about her parents, their life in the village, and the attack by the saurians (which they should naturally assume means the saurian zombies). She's not about to tell the Cast that they're wrong. They'll discover it soon enough, for when the sun sets, a group of robed saurian cultists assault the camp, bloodshed on their minds.

The assault is stealthy, but Perception and Notice Tasks at –2 should allow the Cast to react without surprise (those with Situational Awareness or Fast Reaction Time do not need to roll). During the course of the battle, once it becomes clear the saurians can't defeat the Cast, the cultists drag the young girl away. The Cast must track them to a large building deep in the forest. Odd lights flicker from inside a cyclopean temple, and as the Cast draws near, a simple Perception Test reveals ominous chanting from within.

These are the ruins of an ancient temple dedicated to Tiamat, and her saurian priests conduct a ritual. When completed, this ritual imbues the priestess with Tiamat's power, making her an avatar of the goddess of chaos let loose on an unsuspecting world. The cultists plan to use the girl as part of their sacrifice to Tiamat. It is up to the Cast Members to infiltrate the temple and stop the ritual before the girl is killed (along with the rest of the townspeople) and Tiamat puts in a personal appearance.

Saurian Priestess

Strength 3	**Constitution** 3
Dexterity 4	**Intelligence** 2
Perception 3	**Willpower** 4
Life Points 34	**Speed** 14
Endurance Points 35	**Essence Pool** 19

Skills: Brawling 2, Hand Weapon (Sword) 3, Myth and Legend (Lizardman) 4, Occult Knowledge 4, Rituals (Summoning) 6

Qualities and Drawbacks: Delusions (Delusions of Grandeur), The Gift, Infravision, Inspiration, Minority, Zealot

Metaphysics: Holy Fire, Strength of Ten, Visions

Gear: Two swords D6 x 3(9), leather armor AV D6+1(4)

Elf Elemental Sorcerer

Adept Hero

Str 2 **Dex** 5* **Con** 4
Int 2 **Per** 5* **Wil** 3
LPs 45
EPs 29
Spd 16
Essence 39

Qualities/Drawbacks

Acute Senses (Vision)*
Adversary (Minions of Kali) (–4)
Attractiveness +1*
Delusion (Delusions of Grandeur) 1*
Elf (5)
Essence Channeling 4 (8)
The Gift (5)
Hard To Kill (5)
Honorable (–2)
Increased Essence Pool (4)
Obligation (Battle Kali) (–4)
Socially Inept (–2 with non-Elves)*

Skills

Dodge 3
First Aid 2
Hand Weapon (Long Sword) 3
Hand Weapon (Finger Blades) 2
Myth and Legend 2
Occult Knowledge 1
Science (Animals) 1*
Seduction 1
Smooth Talking 2
Stealth 2
Survival (Forest) 2*

Aspects/Metaphysics

Elemental Fire 3
Elemental Air 3
Shielding 3

* Granted or modified by Elf Quality

Gear

Backpack, Bedroll, Lantern and 6 Pints Oil, Leather Armor, 50-foot Rope, 2 Sacks, Long Sword, Retractable Finger Knives, Tinderbox, 1 Week of Traveling Rations, Water Skin, 10 Gold Pieces

Personality

Things used to be a lot simpler. At first, I was able to ignore the Ahriman/Kali business. I used to sail the seas with privateers, hunting down Tiamat's lizard man pirates. There aren't any zombies on the seas. They don't like water. And on a pirate vessel, being an elemental mage who can launch lightning bolts and rain fire down from the sky comes in very handy, indeed.

Yes, things used to be simple. We'd come into port, I'd manage to seduce at least one serving wench, and we'd drink wine and make merry. Now I will grant you that some of my fellow elves don't look kindly upon this type of behavior, but nobody ever said I was typical.

Then we met the dwarf and the minotaur, and everything changed. I found out about the zombies and the dark gods and what fate awaited the world if we didn't win out over the darkness. Maybe it was that first zombie attack that changed my mind. Or maybe it was the fact that Mitra brought me back from the dead at the behest of her cleric. Either way, I'm indebted, now. I don't like it, but that's the way it is, and though I'd never admit it openly, I like these guys.

Quote

"A little practicality, please . . . oh, isn't she a lovely vision!"

Dwarf Priest of Mitra

Adept Hero

Str 4* **Dex** 3† **Con** 4*
Int 2 **Per** 2 **Wil** 3
LPs 51
EPs 38
Spd 14
Essence 28

Qualities/Drawbacks

Adversary (Demons and Undead) 3†
Adversary (Servants of Kali) (–3)

Dwarf (5)
Essence
Channeling 2 (4)
The Gift (5)
Hard to Kill 2*
Holy Order of Light
Priest (5)
Honorable 2*
Humorless (–1)
Increased Essence Pool (2)
Inspiration (5)
Inspired Invoker†
Negative Buoyancy*
Obligation (Destroy Supernatural Evil) 3†
Resistance (Magic) 1*
Socially Inept (Pugnacious) 2*
Zealot (–3)

Skills

Craft (Weaponsmith) 2*
Craft (Weaponsmith Rune Carving) 4*
Dodge 3
Hand Weapon (Sword) 4†
Hand Weapon (Axe) 3
Myth and Legend (Pantheon of Iurth) 5†
Notice 2
Occult Knowledge 4†
Streetwise 1

Aspects/Metaphysics

Infravision*
Binding
Strength of Ten
Elemental Fire 3

* Granted or modified by Dwarf Quality
† Granted or modified by the Holy Order of Light Quality

Gear

Blessed Long Sword (+1 to hit and damage, cast 10 points of Heal Wounds twice per day), Plate Armor, 50-foot Rope, Holy Symbol, Backpack, 30 Gold Pieces

Personality

My god is Mitra. He lives in the ground. He is strong like the mountain and does not use servants to bring his messages. My power comes from Mitra himself—the power to protect. Mitra protects by killing his enemies before they can strike. My god is stronger than your god.

I know this because I have seen it. I grew up in Under Mountain, what you humans call The City of Smoke and Stone. My father was a maker of weapons. My mother, a potter. When I was a stripling, my cousin Belzak died, and became home to an Asura. He rose up and killed many dwarves, who also rose up—my mother among them. But a priest of Mitra banished the Kali zombies, using holy fire and the strength in his arms. He organized the city's defenses, and led us to victory.

I wanted to be like him, and to kill the demons and undead sent by Kali. My father gave me my sword, which he named after my mother, and I joined Mitra's temple. They showed me the strength in Mitra. Now I wander the land, seeking zombies to kill.

Quote

"In the name of all the gods of light, with the power of Mitra, I banish you back to hell!"

CHAPTER FOUR

Things are not as they once were. The taint of darkness has risen, infecting the land, the oceans—everything. Here in the East, we have not yet felt its touch, but it comes. Make no mistake of that. The power of the Dark Lord Adramalech grows, increasing by miniscule increments, but increasing nonetheless. Who is this Dark Lord, you ask? My child, the Dark Lord is an ancient and evil power, placed deep into torpor thousands of years ago. He was a master of the darkest magicks, and a forger of items of great and terrible power. Once, long ago, he ruled this world with a spiked fist, and many were murdered in his name, to sate his twisted thirst for the souls of mortals and immortals alike.

Out of a great alliance of sidhe, dwarves, gnomes and humans came forth the great warrior king Albrecht the Valiant. Albrecht wielded a sword like no other—a sword forged by the greatest dwarven smiths, enchanted by the wisest gnomish mages and blessed by the most pious sidhe priests—a sword borne with the courage and strength of a human. With this sword, Albrecht was able to shatter the Dark Lord's Apocalypse Blade, which held its master's own life essence, during the final battle. When the dust cleared, no trace of either blade could be found. The Dark Lord was gone, and Albrecht lay mortally wounded. When he passed, it was with a smile on his lips, as if the goddess Danna herself had taken his soul in her tender grasp.

With Adramalech and his blade destroyed, the legions of darkness crumbled to dust. Adramalech's body was never found, though the Elders among the sidhe say he was not destroyed, but only forced into a comatose sleep. So long as the Apocalypse Blade remained safely out of the hands of mortals, the Dark Lord would never awaken.

For millennia the world has remained at peace, but shards of the blade have resurfaced. Now, the Dark Lord has awakened in the South, and his awakening has roused the dead, who walk and murder in his name. His armies spread gradually, threatening to cover the world with a blanket of shadow. But all is not lost—the world is not yet covered in darkness. There yet remains hope, so long as there are those who are willing to stand against the darkness.

The forces of good rush to prepare themselves for the coming conflict, which will change the fate of the world and reshape entire nations. The Dark Lord has sent out his minions, the soul-drinking shedim zombies, to retrieve the pieces of the blade, so that he

might become whole again. Even the sniveling creatures of the deep—goblins and orcs—emerge en masse from their holes to join us against their former master, who has spurned them in favor of his zombie hordes. There are yet those who would wear the mantle of champion, and if they are successful the Dark Lord will be destroyed, and we may know peace. If they fail, there is no telling how many will die or suffer fates far worse than death . . .

Dawn of a Dead Age

Introduction

When people think about fantasy, they usually envision epic fantasy, or "high fantasy." These stories concern themselves with the epic struggle between good and evil, touching perhaps on some primal need for a world in which everything is either black or white. Epic fantasy has a grand scope and tells a tale of earth-shattering events. It has a sense of grand destiny.

In the plot, a small band of heroes (the Cast Members) are pulled into the sweep of history. They participate in events that decide the fate of their land, as they chase about the world in search of powerful objects—rings and swords, tomes of knowledge, or the answer to some riddle. They travel to wondrous places—the ancient sylvan glens of the elves, the white marble city of the High King, the massive underground fortresses of the dwarves. They combat evil personified, some Dark Lord who aims to dominate the world and extinguish the light of good. These somewhat ordinary characters carry a heavy burden upon their shoulders, and must confront forces far more powerful then they are.

Dawn of a Dead Age concerns itself with just such a story, of an ancient and terrible power reawakened, seeking to conquer the world. An ancient artifact of great and dark magic allows the enemy to rise again. Even now, his agents scour the land, looking for it. And it is up to the Cast Members to seek out an artifact of their own which will enable them to stand up to the Dark Lord Adramalech.

The World

Domhain (pronounced DOME-hayn) is a classic medieval fantasy world where powerful kings rule vast kingdoms, doling out lands to lords and vassals, who manage their peasants with varying degrees of success. Castles are dank and cold, even in the fanciest and most well appointed rooms, while peasants live in cottages of timber and daub. Domhain is an peaceful land, and for thousands of years there has been little in the way of true evil to speak of. Occasionally one kingdom makes war against another, or a vassal steps out of line, inciting revolution among his peasants or incurring the ire and wrath of a rival or liege, but for the most part, the world enjoys an age of peace.

Magic is real in Domhain, and every court has at least one wizard. Those who practice magic outside of the courts do well to keep their Art secret, lest they be branded servants of dark powers or worse—a threat to the king. Still, many villages boast midwives and sages, and so long as they maintain a low profile and don't step out of line, they are tolerated and even appreciated, given their skills with herbalism and the healing arts. Few humans are Inspired, as connection with the Tuatha de Dannan, the deific figures of Domhain, remains the domain of the sidhe. Necromancers and spirit mediums are rare, since death magic is the path of Adramelech, the Dark Lord. Because necromancy is a fast way to the stake and flames, mediums are generally tight-lipped about the Art.

Aside from humans, Domhain boasts sidhe (elves, pronounced SHEE), dwarves, and gnomes, and each race maintains its own laws and society. In addition to these common, "fairer" races, goblins and orcs stalk the land. These creatures have been the scourge of the good races for thousands of years, but recently have come to stand alongside the fairer races against the dark shadow, allies of convenience against a horrific foe. In the deserts to the West reside wandering tribes of minotaurs, rarely seen in civilized society but prized in the gladiatorial arenas of the human kingdoms.

The last world-shattering event occurred over five thousand years ago, when the races of the world united against the Dark Lord Adramalech, who at the time ruled most of the world, using his orc and goblin servants to wreak chaos and destruction. Adramalech sent his shedim servants out from Doitcaayr, the Citadel of Shadows, to bring the Dark Lord souls to feed his terrible and eternal hunger. He wielded vast and terrible magic and the most evil of magic swords. Finally, the leaders of the intelligent races of the world met in secret, forging a blade that could once and for all break Adramalech's power. The blade was created by the dwarves, sidhe, and gnomes, and wielded by a human. It broke Adramalech's power, but the unity among the races shattered with it. Now, although there is peace between humans, sidhe, and the rest, there is little contact. The world of men isn't suited for sidhe, and dwarves prefer their mountain strongholds. Gnomes still act as go-betweens for the sidhe and dwarves, and occasionally pop up in human cities.

Now, the time is ripe for the races to once again come together. Adramalech has awakened, spurred on by the discovery of a piece of his sword, and the race for the fate of the world is on.

Cosmology

In epic fantasy, the main characters are drawn into the grand sweep of events. They take part in grand historic eddies that began long before their birth. It is they who write the final chapter of an epic began long ago. In order to understand their role in events, it is important to know the cosmology of the world.

The cosmology of Domhain is based upon the sidhe creation myth. In Domhain's cosmology there is a single mother goddess figure, Danna. Danna maintains servants, the Tuatha de Dannan, the Tribe of Danna, who are her emissaries to the physical realm, but are forbidden to interfere directly with the natural course of events, or directly confront the forces of darkness. There is also a great adversary, the Dark Lord Adramalech, the Shadow in the South. For thousands of years, most have treated the Tuatha de Dannan and the Dark Lord as bedtime stories, though most believe in Danna. Adramalech's rise has shattered the comfort most take in their peaceful lives.

The Beginning

In the beginning was chaos, formed by the destruction of what came before. Danna, called the Power Above and Below, set about creating anew. With a breath and a kiss, Danna blew chaos into order, and formed Essence into physicality. Domhain was born.

Now there were earth, air, fire, water, night and day and stars in the sky, but no life, so Danna sent the Tuatha de Dannan to the world that they might create creatures to populate it. At first the Tuatha de Dannan were lost and confused, uncertain of how to go about using their power of creation. When they came together to sort out their thoughts, from this cooperation sprang the sidhe, wise and possessed of great power, and they helped the servants of Danna to create other creatures, beasts of the land and sea and sky. When all seemed as it should be, many Tuatha de Dannan returned home. Some few, however, remained to live among their beloved sidhe, and watch over them.

The Coming of Others

Thousands of years passed, and the sidhe, immortal and contemplative, made little progress. Danna worried that her new creation might into entropy. The sidhe were beautiful and wise, but their immortality made them loath to rush into change. To resist stagnation, Danna needed other races to challenge the sidhe and bring change. Thus again were the Tuatha de Dannan called upon. From their second attempt at creation sprang the dwarves and gnomes, possessed of qualities that would drive them to evolve. Yet still the sidhe were masters of the world, guiding the other races with great benevolence and wisdom.

As cultures arose and evolved, an alien race came to Domhain. These were the dragons, dimensional travelers who were curious to learn of new cultures. They took on sidhe form and walked among the lesser races. Some dragons became advisors to the sidhe and their allies, while others turned to evil, becoming powerful nemeses. Before long, however, dragons became a fixture in the world and soon it was as they had always been.

The Fall

Eventually, those Tuatha de Dannan who remained in the world abused their powers to enslave and control. They had become worldly, and arrogant in their power to make and unmake reality. The sidhe called upon them to depart. Some Tuatha de Dannan understood and withdrew willingly, to atone for their sins. Others looked inside themselves and saw only darkness. Led by the greatest of their number, the Dark Lord Adramalech, they became the shedim, and sought to conquer the sidhe. While the immortals used their magic, and the dwarves massed great armies to engage the shedim in battle, the shedim

used their now-corrupt powers of creation to breed goblins and orcs to stand against the dwarven armies. The black citadel of Doitcaayr, the stronghold of the Dark Lord, was raised in the South. The Shadow forged for himself a sword into which he placed all his power, so that he could become invulnerable and feed upon the souls of those who fell to it.

The fair races were more than a match for the orc and goblin armies, and it seemed the sidhe and their allies would be victorious. A powerful spell wrought by over one hundred sidhe lords stripped the shedim of their physicality. This was to be the moment of victory for the forces of light. Just as the spell was complete, however, the orcs staged a horrible and brilliant retaliation, breaking through the lines and capturing the sidhe magi. At Doitcaayr, they were tortured, driven mad, murdered, and given to the shedim as new bodies—the first zombies on Domhain.

Without their most powerful magi, the sidhe had few advantages left. Although the people of Domhain fought for their lives, the armies of darkness spread quickly across the world. Even the dragons felt the sting; Adramalech sent his shedim zombies to hunt dragons to extinction, and many left Domhain, seeking less dangerous worlds on which to live. Those few who stayed and survived the purge went deep into hiding to preserve their race.

The Rise of Humanity

The sidhe and dwarves could not battle Adramalech and his minions alone. In desperation, several sidhe and a few dwarves retreated to a remote island to plan and create. The fruits of their labors were a new race—a short-lived and hardy people who fought almost as well as the dwarves, but possessed a brilliant spark of creativity. They could be as vicious as they could be honorable, and possessed a tenacity and thirst for greatness unparalleled in the world. This new race was humankind. The arrogance of the sidhe in creating a race on their own angered Danna, and she stripped them of much of their power and wisdom even as she loved the passion and fire in the souls of creations.

The humans bred quickly and spread across the world. Soon, their natural affinity for war combined with the dwarves' weaponry, sidhe blessings, and gnomish magic drove the orcs and goblins back, and it seemed the forces of light might emerge victorious. A final stand was still to come as the armies of light finally converged upon Doitcaayr.

Victory

Sidhe sages prophesied that it would be Albrecht the Valiant, greatest among men, who would strike the final blow against Adramalech, and they and the other fair races created a mighty sword that could break the Dark Lord's power. Forged in secret in the great dwarven undercity of Tor Merrin, and infused with the magic of sidhe, gnome, and Tuatha de Dannan, this sword imbued Albrecht with the power to stand up to the dark and fallen celestial.

The armies of Domhain rode south toward Doitcaayr, smashing through orc and goblin lines. The shedim retreated toward the Black Tower and their lord. As Adramalech emerged from his citadel to face his enemies, Albrecht strode forward and the battlefield fell still. The two clashed, their swords ringing out across the land. Adramalech found to his horror that the blade Albrecht wielded granted him immunity from the Dark Lord's magic, luck to dodge his blows, and strength enough to injure Adramalech. At last, with a single, mighty blow, Albrecht shattered Adramalech's sword.

A bright flash, like the sun come down to earth, blanketed the battlefield. Adramalech was gone.

Albrecht lay dead upon the battlefield and the undead among the ranks of the Dark Lord crumbled to dust. The orcs and goblins quit the field, retreating to the depths of the earth to nurse their defeat. And the four pieces of Adramalech's Apocalypse Blade scattered to the four winds. Albrecht's sword had vanished, as well. The war was won.

The fairer races went home to rebuild. Many sidhe simply left for a far off land they could still call their own; the humans were now the most populous and dominant race in the world. The dwarves returned to the isolation of their undercities, though their goods remained in demand among the humans and they continued to trade through their gnomish agents. The goblins and orcs brooded in dark places, and plotted their revenge.

The Tuatha de Dannan withdrew, and would no longer use their powers to assist the fairer races. Perhaps this resulted from laws imposed by Danna, or out of fear that should they again use their power, they might fall to darkness once again. Regardless, few Tuatha de Dannan remain in the world, and those who do remain in disguise, acting as advisors and sages, never interfering in the natural course of events.

For millennia, the world has been calm and peaceful. Then the dead awoke.

The Rise

Domhain is a world just beginning to experience the Rise. Pieces of the Apocalypse Blade have resurfaced and the Dark Lord has awakened. Though still insubstantial, he has sent his consciousness across the land to contact his former minions and let them know of his return. Also felt by every sage and sorcerer in the world, those among the wise knew dark times were ahead. But the consciousness of the Dark Lord's thoughts had another, more immediate, and insidious, effect.

The first sightings of the undead came on the outskirts of civilization, in small towns, farms, and villages. Dead relatives suddenly sat up from their daisies of honor and attacked their loved ones, hungry for living flesh. These zombies then slowly made for Adramalech's fortress in the South, awaiting the time to spread across the world.

More shocking have been reports of a new brood of shedim zombies leading the undead hordes in the south. Sidhe scholars had believed the shedim were extinct, and none seem to know from whence these new monsters come. There are rumors they are traitorous sidhe, but these remain unconfirmed.

With Adramalech's return, the orcs and goblins have emerged from hiding to discover their master had turned on them; the only goblinoid soldiers Adramalech appears interested in now are undead, who would not break and run in the face of defeat. Orcs and goblins have been slaughtered to join the ranks of Adramalech's army of the dead; survivors of this holocaust have crawled to the fair races, begging forgiveness for past crimes.

The Rise has become a plague to the people of Domhain, and continues to this day. Loved ones are bound at the moment of death, and burned to ash to prevent their arising. The army of the dead has begun its march from Doitcaayr, and many settlements in the South have already fallen. The shedim and their zombies do not take prisoners, and every soldier who falls in battle arises moments later to join the army of the dead, which grows exponentially in size. Women, children, and the infirm are captured and shipped off to camps, where the shedim butcher them alive to feed their undead troops, in a gruesome preview of what awaits the living if Adramalech's zombie apocalypse succeeds.

Adversaries

Adramalech has many servants under his banner, mostly varied undead culled from all manner of creatures across Domhain.

Approximately a century ago, a sect of sidhe arose, resentful of their loss of dominance to humanity, and Adramalech took notice. Through dreams and visions, Adramalech promised these "shadow sidhe" power beyond their wildest imagining. All they needed do was kill in his name and powers over life and death would be theirs. The shadow sidhe rose up against their race in the forests, but were outnumbered and driven out by the other, untainted sidhe.

The shadow sidhe made their way in secret to the ruins of Doitcaayr, where Adramalech gave them the power they craved, twisted to his ends. The shadow sidhe died, and a new brood of shedim was born, with the power to create more of their kind by killing sidhe, and to raise basic zombies. Shedim rode in search of the Apocalypse Blade, and began to rebuild Adramalech's armies. Their earliest missions, in fact, were "diplomatic" visits to goblin and orc tribes, to inform them that their master had returned. Orcs and goblins came to Doitcaayr in droves, but were slaughtered wholesale to be raised as zombies in the Dark Lord's service. Surviving goblinoids fled north to ally with the fair races they once warred against.

Live shadow sidhe serve in Adramalech's armies, hoping to prove themselves worthy of elevation to shedim. They and evil humans are the only living creatures allowed in the Dark Lord's service. Humans and shadow sidhe in Adramalech's employ are universally necromancers, Inspired of Adramalech, or Zombie Lords, allowing them some measure of control over the hungry dead.

The Dark Lord Adramalech

Adramalech is still trapped in spirit form, and needs his assembled sword in order to reincarnate. Despite this hindrance, he has managed to rebuild his power base through the force of his terrible will. He has created new shedim to lead his armies, and recruited shadow sidhe to serve him. He has raised new armies of undead, mostly from amongst the goblins and orcs he believes betrayed him. But most importantly, he has turned his terrible will to the task of finding his Apocalypse Blade. Shedim agents scour the land looking for information, while Adramalech himself sends forth his consciousness to seek the missing pieces.

Shedim Zombies

Shedim zombies were once sidhe, but have become perverse and twisted. The original shedim were tortured and experimented upon by Adramalech millennia ago, murdered and revived dozens of times, going gradually insane in the process. Finally, their sanity shattered, the demonic shedim possessed the bodies, creating powerful zombies. When Albrecht vanquished Adramalech, the power of the shedim was broken, their bodies crumbled to dust. But the demons lived on in spirit form and have new bodies to inhabit, offered up *voluntarily*, by the shadow sidhe. Currently the shedim are spread throughout the world, searching for the pieces of the Apocalypse Blade.

The shedim drain Essence, but only consume half (see *AFMBE*, p. 155), the other half is transferred to Adramalech to help him reincarnate. Characters who discover this secret may be able to find a way to stall or slow the Rise. Shedim can also feed on Essence drained through their necromantic bolts (Death Lordship 5). Shedim are not bound by Essence Channeling and can use their Soul Sucker Aspect to replenish their Essence Pool. Otherwise, shedim replenish lost Essence at the rate of eight points per minute. Finally, any sidhe who die from this Soul Sucking arise as new shedim zombies. Shedim are powerful zombies, and act as the lieutenants and gen-

Shedim Zombie

Strength 4 | **Constitution** 5 [+2]
Dexterity 6 [+2] | **Intelligence** 3
Perception 2 | **Willpower** 4 [+2]
Dead Points 42 | **Speed** 18
Endurance Points n/a | **Essence Pool** 47

Skills: Brawling 2, Hand Weapon (Sword) 5 [+5], Magic Bolt 5 [+5], Necromancy 5 [+10]

Attack: Broadsword D8 x 4(16), soul sucking (8 Essence loss)

Weak Spots: All [0], Fire [–5], Blessed Weapons (Sidhe) [–1]

Getting Around: The Quick Dead [+10], Climbing [+2], The Lunge [+3]

Strength: Strong Like Bull [+5], Damage Resistant [+5]

Senses: Like the Living [+1], Life Sense [+4]

Sustenance: Weekly [+4], Soul Sucker [+5]

Intelligence: Language [+1], Long Term Memory [+5], Problem Solving [+15]

Special Abilities: Death Lordship 5 [+10], Dragon's Bane Poison Blood (see Dragons, p. 82), Increased Essence Pool [+5], Mystic Targeting [+3], Regeneration (1/Turn) [+5]

Spreading the Love: Only the Dead [–2] (sidhe killed by shedim rise as new shedim, others as regular zombies)

Power: 106

erals of Adramalech's forces. They are not intended as common group encounters, but rather as special "boss" character encounters.

The Walking Dead

Zombies are a recent occurrence in Domhain. The negative energy created by Adramalech's slow awakening has caused many of the recently dead to arise again the world over. Any who are killed by the shedim also rise as zombies, and in this manner the Dark Lord rapidly builds his armies as his forces spread ever further north.

Half the people who die in Domhain rise as zombies within D4(2) minutes of death. Even sidhe can rise as Domhain zombies, if killed by any means other than a shedim soul-sucking attack. Zombies on Domhain use the sidebar stats, but keep any Aspect or Supernatural Qualities they possessed prior to death when they rise. This means Psychic Invokers who rise can still use their Invocations, for example.

Zombies retain memories and values from their prior lives, but lose their ability to communicate and are tragically compelled not only to feed, but also to serve Adramalech's dark aims. These creatures are tortured and pathetic souls, driven to commit acts of atrocity they never would otherwise do. Cast Members with Necromancy and the Death Lordship power may be able to temporarily free these creatures from Adramalech's will, but a weekly effort is required, and the necromancer must roll Willpower and Necromancy against Adramalech's Willpower and Necromancy (D10 + 22)! The Cast Member may add the zombie's Willpower as a bonus to the Test if the creature was good in life. Worse, even when freed of Adramalech's influence, the zombie must feed on fresh meat daily.

Domhain Zombie

Strength 4 | **Constitution** 2
Dexterity 2 | **Intelligence** 2
Perception 1 | **Willpower** 2
Dead Points 34 | **Speed** 4
Endurance Points n/a | **Essence Pool** 13

Skills: Brawling 2, Hand Weapon (choose) 3 [+3]

Attack: Bite D4 x 4(8), claws D6 x 4(12), or by weapon

Weak Spot: All [0]

Getting Around: Life-Like [+3], Climbing [+2]

Strength: Strong Like Bull [+5], Claws [+8]

Senses: Like the Dead [0], Life Sense [+2]

Sustenance: Daily [0], All Flesh Must Be Eaten! [0]

Intelligence: Long-Term Memory [+5], Problem Solving [+15]

Special Abilities: Regeneration (1/Turn) [+5]

Spreading the Love: Only the Dead [–2]

Power: 51

Dracozombies

Dragons who die as a result of shedim soul-sucking attacks (but *not* from shedim blood poison) rise within moments as fearsome creatures known as dracozombies. Dracozombies retain many of the abilities they had in life, but are not quite as powerful, tough, or intelligent. Dracozombies are always completely beholden to the shedim who created them, and one of the most fearsome sights on Domhain is that of a shedim riding the back of a dracozombie.

The Living

Various races make their home in Domhain, struggling against the minions of Adramalech.

Dragons

Dragons are dimensional travelers who adopted Domhain as their home. Millennia ago they were common, painting the skies rainbow hues as the sun glinted off of their red, blue, yellow, green, white, black, even gold and silver scales. Adramalech had dragons hunted to the brink of extinction, seeing the powerful creatures as threats to his rule. Now dragons are rare creatures. Few know the hiding places of surviving dragons, and none reveal such secrets except in the direst circumstances. If a character can convince a dragon to render assistance, the creatures have knowledge and power far beyond those of even the sidhe. The only creatures that dragons fear are the shedim. Dragons who die to shedim soul-sucking attacks rise as undead dracozombies.

Dwarves

Dwarves in Domhain are exactly as described in **Chapter Two: Swords, Sorcery, and Shambling**—subterranean miners and craftsmen, who love a good brew, good song, and a good fight.

Tuatha De Dannan

Tuatha de Dannan are seldom encountered, and when they do appear, they masquerade as powerful wizards rather than show their true angelic form. They are allowed to aid the forces of light in indirect ways, but may not engage in battle with the forces of darkness, though they may defend themselves if cornered. It is unknown whether mystical or divine forces block such interference, or if the Tuatha de Dannan wish to gauge the aptitude of Domhain's people to defend their world.

Dracozombie

Strength 20	**Constitution** 2
Dexterity 12	**Intelligence** –2
Perception 7	**Willpower** 2
Dead Points 98	**Speed** 28, 56 flying [+8]
Endurance Points n/a	**Essence Pool** 41

Skills: Brawling 8 [+12], Dodge 5 [+5], Intimidation 10 [+20], Magic Bolt (Fire Breath) 8 [+14]

Attacks: Bite D4 x 20(40) and claws D6 x 20(60)

Weak Spot: All [0]

Getting Around: Special Dexterity [+32]

Strength: Special Strength [+50], Damage Resistant [+5], Claws [+8]

Senses: Like Nothing You've Seen [+10], Infravision [+14]

Sustenance: Who Needs Food? [+8]

Intelligence: Dumb as Dead Wood [0]

Special Abilities: Acid Blood [+5], Mystic Targeting [+3], Regeneration (1/Turn) [+5], Spew Flame [+20]

Spreading the Love: Dracozombies do not Spread the Love

Power: 219

Dragon

Strength 20
Constitution 15
Dexterity 12
Intelligence 10
Perception 13
Willpower 12
Life Points 98
Speed 54, 108 flying
Endurance Points 146
Essence Pool 132

Qualities: Age 20, Damage Resistance, Fast Reaction Time, The Gift, Hard to Kill 10, Increased Essence Pool 10, Infravision, Inspiration, Life Sense, Mystic Targeting, Natural AV D8 x 5(20), Regenerate (15/Turn), Situational Awareness, Track by Scent

Special Attacks: Spew Flame (30 damage, every other Turn, requires a Dexterity and Magic Bolt Task to hit (Mystic Targeting bonus applies), and can be dodged normally.)

Attacks: Bite D4 x 10(20), claw D6 x 20(60) and tail D4 x 20(40)

Metaphysics: Dragons have access to all Metaphysics, and do not require Essence Channeling. In addition, for five Essence points, they can shapeshift into any living creature. The form can be maintained indefinitely, and changing back costs no Essence. Many are also students of Necromancy (level 5 in all abilities). The most ancient and powerful know all Invocations at level 10, all Miracles, and all Necromancy abilities at level 5.

Skills: Brawling 9, Dodge 7, Hand Weapon (any three) 8, Instruction 4, Intimidation 10, Magic Bolt (Fire Breath) 10, Myth and Legend (Domhain) 10, Notice 8, Occult Knowledge 10, Stealth 5. These are skills of note. Most Dragons will have at least a few ranks in any necessary skill.

Gear: Dragons are said to guard vast hordes of treasure easily equal to a king's ransom.

Weakness: The blood of shedim is poison to dragons. Shedim often coat their weapons in blood before hunting, and hundreds of dragons have fallen to this toxin, which serves two purposes. The first is a corrosive that allows the poison to automatically penetrate a dragon's natural armor. Secondly, the blood is a nerve toxin, Strength 15, which only affects dragons. If the dragon fails its roll against the poison, it suffers a D8(4) loss to Constitution each round for D6(3) rounds. If the dragon's Constitution score reaches zero, the beast dies.

The Affairs of Wizards

Although the Tuatha de Dannan do not meddle in the affairs of mortals in the defense of Domhain, the same cannot be said for affairs of the heart. It is said that those capable of wielding magic possess Tuatha blood in their veins, or themselves might be celestials in disguise. Players who select The Gift Quality for their Cast Members might consider themselves the children of a union between Tuatha de Dannan and mortal.

Tuatha de Dannan possess mastery over all aspects and applications of Essence. All Metaphysics are available to them, and if threatened they bring vast power to bear in self-defense. The few who have revealed themselves claim to be servants of "The Power Above and Below." The sidhe know the Tuatha de Dannan as the Tribe of Danna, who the sidhe presume to be this Power. Tuatha de Dannan enter into conflict so rarely that statistics have not been provided for them, though they should at least be on par with ancient dragons.

Gnomes

Gnomes serve as go-betweens and mediators for the other races; easygoing and cheerful, they make ideal dignitaries. There are two general "subspecies" of gnome—forest gnomes and mountain gnomes—although the differences are cosmetic, based on the locale of the gnome's home community. Forest gnomes live deep in the forests and get along well with sidhe, while mountain gnomes live among the dwarves. When not earning their keep as traveling merchants, entertainers, and diplomats, gnomes can be found tinkering with whatever inventions currently occupy their attention.

Humans

Humans push themselves hard to achieve greatness, and many of the greatest heroes in the world are human. Unfortunately, the very qualities that drive humanity towards greatness may also be the downfall of the race. Humans are quarrelsome and willing to go to war over simple differences in philosophy. In fact, humans and shadow sidhe are the only living creatures Adramalech allows to serve in his army. Still, it was a human arm that shattered the Apocalypse Blade those thousands of years ago, so hope is not lost for humanity.

Orcs and Goblins

Once the core of Adramalech's forces, the Dark Lord has turned from the orcs and goblins in favor of the undead, and now his former servants seek revenge. Recently, both races have joined the fight alongside the fair races, proof that goblinoids can turn their backs on evil if they so choose. However, old habits die hard, and goblins and orcs are wily and deadly creatures, not to be taken lightly.

Sidhe

Sidhe are tall, slender, and noble, and view the other races of the world as children in need of their guidance. As a result, they act haughty and condescending. The sidhe are born of nature, and refer to themselves as *Clann Aírune*, which roughly translates to "Children of the Forest." The sidhe tongue is as close to a universal language as exists in Domhain, though the version spoken by humans is tainted by dialect and slang. Sidhe only die through violent means, and the death of a sidhe is mourned by all her kind. Millions of sidhe perished in the first war against the Dark Lord, and the race has never fully recovered; their numbers continue to dwindle. Tired of the world, many sidhe journey to a distant island paradise where they can live peacefully until the end of time. However, the Dark Lord's arms may

Shadow Sidhe

Shadow sidhe have turned from Danna and been stripped of their natural Gift and Inspiration Qualities. Most shadow sidhe are base and evil creatures, though a few rare individuals seek to repent and redeem themselves. Sidhe can sense when one of their kind has Fallen, which makes it difficult for shadow sidhe to pass among the fair races. If the ZM decides to allow shadow sidhe characters, they are created as standard elves (see p. 22), though if Inspired only gain miracles from Adramalech.

stretch even to this sidhe retreat, and many again take up arms to combat the threat of the Shadow in the South.

Sidhe

5-point Racial Quality

Prerequisite: The Gift

Sidhe gain +2 to Dexterity, the Acute Senses (Vision), Attractiveness +1, and Inspiration Qualities, +1 level in the Science (Animals) and Survival (Forest) skills, Communion 1, as per the Invocation (this is an exception to the rule forbidding Invocations and Miracles, and the sidhe can take no other Invocations, though they can improve Communion). On the downside, they have two levels of Socially Inept, as standard elves, as well as a two-point Delusion (Delusions of Grandeur), a four-point Adversary (Minions of Shadow), and a one-point Honorable Drawback.

Other Monsters

Any creature the ZM can think of could be used in this setting. Be creative, and use the statistics provided for various creatures throughout this and other AFMBE books to draw up stats for new monsters. To this end, we highly recommend Atlas of the Walking Dead, which contains a wealth of undead and optional rules ideal for Dungeons and Zombies. While Domhain has an epic storyline, there can be other adventures in the world. There are thousands of years between the end of the first war with Adramalech and his reawakening. During this time there are evil wizards to overcome, ruins to be explored, and political intrigue to be had. An example of an improvised monster, a werewolf in beast form, appears nearby.

Werewolves (Beast Form)

Strength 4 **Constitution** 4
Dexterity 4 **Intelligence** 1
Perception 4 **Willpower** 2
Life Points 50 **Speed** 16
Endurance Points n/a **Essence Pool** 15

Skills: Brawling 5, Tracking 3

Attack: Claws D4 x 4(8) and bite D4 x 4(8) plus infection

Special Abilities: Ambidexterity, Damage Resistance (normal weapons). Werewolves suffer only half damage from normal weapons; however, fire and silver deal double damage to them, and magical weapons and attacks affect them normally. Werewolves can infect a human with their bite. Each time a Cast Member is bitten, the ZM should secretly roll a Difficult Constitution Test at –4 to determine whether lycanthropy was contracted. Eating a sprig of wolfsbane within 24 hours of being bitten grants the Cast Member another Test (ZM makes the roll secretly) at no penalty, but the Cast Member eating the sprig must roll a Simple Constitution Test or become ill with vomiting and nausea for D4(2) hours. Those infected transform into werewolves during the three nights of the full moon each month and rampage under the control of the ZM.

The Story

Unlike many other Deadworlds, where the ZM is presented with several options for using the material, Dawn of a Dead Age is concerned with an epic story—the battle of the forces of good against Adramalech. Thus, the story should follow the format of the epic, as outlined by Professor Joseph Campbell. This he called the Hero's Journey, and summarized the major elements common to the mythic quest.

Much has been written over the years about Campbell's Monomyth, the story structure upon which tales ranging from Perseus to Star Wars are based. The Zombie Master should be aware of this structure, and present Dawn of a Dead Age appropriately. You don't have to be an expert on Professor Campbell's work, though you might enjoy reading *The Writer's Journey* by Christopher Vogler, which distills Campbell's work for the aspiring storyteller.

The Ordinary World

Dawn of a Dead Age begins in a world familiar to the Cast Members, the ordinary world of a fantasy setting. Although in this epic story the Cast Members quest to save Domhain from Adramalech's grasp, the story should begin before they ever learn about it. The ZM should run one or two game sessions without any mention of zombies or Adramalech, so they can get a feel for their characters and the setting, and thus become familiar with the "ordinary world" of this fictional setting.

All manner of adventures could be had among the peoples, towns, and ruins of Domhain before the Rise. The ZM should run through one or two adventures common to fantasy roleplaying—a dungeon crawl or an assault on orc raiders. The goal is to get the players to forget they are playing a game of fantasy horror, so no mention of zombies should be made. They might even suspect they are playing a **Unisystem** fantasy game instead of *AFMBE.*

On one of their adventures, the Cast should uncover a curious relic—the pommel and cross guard of an apparently shattered sword, kept in a velvet-lined, wooden box. This might be among the treasure of some fell creature, for example, or among the prized possessions of some necromancer. Indeed, this necromancer could be an agent of Adramalech, who uncovered this first piece of the Apocalypse Blade, realized its importance, and planned to bring it to the South. The Cast should learn none of this, however; to them, it should simply be a mysterious broken sword.

Alternatively, one of the Cast Members might inherit the pommel of the Apocalypse Blade as a family heirloom, or among the reward for some service they provide ("thank you for saving our town, here is a sack of gold, and this ancient relic"). Unwrapping it somehow awakens its power. Either way, give no hint of the pommel's importance, at least not yet.

The Call to Adventure

Once the Cast has the shard of the Apocalypse Blade in their possession, zombies attack the heroes. This should appear to be a random encounter of some kind, perhaps after they make camp for the night. The zombies do not pay particular attention to the Apocalypse Blade, however. They have simply been attracted by its dark power, and have not been sent to retrieve the relic for Adramalech.

The next time they enter civilization, a Tuatha de Dannan disguised as a human sorcerer comes to the Cast with a mission. While they rest and make merry in a tavern, a mysterious stranger approaches them. He seems to know at lot about them, which should make the Cast a little uncomfortable, and he also seems to know about the relic they carry. He drops ominous hints about its power and history—"You know not what you carry, for if you did you would not rest so comfortably," and the like. For more action oriented groups, a band of ne'er-do-wells might make trouble, prompting the Tuatha de Dannan to step in and send an empowered servant to save them (like a certain Jedi in a certain cantina). These thugs sense the power of the relic, perhaps, and attempt to make trouble, or they might be agents of Adramalech.

The Tuatha de Dannan, who calls himself Gadreel, tells the group about the Adramalech's history once they are in private. He refuses to take the pommel for himself, and instead charges the Cast to find the other pieces of the Apocalypse Blade, at which point he will again contact them. Unfortunately, he does not know where the other shards of the shattered sword are. Throughout the rest of the epic, Gadreel can appear periodically to help the Cast at desperate times, or to provide vital clues when they are stumped. Similarly, the ZM can introduce other characters who assist the Cast in Gadreel's name (a good way to provide skills or abilities the Cast Members lack).

Moving Along

One way in which the ZM can get the Cast to move from encounter to encounter is to treat the shards of the Apocalypse Blade as a kind of divining or dowsing rod guiding them to other pieces. They might simply find themselves moving in the right direction, or the character carrying the pieces might have visions and strange dreams involving their next destination.

Crossing the Threshold

This is where the Cast sets out on their journey, and discovers the nature of the evil confronting them. This is where the story really takes off, and the Cast enters the special world of the epic. If they refuse Gadreel's call to adventure, the Cast faces increasingly brazen and deadly zombie attacks until they set out on their quest.

In order to demonstrate the stakes both they and the world face, the next encounter should involve the shedim. While they travel, they are chased by a shedim riding a dracozombie and accompanied by Domhain zombies. Perhaps they are attacked by waves of zombies after they have made camp for the night, or zombies surprise them on the side of the road.

The ZM should overwhelm the Cast, with five or six zombies for each character, and the shedim and dracozombie should pose a serious risk to them. They should be hopelessly outnumbered as the battle begins. The goal here is to get them to flee. During their flight, the Cast stumbles upon sidhe ruins in the forest.

The ruins radiate a sense of tremendous age, and Gifted Cast Members sense they are in a place of power that was once a holy site. The zombies and shedim cannot enter the ruins, so for the time being they are safe. Suddenly, they are surprised by the sidhe who maintain the site as one of their havens.

Initially, the sidhe simply provide shelter, food, and healing to what they perceive to be weary travelers. The leader of the community wants to know why one of Adramalech's fell servants chases the group, offering a perfect opportunity for the Cast to reveal their mission. If they are reluctant, as they might be, the sidhe leader drops loud hints that he senses the reason—as a Gifted character, he can perceive the supernatural power of the Apocalypse Blade. Once they explain Gadreel's mission, the sidhe divulge two things: First, the servants of Adramalech seek the Apocalypse Blade, too; second, they have a piece of the blade in safekeeping. The sidhe turn it over to the Cast once they are sure they intend to destroy the blade (though they do not know how).

Finally, if the Cast behaves well around the sidhe, they can later call on them for assistance (which becomes important later on in the epic).

Allies and Dangers

This is the meat of the Epic campaign. Here, the Cast journeys from place to place, making allies and facing various dangers. Throughout, it is up to the ZM to link the various encounters together, though commonly the Cast should stumble upon the other pieces of Adramalech's sword by accident.

Roskildeland

Beyond the eastern forests lies a great mountain range, where rest the ruins of the City of Roskildeland. Once the greatest dwarven city in the East, these dark caverns have fallen to ruin and been overrun by orcs and goblins. More recently, a plague has ravaged the inhabitants, leaving the tunnels ridden with zombies, and the few surviving orcs and goblins fight a losing battle to keep the undead hordes at bay.

The Cast could end up in Roskildeland as they make their way through Domhain. For example, a dwarf Cast Member might mention they are close to the ruins, and he has an uncle who fights to reclaim it from goblinkind; perhaps they can find hospitality there. On the other hand, the Cast might find the path they're taking blocked by several shedim, and attempt to avoid them by traveling through the underground ruins.

Remember, Adramalech has targeted the orcs and goblins like the other races of Domhain, so they are not necessarily hostile. This can make for an interesting encounter, as the Cast makes certain assumptions and the orcs and goblins try to overcome their stereotype. If the ZM uses the "dwarf uncle" hook, this Supporting Cast Member could help smooth things over. For their part, the goblinkind initially watch the Cast from the shadows. If things go badly, don't be afraid to have a fight or two before some peacemaker on the goblin side steps in.

If everything has been smoothed over, and the orcs and goblins demonstrate their good intentions, the Cast is given permission to make their way through the ancient dwarven city. They even provide a goblin guide to show them the way to the other side of the mountain. Along the way, which should take several days worth of travel, the Cast stumbles upon the lair of an insane dragon deep in the mountain. This beast guards the crosspiece of the Apocalypse Blade as part of its treasure horde.

As a final note, if the Cast works well with the goblins and orcs (and any dwarves that may be present), they can later call on them for assistance (which becomes important later on in the epic).

Goroth Desert

In the western deserts, the Cast stumbles upon the camp of some minotaur nomads. The minotaurs of the west travel across the barren, rocky landscape chasing herds of acuna (a kind of giant lizard). They live in domed tents of hide and wood always arranged around a central, community fire.

The minotaurs are wary at first; they know people from the east come to kidnap minotaurs and sell them into slavery. If the Cast is not cautious, they could end up being attacked. At first, the minotaurs send them away, and make veiled threats, but they do not attack unless they themselves are attacked. The Cast must somehow gain their trust (a successful Intelligence and Storytelling Task could work; the minotaurs like a good tale). If convinced of the party's good intentions, the minotaur warriors take the Cast to see their shamaness.

Griffon

Strength 9 | **Constitution** 7
Dexterity 5 | **Intelligence** 1 (animal)
Perception 5 | **Willpower** 5
Life Points 106 | **Speed** 34, 59 flying
Endurance Points 94 | **Essence Pool** 32

Attack: Bite D8 x 10(40) and talons D6 x 9(27)

Skills: Brawling 2, Dodge 1, Notice 3

Special Abilities: Beak (Bite), Enhanced Sight, Fast Reaction Time, Flight, Natural Toughness, Nerves of Steel, Talons

The shamaness is ancient and feeble, and lives in a darkened tent inhaling the fumes of strange-smelling incense. When they enter, she appears to be in a trance. She says the Cast Members are great warriors, and she has foreseen their arrival. In order to find what they seek, they must travel to the Valley of Bones, where lives the griffon. At this, the assembled minotaurs murmur with concern and anger—the griffon has killed many of their kind.

With the shamaness' words still ringing in their ears, the minotaurs expect the Cast to travel to the Valley of Bones and bring back proof of their victory. They give the Cast no choice in the matter, and send one of their kind to serve as guide. The Valley of Bones, which gets its name from the bones of the griffon's meals littering the valley floor, lies three days' travel to the northwest.

This is a straight up battle between the Cast and a griffon. While they travel along the valley floor, it swoops down and attacks them. The particulars of the battle are left to the Zombie Master's discretion, though it continues to attack until either one of the Cast Members are dead (which it carries off to its lair as a meal) or it is defeated.

There is no piece of the Apocalypse Blade in the monster's lair, which rests high up on a mountain peak. When they return to the minotaur camp with proof of their deed, however, the shamaness produces a bundle of reptile hide wrapped around a piece of the Apocalypse Blade. Again, when unwrapped, the shard awakens. As they depart, she tells them they bear a terrible burden, and the world rests heavily upon their shoulders.

If the Cast handles themselves well with the minotaurs, they can later call on them for assistance (which becomes important later on in the epic).

The City of Narendil

Narendil is the capital of a human kingdom, a bastion of good ruled over by the High King Corriden. It lies in the center of a vast, grassy plain, from which the valiant horsemen of Narendil patrol the surrounding countryside. Narendil represents everything good and noble and wise about humanity, and it is called the Light of the East. Unfortunately, it is also the hiding place for the final piece of the Apocalypse Blade, the gems that go in the sword's pommel and cross guard. These have been the heirlooms of the Royal House of Narendil for generations, kept in safekeeping by her kings. Adramalech has learned of the jewels from spies and sent the shedim to recover them. An army of undead lays siege to the city in order to claim it for their own.

The Cast discovers this predicament while they travel through the kingdom. From many miles off, they can see the proud spires of the city jutting into the sky, and the black stain of zombies surrounding the city's walls like swarming ants.

On the one hand, the Cast may assume they cannot help Narendil and attempt to avoid the army. On the other, they might correctly figure out that this is where they need to go next. Either way, no matter what they decide, a band of scouts from the city ambushes the Cast. The scouts are not mounted, but instead hide under canvass tarps disguised with tall grass in order to surprise their prey. They capture the Cast, rather than kill them. It is important for the scouts to succeed, so the ZM should be careful in running this encounter. A bunch of dead scouts or Cast Members does no one any good.

The leader of the scouts, a man named Jarradan, interrogates the group personally. Once he is satisfied they are not servants of the Dark Lord, he advises them to avoid the city, for it is besieged by the forces of darkness. If the Cast asks whether he knows the reason for this, Jarradan answers only that the shedim look for something within the city walls. Should the Cast Members stress the importance of their getting inside the city, Jarradan agrees to take them through a secret passage they use. Along the way, they should encounter at least one band of zombies, and have to either fight or sneak past them.

The Cast encounters King Corriden and he proves to be a honorable and heroic man. They should make their mission known to him. At this point, the High King reveals the final pieces of the Apocalypse Blade—three gems kept in a simple velvet pouch. They are black, but suddenly glow with an inner fire once brought before the party (and the other shards of the blade). The King commands Jarradan to guide the Cast beyond the city walls.

If the Cast acquits themselves well in Narendil, they can later call on King Corriden for assistance (which becomes important later on in the epic).

The Supreme Ordeal

By now, the Cast has all the pieces of the shattered Apocalypse Blade, and they have all awakened. It's time for the final confrontation.

At this point, Gadreel promised to appear to the Cast and tell them what they're supposed to do next. He does not. They might suspect the sorcerer cannot get through the shedim blockade and agree to let Jarradan lead them beyond the kingdom's borders. Either way, they have to get out of the city, because the forces of darkness surround them; if they remain in the city when it falls to the shedim, they will almost certainly lose the sword.

Unfortunately, the shedim besieging Narendil sense the power of the Apocalypse Blade shards and immediately give chase. The ZM should let the Cast get beyond Narendil's walls and stage a few close calls with zombie outriders and stragglers. Then, suddenly, dracozombies take wing and chase after them. This should be a harrowing pursuit across open ground, as the shedim (there should be more than one) wheel and dive with their mounts, and scouts fire arrows to keep them at bay. At a dramatically important moment, the shedim land their beasts to cut off the Cast's escape route. It will have to be a fight.

The shedim must end up with the Apocalypse Blade, so the ZM shouldn't hold back. Let one or more Cast Members die if the fates decree. This is supposed to be the moment when the heroes face their supreme challenge—the possibility of their death. The shedim keep coming until they have the blade; simply overwhelm them with forces they cannot hope to combat. Once the shedim have the pieces of the Apocalypse Blade, they lose interest in the Cast, and wing their way south toward Doitcaayr.

Albrecht's Tomb

Some Zombie Masters might prefer there to be some kind of threat to oppose the Cast Members in Albrecht's tomb. Rather than zombies, this kind of opponent traditionally takes the form of some outward manifestation of the main characters' inner demons. They must prove they understand the nature of the threat confronting them, or prove they have mastered themselves before going on to conquer the main antagonist. The Cast Member might have to fight doppelgangers of themselves, or defeat an animated Albrecht, or best Gadreel. Alternatively, they may be required to answer some kind of riddle, the answer to which lies in information they've learned along the way.

The Road Back

It is a dark time for the Cast. They have lost the Apocalypse Blade to the forces of evil, and one or all of them may be dead. Things look pretty bleak for Domhain.

Now is when Gadreel reappears, striding through the site of the previous battle. Any dead Cast Members awaken to find him standing over their bodies (he's a celestial, after all, and restores them to life). He knows the Cast Members have failed, but asks them to take heart. There is yet something the Cast can do. Gathering and neutralizing the shards was the best means to Adramalech defeat, but now that that avenue is closed, Gadreel has been granted new information. He then relates the story of Albrecht and his sword. Gadreel sends them to recover this sword from its hiding place in the center of the earth.

Center of the Earth

Somewhere within the belly of the world, the sword of Albrecht lays waiting to be found. Gadreel travels with the group, leading them to the entrance to the underworld located equidistant from the lands to the North, South, East, and West. Hidden beneath a massive oak tree lies a stairway which leads down to a massive labyrinth of crypts and hallways. At the center of this labyrinth is Albrecht's tomb. The sword itself has somehow found its way back to its original wielder, and lies upon his chest within his sarcophagus. Gadreel declines to accompany them.

The Cast likely suspects attacks by zombies, shedim, or guardian creatures. These do not take place, which should keep the group on edge. Adramalech marshals his forces to the south at his citadel, and the calm before the storm should tip the Cast Members off that something big is about to happen.

The Sword of Albrecht

This powerful magical broadsword deals D12(6) x Strength damage, and drains D10 Essence points from its victim per successful hit. It grants the wielder an Armor Value of D10(5), which adds to normal armor, and three levels of the Good Luck Quality. Finally, the character wielding the sword is immune to all of Adramalech's Metaphysics.

In the end, the Cast emerges from the center of the world with Albrecht's sword in their possession.

The Final Conflict

At this point the heroes have returned from the special world carrying whatever they were supposed to find. They have faced various challenges, and are now ready to confront evil on its own terms.

Emerging from the underworld with Albrecht's sword, Gadreel charges them to defeat Adramalech for the final time. They must travel south, to the citadel of Doitcaayr. This alone might require several adventuring sessions, as the Cast marshals an army from amongst their newfound allies (the sidhe, dwarves, orcs, goblins, minotaurs, and humans they encountered in their travels) in order to fight their way through Adramalech's forces.

At the massive obsidian gates that form the border of Doitcaayr, the final battle takes place. The ZM could describe the clash of mighty armies as the Cast fights their way to the borders of Adramalech's land. Suddenly, the colossal doors swing slowly open, and the Dark Lord strides out onto the field of battle.

Only one Cast Member can wield Albrecht's sword, and this is the only way to defeat the newly corporeal Dark Lord. This character becomes the champion of Domhain, as Albrecht was before. While the other Cast Members are relegated to the sidelines in this fight, they could still provide some assistance in the form of Invocations and Miracles used to help the champion, and could fight to keep the zombies and shedim at bay while the champion battles Adramalech.

The Aftermath

Once the physical form of Adramalech has been killed, the Cast must journey into Doitcaayr and destroy the sword in the furnace where it was forged. Once Adramalech falls, the majority of Domhain zombies and shedim collapse and turn to dust, though a few may remain to be mopped up by the Cast on the way. Once they drop the sword into the heart of the volcano, the Cast succeeds and the story is over.

If they fail to defeat Adramalech, this means the end of everything. His zombie army, led by his shedim lieutenants, sweeps across the land. Cue survival horror mode.

The Dark Lord Adramalech

Strength 10	**Constitution** 7
Dexterity 8	**Intelligence** 10
Perception 10	**Willpower** 12
Life Points 108	**Speed** 30
Endurance Points 92	**Essence Pool** 107

Qualities: Cruel 2, Damage Resistant, Delusions (Delusions of Grandeur), Essence Channeling 15, Fast Reaction Time, The Gift, Hard to Kill 10, Increased Essence Pool 10, Mystic Targeting, Regenerate (7/Turn), Obsession (Rule the World), Situational Awareness

Skills: Brawling 9, Dodge 7, Hand Weapon (Sword) 8, Intimidation 10, Myth and Legend (Domhain) 10, Necromancy 10, Notice 8, Occult Knowledge 10, Stealth 5. These are skills of note; Adramalech can possess whatever skills the ZM requires.

Metaphysics: Adramalech possesses all Necromancy powers at level five.

Gear: Apocalypse Blade D12 x 10(60), plus each hit drains D10 x 3(15) Essence which Adramalech absorbs into his own Essence Pool, plate armor AV (D8 + 3) + 8 (20)

Notes: Adramalech is immune to attacks from all weapons other than the Sword of Albrecht, and the only Metaphysics that affect him are Soulfire Blast, which deals half damage, and Necromantic Bolts, which inflict full damage. Adramalech is a fallen Tuatha de Dannan, and seeks to absorb all the other Tuatha de Dannan into him. The Apocalypse Blade can kill a Tuatha de Dannan (including Adramalech) in one blow, transferring all of its Essence and power to the wielder, but driving him mad in the process, affecting him with Adramalech's Mental Drawbacks. Basically, any Cast Member who uses the Apocalypse Blade against Adramalech will become Adramalech.

Breaking the Apocalypse Blade is possible, though does not have the same dramatic effect it had previously; Adramalech has learned from past mistakes and keeps much of his own power within him now. However, shattering the blade halves all of Adramalech's attributes, negates his Damage Resistance and Regeneration, and renders him vulnerable to all normal attacks. The Apocalypse Blade is only vulnerable to the Sword of Albrecht, and even against this sword it has AV 10 and DC 50.

Sidhe Woodland Protector

Inspired

Str 4 **Dex** 5* **Con** 3
Int 3 **Per** 4 **Wil** 4
LPs 47
EPs 38
Spd 18
Essence 24

Qualities/Drawbacks

Acute Senses (Vision)*
Adversary (Minions of Shadow) 4*
Attractiveness +1*
Cruel (–1)
Delusions (Delusions of Grandeur) 2*
Delusions (Prejudice against Dwarves) 1
Fast Reaction Time
Gift
Hard to Kill 3
Honorable 1*
Inspiration*
Obligation (Companions) (–3)
Obsession (Defeat Evil) (–2)
Ranger (5)
Sidhe (5)
Situational Awareness†
Socially Inept 2 (from Ranger, replaces Sidhe)
Zealot (-3)

Skills

Climbing 2
First Aid 2
Hand Weapon (Long Bow) 3
Hand Weapon (Sword) 3†
Martial Arts 1
Myth and Legend (Sidhe) 2
Notice 3†
Questioning 1
Riding (Horse) 2
Science (Animals) 1*
Stealth 3†
Survival (Forest) 3*†
Tracking 3†
Unconventional Medicine (Herbalism) 2

Aspects/Metaphysics

Communion 1*
Blessing
Divine Sight
Touch of Healing

* Granted or modified by Sidhe Quality
† Granted or modified by Ranger Quality

Gear

Backpack, Bedroll, Leather Armor, Long Bow, 2 Short Swords, Quiver with 20 Arrows, Tinderbox, 1 Week of Traveling Rations, Water Skin, 40 Gold Pieces

Personality

I am young by the standards of my people, though bordering on ancient by human standards. I have spent all of my long days living beneath the trees of my peoples' forest, smelling the jasmine in spring and reveling in the chill of the autumn air. I defended the borders of our lands from human kind, who breed like rodents and build castles of brick and stone. The world had become theirs, and we sidhe only wanted to live in peace until the time when we would make our journey to the far shores. There, we could live in harmony until the world's end. I looked forward to my time, when I could put down the bow and live in peace.

Then, the Darkness arose again. The first signs came when the deceased beasts of the woodlands rose again, and attacked our people. As though on cue, some among us rose up and rebelled against our ways and everything that we are. We knew immediately what had happened. Adramalech had reawakened, and the shadow sidhe hearkened to his call. Soon enough, the shedim will ride again, leading armies of zombies across the land. And I must put thoughts of the far shores and peace out of my mind.

Quote

"I sense a fell presence in the air. We are not alone."

Minotaur Ex-Gladiator

Talented Hero

Str 6* **Dex** 3 **Con** 5*
Int 3 **Per** 3 **Wil** 3
LPs 84
EPs 53
Spd 22
Essence 26

Qualities/Drawbacks

Acute Senses (Smell/Taste)*
Attractiveness –2 (–2)
Emotional Problems (Fear of Commitment) (–1)
Fast Reaction Time*
Hard to Kill 10*
Honorable 3*
Humorless*
Mental Problems (Prejudice against Humans) (–1)
Minority*
Minotaur (7)
Nerves of Steel
Showoff (–2)

Skills

Brawling 3*
Climbing 3
Dodge 3
First Aid 3
Gambling 1
Hand Weapon (Short Sword) 4
Hand Weapon (Spear) 4
Intimidation 3
Notice 3
Running (Marathon) 1
Shield (Small) 4
Storytelling 2
Survival (Desert) 2
Tracking 1
Weight Lifting 2

Aspects/Metaphysics

Infravision*
Horns D10 + 5(10) (stabbing)*
Scent Tracking (as Zombie power) (3)

* Granted or modified by Minotaur Quality

Gear

Backpack, Bedroll, Leather Armor, 50-feet Rope, Short Sword, Long Spear, Tinderbox, 5 Torches, 1 Week of Traveling Rations, Water Skin, 20 Gold Pieces

Personality

Do not talk to me. I do not talk well. I was a hunter and warrior among my people, chasing game across the barren, rocky deserts of the west. I was known to my people as an honorable being, and I gained much respect. I felt the hot wind in my mane, and bellowed the war cry in freedom. Now, I live among the honorless humans of the East, taken as a slave to work in the mines. My broad back bent under the weight of heavy rocks. My strength was put to pushing boulders. Sometimes, my taskmasters bade me fight others of my kind for their amusement. One day, I turned my sword against them, and escaped.

Now, the dead walk the land again. I hear frightened whispers in the taverns. The sages tell us of a dark time ahead, come from the mists of the past. I do not know about such things, of this Adramalech and his shedim warriors. All I know is battle. The people who have befriended me—a band of adventurers—talk about joining the battle. I will go with them. I will not be a slave again.

Quote

"What I do best isn't very nice."

CHAPTER FIVE

Guinevere sat on her throne, dressed in a silken gown once the color of the summer sky, now faded to gray. Lace had crumbled, silk had torn, pearls had gone missing. Her face, once joyful and carefree, was pale and gaunt. She stared blankly at the ground, as though her very soul had drained away. Percival heart stopped in his chest as the terrifying thought pierced his mind: *the Queen is dead*. Then he caught the almost imperceptible heave of her bosom and rushed forward. He dropped to his knee, and kissed her hand, not realizing she had not offered it.

"My lady, I have heard the call in my dreams that the knights have gathered for a final quest."

"Percival," Guinevere showed the barest hint of recognition. "The Grail . . . have you brought it?"

Percival swallowed hard. "No, my Queen, do you not remember? We failed, and the King sent us away. For a time it seemed the land would recover, but what I have seen makes my heart heavy."

"Yes," the Queen mumbled, memories lit up one by one behind her sad eyes, "the failure of the quest broke us. Percival . . . is that you?" She reached for his weather-beaten face.

"Yes, my Queen! It is. The King . . . where is he?"

For a moment, Guinevere's face lit up with warmth. Then her features twisted into a grimace of pain and fear. "You must leave here at once. You are not welcome."

"But, Queen Guinevere, I heard the King's call. He bade me come!"

"The King did not call you here. Begone from this place!"

"My Lady—"

"Heed my command, Sir Knight. Leave, and never return."

"No," said a voice from behind Percival. "Let him stay. All of the King's knights are welcome here."

Percival lifted his head and looked Guinevere directly in the eye. "I know that voice," he choked.

"I tried to tell you," Guinevere said, tears welling, "tried to tell you to leave. Percival, I am so deeply sorry."

"Things aren't supposed to be this way, my Lady." Percival stood, and ran his hands down the front of his tarnished armor, as though trying to smooth it out.

"Is that a fact?" said the voice.

"Indeed," he said, turning. "You, Mordred, are not supposed to be here."

"Shows how informed you are of current events," Mordred said. "You may address me as 'Your Highness.'"

Percival drew his sword. “I shall die before I bend knee to you, traitor.”

“So be it,” Mordred said. The hollow echo of armored footsteps rang throughout the hall. A fetid stench filled Percival nostrils, blinded his watering eyes.

“Fear not, my Lady,” Percival said, “I will prevail, and take you from here.”

Guinevere laid a hand on Percival shoulder and whispered, “Percival, I chose this life.”

Aghast, Percival opened his mouth to demand an explanation, but was silenced as the knights emerged around the room, clad in armor tarnished and black. Their gaunt, gray skin stretched tightly over bone, their eyes sunken into their sockets.

“God have mercy,” He whispered. “Galahad . . . Kay . . . Bedevere . . . this cannot be!”

Mordred sneered. “But it is. The knights are mine. Behold the Death of the Round Table.”

DEATH OF THE ROUND TABLE

Introduction

Arthur, Morgan, Merlin, Guinevere, Lancelot—names synonymous with the romantic image of medieval times. Chivalry sprang from these legends and the players take on roles that grace almost every fantasy tale. Everyone knows of Arthur, the boy who pulled the sword from the stone, united the Britons against the Saxons, and founded Camelot. His exploits and those of his Knights talk of Excalibur, the Holy Grail, and events like the creation of Stonehenge by Merlin.

There is a darker side to the legends all too easily forgotten. Arthur's story ends in tragedy. His knights are victorious in their final stand, and Mordred is killed on the Plain of Salisbury, but Arthur dies at the same time. Camelot is broken by Lancelot and Guinevere's betrayal, and the Britons fall to the Saxons in the end. Like many tales, King Arthur's story ends in bloodshed. Add zombies to the mix and it just gets worse.

In historic fantasy, writers combine fact with fiction. Shakespeare did with his plays, and one of the writers most associated with the tales of King Arthur, Geoffrey of Monmouth, did it, too. He took an ancient Celtic story and embellished it to please his Norman readers. This melding of the factual with the fantastic has gone on for centuries, and continues to this day. In more modern times, writers have re-imagined tales from old, giving them a new twist to suit the day. And none has been more popular for this treatment than the Arthurian tales.

The Arthurian Tradition

The tales of the Knights of the Round Table fill volumes. One of the first tellers was a bard named Geoffrey of Monmouth. His story purported to tell the history of Britain's first king, Arthur. Perhaps it was based on history, but Geoffrey wrote his account many years after Arthur lived. Sir Thomas Mallory cemented Arthur's legend in his retelling of the tale. And like others to come, he added what he liked and left the rest behind. It's hard to tell, definitively, whether or not the characters in the Arthurian legends are indeed genuine, or based on religious icons, political necessities, or fanciful dreams, or a mix of them all.

No matter who tells the tale, certain elements remain central to the Arthurian legends—courtly love, chivalry, and the Holy Grail among them. It's important for Zombie Masters to be familiar with these in order to run a plausible Arthurian campaign.

The Historic Arthur

If we are to believe Arthur was an actual person, his life was very different from the way most readers envision it. Some historians believe Arthur was chief of a Celtic tribe who managed to carve out an "empire" from among the surrounding warring tribes. This places the time frame for King Arthur much earlier than in the common belief (some estimates place this as much as 400 years before Geoffrey of Monmouth wrote his tales). Games set in the period of an historic Arthur would be much different from the common perception—they would be set primarily in southern and central England, there would be no concept of courtly love or chivalry, and the tone would be definitely more barbaric or primitive.

On the other hand, many players envision the Arthur fictionalized in the writings of Chretien de Troy and Thomas Mallory. In this, the authors were writing about an historical period (likely having heard oral tales of the real Arthur) and embellished with elements they could see outside their windows. This is where the ideas of jousting, and feasting, and courtly love come from. Knights wore shiny plate armor and gallivanted about. Women waited patiently for their heroes to return, perhaps doing a bit of needlepoint to pass the time. The scope widens to include Normandy, Denmark, and France. In these kinds of games, the setting reflects the world of the 12th century, and a majority of adventures will be played this way.

But Arthurian legend has not been limited to a handful of authors writing hundreds of years ago. It has been re-imagined in every generation. It has been retold with women as the central characters. It's been set in the far future and on other planets. It's even been told from Mordred's point of view. So the Zombie Master is not limited to a historically accurate portrayal of Arthur's world, and should decide beforehand whether the campaign will be historically accurate or highly fictionalized.

People and Places

Obviously, a game set in King Arthur's time takes place on Earth, rather than on some imagined world, so there is no need to detail fictional places and cultures. While centered on the British Isles, the legends range all over Europe—France, Normandy, Germany, and so on. Many of the quests the Cast Members pursue will take them to places with which they are already familiar—if not by experience than through history—so the ZM need not worry about devising fictitious lands. Although the setting should be familiar to players, try to keep an air of mystery and magic. Throughout Arthurian Europe are mysterious locales such as Avalon, the Celtic otherworlds, and the Castle of the Fisher King. Mixing the fantastic with the mundane is important to the feel of an Arthurian setting (it served Geoffrey of Monmouth well, so why not you?). A little research into the time period (either 5th or 12th century) wouldn't hurt, either, when dealing with this kind of setting.

Generally, there are no elves or dwarves in Arthurian legend, though this depends on the timeframe of the campaign. Set in an "historic," more Celtic time, beings from the otherworlds might put in an appearance (and perhaps join the Cast), though this should be rare. The Lady of the Lake and Nimue are fey creatures, and sometimes a questing knight ventures into their lands, but players and ZMs need not worry about their culture or politics. On the whole, all characters are human. Some, like Merlin, are supposedly part demon, and there are conflicting tales of dragons, though these are mentioned as asides. In general, however, all of the Cast's concerns in an Arthurian campaign will be human.

Likewise, types of characters in an Arthurian game are somewhat different. The Paladin Quality should be restricted to the truest and bravest of knights, never to starting Cast Members. Other Profession Qualities in **Chapter Two: Swords, Sorcery, and Shambling** may be inappropriate to a game, like the Swashbuckler; the ZM can disallow them if this is so.

The Code of Chivalry

Even though the story of Arthur predates the Code of Chivalry, the two have become inextricably merged. Chivalry, as espoused by Sir Thomas Mallory in his definitive telling of the Arthurian tales, demands a strict adherence to a code of behavior. All knights, in order to be considered honorable gentlemen, were expected to adhere to this code of ethics. Sir Thomas Mallory lays out the code in six core tenets. Later authors added other embellishments, which have merged over the years with the chivalric ideal.

The chivalric code likely emerged as a way in which to control the aggressions of many young noblemen. Rather than marching off to war, their energy was channeled into ritualized combat, known as tilting or jousting. As with any ritual, there had to be rules.

Mallory's Code of Chivalry

- Never engage in acts of rage or murder.
- Always be mindful of treason.
- Never be cruel, and always offer mercy to those who beg it.
- Always render aid and assistance to ladies, gentlewomen, and widows in need.
- Never force oneself upon a lady.
- Choose one's battles wisely. Never fight for anger, love, or unjust causes.

Later Additions to the Code

- Never lay down arms.
- Seek out wonders.
- Defend the weak with all one's strength.
- Be willing to lay down one's life for the security of king and country.
- Never break an oath once given.
- Always be pious and faithful.
- Always be courteous and hospitable to the best of one's ability.
- Always be honest and truthful, even if it means dishonor.

Breaking the Code

Characters who break the Code should be penalized experience points based on the severity of the violation. Minor violations like losing one's temper might cost one point. Serious violations, like assaulting a woman in a fit of rage while uttering insults at the King should be worth five or more points . . . and probably death. The exact penalty is up to the ZM, just keep in mind that the Cast should see Arthur as the true king; insulting Mordred should not be considered treason.

Belief Structures

Arthurian tales and chivalric tales are not necessarily the same thing, even though they are conflated in the minds of many. The concept of good and evil likely did not exist in the world of the Celts. They moved through a world of symbolism and nature, in which everything had a positive and a negative side. Even their gods were not necessarily "good" or "evil," but rather the embodiment of natural forces. Christianity, however, drew a bright line between good and evil, God and the Devil. This dichotomy would have a profound effect on the Arthurian tales.

Because the Arthurian legends are a later, Christianized retelling of a Celtic story, the two belief structures have become mixed, placing god-fearing knights alongside faeries and giants. Although Arthur and his knights were Christians who engendered all the positive aspects of the faith, they also held counsel with those who in other tales would be considered heathens in league with the Devil. But in Arthurian legend, magic was not always the tool of Satan; it could be a force for good or ill, and even Merlin, with his druidic powers of prophecy and magic could be made to serve a Christian king. Thus, the Gift Quality and all types of Metaphysics should be made available to players, but require good background stories.

Magic and Metaphysics

There are two groups of magic wielding characters in the Death of the Round Table: Sorcerers and Druids.

Druids

The druids were a society of Celtic mystics who acted as lawmakers, judges, teachers, historians, and leaders. Such a lofty position required years of training as guardians of the oral tradition and as religious leaders. Druids hailed from Ireland, the one area of Europe the Romans never invaded. Although druids engaged in human and animal sacrifice, they were not the evil murderers Christian scholars painted them. Their animistic faiths required sacrifice to maintain the prosperity of all and many offered up in sacrifice may have been voluntary subjects.

The druids served as the priesthood for the local Celtic population, and as such should be Inspired characters.

Sorcerers

Because the Church believed that all who dabbled in magic were in league with the forces of darkness, most magic users were looked upon as people with ties to the Devil. Merlin was thought to have some degree of demonic heritage, and in this manner a person is granted access to special powers and magic (The Gift Quality). Rarely does the subject know the specifics regarding their lineage; it is simply assumed that the sorcerer's magic comes from his demon blood. This does not automatically make the character evil, and some sorcerers fought on the side of justice, like Merlin.

Faeries

The Arthurian tales are suffused with creatures of myth and legend, either lifted from earlier, Celtic, accounts of Arthur's time or placed there by later authors to add a bit of the fantastic—giants, dragons, unicorns, and so on. Knights continuously ventured into and out of the realms of faerie, as a part of some quest. Certainly the most well known of these figures is The Lady of the Lake, who gave Arthur his sword and raised Lancelot. While Zombie Masters may choose to allow players to create Fey Cast Members, it's best to leave these creatures on the fringes of play, unknown wild cards in their stories.

Tragic Love

Alongside the rise of the chivalric code came the concept of courtly love. The idea was that love was a noble feeling, akin to a religious experience. That is to say, it was platonic love, which was much different from amorous love in that there could be no sex involved. The woman, as the object of these feelings, became a superior being who could only be approached reverently. Courtly love was to be borne by the knight like an illness, who became a servant and champion of his lady. He had to prove himself noble and great in both word and deed. Knights carried their lady's favor, a kerchief or flower, into battle. They pursued quests in her name and defended her honor. Cast Members, especially knights and paladins, should have their own courtly lovers to give them someone to fight for and urge them on to greatness.

In the King Arthur legends, the concept of courtly love becomes tragic love in the relationship between Sir Lancelot and Queen Guinevere. This has been portrayed many ways in the different retellings—a passion play warning against adultery, an illustration of the superiority of courtly love, a tragedy of young lovers betrayed . . . In fact, Arthur's story is filled with lust, jealousy, rape, betrayal and all the other things that make a good afternoon soap opera. Arthur was conceived through deception; his father Uther had fallen in love with Ygraine, wife of the Duke of Cornwall, and Uther conspired to have the knight killed and take the woman for his own. In many tales, Mordred is conceived when Morgan le Fey disguises herself as Guinevere to sleep with Arthur, and in still others Guinevere has affairs not only with Lancelot, but with Mordred as well.

The Grail Quest

The Grail quest is a central element of the Arthurian tales, a physical representation of the quest for the spiritual. Scholars generally agree that the Grail is the Christianized version of the much older Celtic *graal*, described variously as a serving plate, bowl, or shield capable of producing unlimited quantities of food and regenerating life. It came to be wrapped up in Christian mythology as the cup passed around at the Last Supper and used to catch Christ's blood at the crucifixion. As a search for a holy relic, the quest challenged knights to practice what they preached—only the pure of heart, those who adhered to the Christian faith and chivalric code, could claim the cup for their own. Lancelot could only catch a vision of the Grail, but never claim it, because of his adultery with Guinevere. Sir Bors, on the other hand, successfully rebuffs the advances of a clutch of maidens in a castle, and eventually wins through. In this way, the pursuit of the Holy Grail—the challenges, the traps, the fights—externalized the pursuit to live a holy (or spiritually pure, or righteous) life.

The Knights of the Round Table were consumed with this quest for Christ's Cup, most likely because of the glory and honor that would be heaped upon them should they succeed. Naturally, these are the wrong reasons to be searching for a holy relic, and they mostly failed. For our purposes, the Zombie Master can start off practically any story by dropping a few not-so-subtle hints about the Grail to trigger a stampede out the castle gate.

The Fisher King

The Fisher King is perhaps the most mysterious and interpretable element of Arthurian legend. His earliest appearance is in Chretien's *Percival*, in which the young knight encounters a fisherman who lives in a castle. This "fisher king," Percival discovers, is crippled. While visiting with him the Grail Procession enters the room, but Percival, told by his mentor that a knight does not ask too many questions, says nothing. It is only after he leaves that Percival learns that he failed to ask the vital question that could heal the Fisher King and prevent the land from falling to waste.

Since this version, the Fisher King's role, and who and what he represents, had differed. Sometimes he is the guardian of the Grail, sometimes he only knows its location. But certain central facts remain the same. With the Fisher King infirm, the land around him also falls to ruin (highlighting the mystical connection between a king and his land that foreshadows the end of Camelot). In order to complete the quest, the hero must demonstrate the ability to differentiate between honor as slavishly following a code, and honor as stoutness of heart and soul. The Fisher King tests the hero's mettle, devotion to Chivalry, and understanding of the chivalric code.

Failure of the Dream

For whatever reason, the Arthurian tales have come to embody the idea of utopia, and the failure of the dream, particularly in contemporary times. Arthur's reign is an idyllic time, and Camelot is heaven on Earth. Perhaps this was true in the historical Arthur's day, as he carved a unified kingdom from a mass of warring Celtic territories. But in every telling of the tale, this utopia fails as it is wracked by betrayal (the Lancelot/Guinevere/Arthur love triangle) and external threats (Mordred and Morgan le Fey).

Humanity is inherently flawed, tainted as it is by original sin, and thus attempting to force such ideal nobility upon it rarely turns out for the best. There can be no heaven on Earth, for heaven is the kingdom of the divine. This lends the Arthurian legends a tragic air, as everyone sees the handwriting on the wall—except for Arthur. But as in all great myths, the stories promise a return of Arthur and Camelot and better days ahead.

Female Cast Members

The Arthurian tales are blatantly patriarchal. It is historical fiction rooted in the values of a male-dominated historical context. Most of the Cast Members in an Arthurian fantasy game are going to be male. This is not to say, however, that there is no room for female questing characters. Women need not be relegated to sitting in castles, waving handkerchiefs while their champions ride off.

In Celtic society, men and women were perhaps more equal than in any other society in history. While true that among the Celts the men traditionally served as warriors, there were respected female Celtic warriors as well. Celtic women held important voices in the community, and could serve in druidic circles. There are several strong female Arthurian characters—Guinevere and Morgan le Fay, for example—that build on this Celtic tradition.

Female Cast Members could act in healing, magical, and advisory capacities in order to maintain some historical accuracy during the later chivalric period. On the other hand, it's also possible to throw historical accuracy out the window in favor of an alternate reality where women commonly rise to knighthood. Even in the real world such things, while rare, were not unheard of. Joan of Arc was a woman, after all, and she led an army to victory for France.

The Story

Arthurian scholars will notice in some places a drastic alteration from traditional Arthurian "canon." This is deliberate, and it is a part of the Arthurian tradition to alter the myths and legends to suit the storyteller's needs. Thus, this Deadworld takes the Arthur and Grail legend and turns it on its ear. What if the Grail quest failed? What if Mordred's coup was successful? These are the alternate angles Death of the Round Table seeks to explore.

Background

In the later years of his reign, Arthur's court fell into despair. The land was at peace, and had been for years. As a result, Camelot became decadent, lazy, and careless. Guinevere and Lancelot's affair was public scandal, ending with the greatest of Arthur's knights banished in disgrace. Guinevere was sentenced to death, and rescued by Lancelot, who returned with a small unit of loyal followers of his own. The act both served the King's honor and saved the Queen's life, and Guinevere later returned to Arthur's side. The two became distant and the Queen was rarely seen except at formal gatherings. As Arthur's dream became more corrupt, the king became weakened and ill. With him, the land fell into darkness. Plants died, rivers stagnated, and soil would no longer support crops. The greatest king ever to sit the throne of Britain saw his kingdom threatened with death and obscurity. He called upon his Knights of the Round Table to hold counsel and find a solution.

Galahad reasoned that the King was connected the land, and if one was healed, so would the other. The question was how? As the Knights debated, a shimmering image of a golden, jeweled goblet appeared, hovering in the center of the room. The power and aura of the image was such that all present knew immediately what it was. Before it vanished, a voice rang out, asking "Whom does the Grail serve?"

If the Knights could bring back the Grail, the king and land would recover. Eventually, Sir Galahad found the Grail, but died in ecstasy upon viewing it. Unfortunately, final death was not for Galahad. Morgan le Fay had spied upon the council of knights and followed Galahad, knowing he would be the one pure enough to find the Grail. She seized the holy cup and and bore it with Galahad's body to her lair. Morgan was able to tap into the artifact's power and corrupt it to her own ends. The Holy Grail once bestowed eternal life on all who drank from it; now it would bestow unlife, creating zombies subservient to Morgan and her bastard son, Mordred. Galahad became the first victim of the Grail's dark power.

Next, Morgan lured her old mentor Merlin to her cave, where she used ancient and powerful magic to trap the wizard in walls of carbon and quartz. Finally, she sent Mordred to Camelot with news of an approaching Roman army on the mainland. Arthur, who had sent his knights away in disgrace after their failure to find the Grail, took heart at a new quest, gathered his armies with renewed strength, and rode forth, the land healing as he rode. Mordred convinced Arthur to leave Camelot in his care. With the help of Guinevere's insecurities and Morgan's dark magic, Mordred seduced the Queen into an affair, and then a wedding. He had usurped the throne.

On the mainland, Arthur found himself facing not an army of Romans, but an army of zombies, raised by Morgan to devastate the king's knights, and Arthur realized only too late he had been duped. The king was never heard from again, presumed defeated and carried away to Avalon.

Using magic and treachery, Mordred called the Knights of the Round Table home one at a time, had them killed, and then raised them with the Grail. Camelot belonged to Mordred and Morgan, as did Guinevere and the Knights of the Dead Table. There is now no one left to take up the mantle and save the Dream . . . or is there?

The Rise

Morgan and Mordred's unnatural crimes have had a horrific effect upon the land. As Morgan traveled across Europe with the Grail, she left a trail of taint behind her that rendered the land barren, and began a plague not unlike the Black Death that would later ravage the continent. The plague is transmitted by rats, and by the eating of diseased livestock, and is fatal in almost all cases, causing a wasting sickness that kills within days. Worse, about three quarters of plague victims rises again as a zombie under Mordred and Morgan's control. These zombies are fast, vicious, and utterly ravenous. Anyone bitten by these zombies rise up within five minutes. A Cleansing Invocation can stop the change, but requires three Success Levels on the Invocation Task, and costs Essence equal to the damage dealt by the zombie's bite. Worse, all zombies carry the plague—anyone who makes physical contact can contract this Strength 8 Terminal illness (see *AFMBE*, p. 108). A simple Cleansing does not stop the disease, though some kind of cure disease Invocation Task (say, Cleansing at a –6 penalty) could do the trick.

Worse, Morgan and Mordred have corrupted the holy chalice to a diabolic end. Any knight who drinks from the cup becomes a special type of undead, far more powerful and deadly than a normal zombie. These zombies are easily a match for a regular Cast Member. All twenty-five Knights of the Round Table have been forced to drink from the cup, except for Lancelot. Note that the Knights' Dead Points apply only to Cast Members wielding blessed weapons (see p. 49). Their fire Weak Spot is special; Knights of the Dead Table have Weak Spot: None against normal weapons and fire-based attacks (see *AFMBE*, p. 148), but fire damage is doubled towards destroying the body.

Arthurian Zombies

Strength 2 **Constitution** 2
Dexterity 3 **Intelligence** 1
Perception 3 **Willpower** 2
Dead Points 15 **Speed** 18
Endurance Points n/a **Essence Pool** 13

Skills: Brawling 3 [+1], Hand Weapon (club, spear, or sword) 3 [+3]

Attack: Bite D4 x 2(4) (+6 per Turn), claws D6 x 2(6), or by weapon

Weak Spot: Spine [+5], Blessed Objects [–1], Fire [–5]

Getting Around: The Quick Dead [+10], Leaping [+3], The Lunge [+3], Climbing [+2]

Strength: Dead Joe Average [0]; Claws [+8], Teeth [+4]

Senses: Like a Hawk [+2], Scent Tracking [+3]

Sustenance: Occasionally [+2], Blood [–2]

Intelligence: Tool Use 1 [+3], Teamwork [+4]

Spreading the Love: One Bite and You're Hooked [+2]

Special Features: Diseased Corpse [+3]

Power: 55

Knights of the Dead Table Zombies

Strength 7 **Constitution** 2
Dexterity 3 **Intelligence** 1
Perception 7 **Willpower** 2
Dead Points 46* **Speed** 18
Endurance Points n/a **Essence Pool** 22

Skills: Brawling 2, Sword 5 [+5]

Weak Spot: None [+10]; Blessed Weapons [–1]*; Fire [–5]

Getting Around: The Quick Dead [+10], Climbing [+2], The Lunge [+3]

Strength: Monstrous Strength [+10], Damage Resistant [+5]

Senses: Like Nothing You've Ever Seen [+10]; Life Sense [+14]

Sustenance: Who Needs Food? [+8]

Intelligence: Language [+1], Tool Use 1 [+3], Teamwork [+4]

Special Abilities: Regeneration (1/Turn) [+5]; Noxious Odor [+5]

Spreading the Love: Knights of the Dead Table do not Spread the Love.

Power: 94

Gear: Longsword D8 x 7(28), plate and mail armor AV D8 x 2 + 8(16)

The Holy Grail

It cannot be stressed enough how vital the Grail is to the medieval perspective. Wars were fought in its name; it is the ultimate symbol of purity and the divine. In the Arthurian tradition, even those of pagan backgrounds are steeped in Christian mythology, and the Grail stands as a symbol to them as much as it does to Christian characters. Tell the players to reflect on what the Grail means to their Cast Members, and occasionally remind them to think on this. It will become important later.

Uncorrupted, the Grail is an Essence battery that never runs dry. Drinking from the ever full cup can grant the drinker his Willpower or Essence Channeling x 10 (whichever is greater) in Essence points, can heal any disease or injury (including age), or can grant any Miracle. However, the Grail is tainted, and performs a very different function, turning dying men and women into hideous Knights of the Dead Table, beholden to Mordred and Morgan. No plant can grow or live within 100 yards of anywhere the tainted Grail travels, and food and drink spoils within minutes of exposure. Worse, it taints the bearer's psyche such that whenever an opportunity arises to act in a cruel, selfish, or evil manner, the bearer must make a Difficult Willpower Test to resist the urge. Each time this Test is failed, the next Test suffers a –1 to the roll, cumulative with any other penalties from failed tests. Voluntarily succumbing does not accrue penalties to future Tests.

Stage One: Humble Beginnings

The adventure begins as the Cast, young, rootless nobles and humble commoners, are called by visions or dreams to a seedy pub in London. The visions come from Merlin, his powers diminished such that he can do little more than guide the Cast to seek out Sir Maximilian, a minor knight who never attended the Round Table. Maximilian has been in hiding since Mordred's coup, and has decided to put together a quest to find the King and put right what has gone wrong. He has spent the last several years traveling the land, looking for suitable candidates.

Sir Maximilian

Strength 1 **Constitution** 3
Dexterity 1 **Intelligence** 4
Perception 3 **Willpower** 2
Life Points 26 **Speed** 8
Endurance Points 23 **Essence Pool** 14

Qualities and Drawbacks: Adversary (Morgan and Mordred) 3, Attractiveness –1, Charisma +1, Honorable 2, Nerves of Steel, Physical Disability (Advanced Age), Recurring Nightmares, Resources (Wealthy), Situational Awareness, Status 2 (Noble)

Skills: Bureaucracy 3, Hand Weapon (Long Sword) 4, Notice 3, Riding (horse) 3, Smooth Talking 5, Streetwise 2, Storytelling 3

Gear: Worn long sword D6(3), worn chain mail armor AV D4 + 6(8)

The knight is too old and infirm to undertake the quest himself, but serves as guide and mentor for the Cast, providing advice and information. Maximilian is not aware that Morgan and Mordred possess the Grail, only that Mordred has usurped the throne and a plague of zombies coincided with this event. He believes the quest is to find the Grail, for only once they have the cup can the heroes restore the land and set the kingdom to rights. As with all great quests, this one starts with a single step. Maximilian knows the last known location of Sir Galahad was outside of Bordeaux, France, and sends the Cast there to retrace his steps.

As the Cast and Sir Maximilian leave the tavern, zombies accost them. There should be one for each member of the Cast and one for Maximilian; after the battle, a local healer can use Cleansing on anyone who gets bitten while she prattles on about the plague racing across the land. No Cast Member should die during this assault; it merely sets the stage for what is to come.

Stage Two: The Quest

In this stage, the Cast undertakes their Grail quest. Throughout the length of the quest, the ZM should work to guide Cast Members along the Hero's Journey with opportunities to shine whenever possible. Encounters with zombies should spice things up and provide opportunity for heroism. The Grail quest is the outward expression of the pursuer's dedication to his faith and beliefs, and encounters should be tailored to challenge each Cast Member in some way (a test of honesty, a test of bravery, and so on). Guide each character as seems most appropriate. It also never hurts in this type of story to set up a courtly love for one or more Cast Members to inspire them to overcome insurmountable odds.

Stage Two involves the majority of the Heroes' Journey for the characters. There are several encounters and pieces that should be worked in. These scenes are described briefly below, but it is for individual ZMs to determine how they fit together. Wherever the Cast goes, however, zombie servants of Mordred and Morgan await them. It doesn't take long for the villains to get wind of the new quest. Each time the Cast overcomes a hurdle or makes a new major discovery, a zombie attack should coincide. The attacks should get bigger and more deadly as the Cast nears their goal, with the Knights of the Dead Table showing up later in the campaign, leading hordes of lesser zombies.

The Fisher King

The Cast should retrace Sir Galahad's steps. This gives the ZM the opportunity to challenge them with some minor tests along the road. An ugly hag might ask for assistance from the "knights," only to reveal she is a lovely sorceress in disguise (in order to test their commitment to the chivalric ideal). Or the ZM could waylay the Cast with a fantastic monster (like a dragon, see p. 83) in order to test their bravery. It should be several days before the Cast arrives at the borders of the Fisher King's lands.

The area around the Fisher King's castle was once lush and green, but now is dying (like much of the land in England). They should have no problem coming up to the castle walls and gaining entrance to the Fisher King's throne room. He appears as an aged and mortally wounded cripple who yet manages to retain his regal stature. He should remind the Cast of King Arthur in bearing and demeanor, and perhaps even slightly in appearance. The Fisher King, though mortally wounded, still remains a gracious host, and offers food and drink.

As the guardian of the Grail, so long as it remains in the possession of Mordred and Morgan, the Fisher King is powerless. He cannot rise from his dais to help the Cast, as result of his grievous wounds. Moreover, he cannot heal his own land, or that of England, without the Grail. No amount of question asking (remember Percival mistake) will reveal the Grail. He cannot help them.

But the Fisher King can provide information. The Grail is gone, taken through treachery and deceit. He cannot reveal the identity of the thief, but will say that it was an evil sorcerer who twisted the purpose of the holy artifact. It must be returned to the Grail Castle in order to be purified.

As the Cast leaves the castle, hit them with a zombie attack.

Lady Guinevere

Strength 2 **Constitution** 2
Dexterity 2 **Intelligence** 4
Perception 4 **Willpower** 3
Life Points 26 **Speed** 8
Endurance Points 26 **Essence Pool** 42

Qualities and Drawbacks: Adversary (Morgan and Mordred) 3, Attractiveness +3, Charisma +2, Emotional Problems (Guilt Complex), The Gift, Inspiration, Increased Essence Pool 5, Recurring Nightmares, Status 4 (Former Queen)

Skills: Bureaucracy 5, Craft (Needlepoint) 3, Dancing (Court) 3, Hand Weapon (Knife) 2, Myth and Legend (Christianity) 5, Myth and Legend (Druidism) 5, Occult Knowledge 3, Rituals (Christian) 4, Rituals (Druidic) 3, Seduction 4, Smooth Talking 2

Gear: Small knife D4 x 2(4)

Miracles: Blessing, Communion, Visions

Guinevere

At this point, the Cast may feel dejected; they've just run into their first roadblock. That is, until they hear Queen Guinevere has escaped Mordred's clutches and fled her island nation for the protection of a convent. How they gather this information is left to the Zombie Master, as are the means by which they learn the location of her hideout.

Guinevere is in seclusion in a convent outside of Paris, where the holy might of the divine can protect her from Mordred's undead. Along the way, the Cast should confront a band of zombies sent to stop them. Once they arrive, they must give the head of the order a convincing enough tale before the exiled Queen deigns to see them. She keeps to her cell, praying for salvation most of the time, and looks haggard, though at peace.

Thanks to her impious relationship with Mordred, she knows about the failure of Galahad's quest, as well as Morgan le Fay's success—the sorceress has the Grail and is the true power behind the coup against Arthur. She also knows the location of the Crystal Cave, Morgan's seat of power. Finally, Guinevere managed to escape with Excalibur, which she keeps locked in a chest beneath her bed. Cast Members who are true and just, or remind her of Arthur, Percival, or Lancelot, may be loaned the use of the weapon (see p. 108).

Until now, Guinevere has been under Mordred's protection (he loves her), and he has been content to leave her alone. But the moment she helps his enemies, Mordred sends his zombies to destroy her. It turns out the convent is no protection against the zombies after all. The Cast must defend their Lady, who is still the Queen of England, and if they acquit themselves well she may turn over Excalibur.

Lord Lancelot

After his rescue of Queen Guinevere from the executioner's axe, Lancelot went into self-imposed exile on his lands in France. There he has stayed, tending to his fiefdom and brooding.

The Cast might seek out Lancelot after their encounter with the Fisher King (before they learn about Guinevere's seclusion) since he is the last surviving member of the Round Table. Alternatively, knowing Lancelot is a brave soul, they may seek him out to gain his aid.

When they arrive at his castle, Lancelot willingly grants them an audience; despite his exile, he remains interested in news from England. Through talking to him, they learn that he has recently received a call to return to Camelot from his love, Guinevere. If the Cast has recently come from her, they can inform Lancelot that the message is false, likely sent by Mordred to lure Lancelot out and make him a Knight of the Dead Table. Otherwise, Lancelot might actually answer the call and die as a result. Finally, Lancelot can also grant knighthood to characters who prove themselves worthy; this is the only way that the Cast can seek out the Lady of the Lake.

The Zombie Master can play Lancelot any number of ways. He could consider himself betrayed by the Round Table and refuse to come to its rescue. He might swear to ride to Camelot's aid and make plans to raise an army from among his vassals. Either way, Lancelot recommends the Cast make their way to the home of his mother, the Lady of the Lake, to seek her help.

The Lady of the Lake

The Lady of the Lake is the mysterious being who imparted Excalibur to Arthur, and who raised (some say bore) Lancelot. This powerful faerie woman gets her name from her home, a kingdom beneath a lake. Lancelot du Lac knows where lies her magic spring, and he can direct Cast Members to her. She never appears in person; only her arm, clad in shimmering gossamer and white scale mail, arises from the pool of water deep in the forest. She sometimes speaks into the minds of worthy knights.

Sir Lancelot du Lac

Strength 6 **Constitution** 6
Dexterity 5 **Intelligence** 3
Perception 2 **Willpower** 3
Life Points 73 **Speed** 22
Endurance Points 50 **Essence Pool** 25

Qualities and Drawbacks: Attractiveness +4, Charisma +1, Emotional Problems (Guilt), Fast Reaction Time, Hard to Kill 5, Honorable 3, Paladin (Fallen), Resources (Rich), Status 4 (Manor Lord)

Skills: Bureaucracy 5, Dancing (Court) 5, Dodge 3, Hand Weapon (Long Sword) 5, Intimidation 3, Martial Arts 2, Myth and Legend (Christianity) 3, Occult Knowledge 1, Riding (Horse) 5, Seduction 2, Shield (Medium) 5, Streetwise 1

Gear: Long sword D6 x 6(18), plate armor AV D8 x 3 + 8(20), medium iron shield, war horse

Morgan Le Fay

Strength 2 **Constitution** 3
Dexterity 3 **Intelligence** 5
Perception 4 **Willpower** 5
Life Points 245 **Speed** 12
Endurance Points 35 **Taint** 72

Taint is the opposite of Essence, a force of entropy and decay, and is the energy upon which Morgan calls to cast her spells. She can draw Taint from her own pool, or draw and Taint the Cave's 150 Essence. Taint has granted her unnatural longevity, but projects an aura of death and corruption about her. Any who come near Morgan must pass a Fear Test at –3 as a result.

Qualities/Drawbacks: Accursed 2 (Aura of Death), Attractiveness +2, Charisma +2, The Gift, Hard to Kill 5, Immunity to Damage (cannot be harmed by physical attacks), Increased Taint Pool 10, Taint, Taint Channeling 10

Skills: Bureaucracy 5, Hand Weapon (Knife) 2, Intimidation 4, Myth and Legend (Christianity) 2, Myth and Legend (Druidism) 6, Occult Knowledge 5, Rituals (Christian) 3, Rituals (Druidic) 5, Seduction 4, Smooth Talking 2

Metaphysics: In the Crystal Cave, Morgan possesses all Necromancy and Invocations at level 5. Outside, all abilities drop to level 4. She is also a Zombie Lord and has Might of the Dead, Seal the Dead, and Rule the Dead (see *AFMBE*, p. 209).

Gear: Ceremonial dagger D4 x 2(2), short sword D6 x 2(6), chain mail armor AV D6 + 6(9)

If sought out for assistance, the Lady of the Lake rewards worthy Cast Members knighted by Lancelot with a blessed sword of their own. Such blades are potent against the Knights of the Dead Table and Mordred. It should be noted that no matter how bad the zombie plague gets, the Cast never encounters zombies at the Lady's glen. Her purity keeps them utterly at bay, and the Cast can always find safe haven here.

Blessed Swords

Swords blessed by the Lady of the Lake add +2 to all combat Tasks and to base damage. They cannot be broken, and inflict full damage against Knights of the Dead Table (Damage Resistant Aspect is inapplicable).

The greatest of these swords, Excalibur, adds +4 to all combat Tasks, +2 to all Fear Tests, and adds +2 to the Armor Value of any character wielding the blade. The sword's damage multiplier is increased by one against Knights of the Dead Table and Mordred (before slashing doubling).

Stage Three: The Crystal Cave

At this stage in the story, the Cast should seek out Morgan to cut off the evil plaguing Camelot at its source. If the Cast visits all three of the important players in this drama, they should know the Grail resides with Morgan, that she holes up in the Crystal Cave, and they should have sufficient magic to combat her.

The Crystal Cave is a hidden labyrinth of quartz and semi-precious gemstones located in Ireland. In order to gain entrance, the Cast must do battle with a small army of zombies (perhaps even one or two Knights of the Dead Table). Once inside, they find Morgan, and Merlin trapped in a prison of crystal. The Cast must confront Morgan and her zombie slaves.

The witch is powerful here, surrounded by crystals radiating magical energy. She is a potent foe with a potent weakness. She is immune to all attacks, but the cave is not, and every time the Cast strikes a crystal

Sir Mordred, Usurper of Camelot

Strength 6 **Constitution** 6
Dexterity 5 **Intelligence** 2
Perception 2 **Willpower** 3
Life Points 273 **Speed** 22
Endurance Points 50 **Essence Pool** 24

Qualities and Drawbacks: Charisma +1, Cruel –3, Fast Reaction Time, Hard to Kill 5, Status (Usurper King) 4, Resources (Wealthy)

Skills: Bureaucracy 2, Dodge 4, Hand Weapon (Long Sword) 5, Intimidation 4, Martial Arts 2, Myth and Legend (Christianity) 2, Occult Knowledge 2, Rituals (Christian) 3, Rituals (Druidic) 3, Riding (Horse) 5, Seduction 4, Shield (Medium) 5, Smooth Talk 3

Metaphysics: Mordred is a zombie lord and has Might of the Dead, Seal the Dead, and Rule the Dead (see *AFMBE*, p. 209).

Gear: Long sword D6 x 6(18), plate armor AV D8 x 3 + 8(20), medium iron shield, war horse

in which Morgan's image appears, the witch takes full damage from the hit. A Difficult Perception Test reveals that when Morgan uses Metaphysics, her image appears in the crystal formations. Also, outside the cave she is vulnerable to normal attacks. Once she reaches zero Life Points, Merlin's spirit breaks free. A red and green glow surrounds Morgan, and Merlin's voice rings out, chastening her for abusing the powers he taught her. She is consumed by the spirit of her mentor, aging rapidly before the Cast's eyes, and eventually crumbling to dust. The cave collapses around her, and the Cast must beat a speedy retreat; a few Simple Dexterity Tests would not be out of line as the Cast dodges falling stalactites.

Upon exiting the cave, the spectral form of Merlin appears and informs the Cast that Mordred still lives. In order to defeat him, they need significant help. He sends the Cast Members on a journey to Avalon to seek out Arthur himself!

Stage Four: The Isle of Avalon

In order to defeat Mordred, the Cast must have the help of King Arthur, who lies wounded in the mystical realm of Avalon after his defeat at the hands of his enemy.

Avalon's entrance lies beneath Glastonbury Abbey, guarded by yet another horde of zombies. Its location can be pieced together from clues given by Lancelot, Guinevere, and the Fisher King. Mordred is frightened, now, and every zombie encounter should include at least one Knight of the Dead Table. Only a knight wielding a weapon blessed by the Lady of the Lake can open the gate.

Beneath the Abbey, the Cast comes upon a vast lake with a white ferry awaiting them. No matter what they do, the ferry does not leave the shore (no matter how hard they row) because it is magically anchored there. The question, "Whom does the Grail serve?" rings out. The correct answer, "Arthur, true King of Britain, and the Lord God above" (or some form of that) allows them to take the ferry across the lake to Avalon to meet King Arthur. Lying upon a dais, wounded like the Fisher King, Arthur cannot yet return to the world of mortal men but can aid the Cast. He orders the fairy women to bind their wounds, offers them food and new armor, and if they have proven themselves worthy, dubs them Knights of the Round Table (they may now select the Paladin Quality). If the Zombie Master wishes to grant the Cast Members additional magic items, now would be the time to do it.

He next informs the Cast that all the assistance they need shall be awaiting them upon their return. They must defeat Mordred and his army of the dead, and return the Grail to its resting place, where it and the land can be healed. Arthur then sends the Cast home, wishing them God's blessing in their final battle against the darkness.

Stage Five: The Final Battle

Back in the mortal realms, the Cast finds Lancelot waiting, his army behind him. He has heard Arthur and come to the Cast's aid, to lay siege to Camelot, and emerge victorious or dead. All the remaining Knights of the Dead Table must be destroyed, and Mordred must be killed, then the Grail must be returned to the Fisher King if the land is to be healed. The details of this battle are left to the ZM, but there are many factors to consider. Who will face Mordred? Will it be one of the Cast, or Lancelot? Mordred is not above using the Cast's chivalry against them, begging for mercy that he knows they cannot refuse. Does he live to try again later? Suppose he escapes, and manages to somehow revive his mother as a zombie. Together, the two of them could lay siege to the reunited Camelot, leading to further adventures later on.

This stage of the campaign is cinematic in nature, and action packed. It should bring to a completion the Hero's Journey of the Cast, for good or for ill, and provide closure to their epic tale. In the tradition of all great cinema, it should leave room for a sequel if the audience demands it.

Knight Errant

Survivor

Str 4 **Dex** 4 **Con** 4
Int 3 **Per** 2 **Wil** 3
LPs 57
EPs 38
Spd 16
Essence 20

Qualities/Drawbacks

Adversary (Zombies) (–3)
Ambidextrous (3)
Fast Reaction Time (2)
Hard to Kill 5 (5)
Honorable (–3)
Nerves of Steel (3)
Situational Awareness (2)

Skills

Bureaucracy 3
Dancing (Court) 3
Dodge 3
First Aid 1
Hand Weapon (Crossbow) 3
Hand Weapon (Long Sword) 4
Intimidation 3
Language (French) 2
Martial Arts 3
Notice 3
Riding (Horse) 3
Rituals (Christian) 1
Shield (Medium) 3
Writing (Poetry) 3

Gear

Backpack, Crossbow, Long Sword, Medium Iron Shield, Chain Mail, Tinderbox, 1 Week of Trail Rations, War Horse, Water Skin, 10 Silver Pieces

Personality

I spent my early days as squire to Lancelot, greatest of Arthur's knights. When my liege was disgraced, I found myself alone and without a lord. No one wished to take on the boy who had served a betrayer of Camelot. And yet, I had my years of training. I was ready to go out in the world and make my own way. Thus did I enter the chapel, take a knee, and swear before God to uphold the standards of chivalry, of righteousness, and of justice.

One dark day, my quest did bring me back to Britain, to a small plague-wracked village. I did what I could to give succor and aid to the women and children, while helping the men clean the town of the bodies of the deceased. The work of a knight errant, you may not realize, is not entirely based upon prowess in battle. As it turned out, however, my martial skills were indeed called upon that day as the hundreds of bodies in the mass graves outside the village stood again! A more horrific sight I have never beholden, but we fought valiantly and put down the insurrection.

One day, perhaps, I shall at long last find my way into the service of a worthy lord, and complete my long journey.

Quote

"Cretin! Apologize to the lady, or draw thy sword!"

Young Druid

Inspired

Str 2 **Dex** 4 **Con** 3
Int 3 **Per** 3 **Wil** 5
LPs 30
EPs 35
Spd 14
Essence 40

Qualities/Drawbacks

Gift (5)
Increased Essence 4 (4)
Inspiration (5)
Nerves of Steel (3)
Honorable (–2)
Obligation (Protect the Forest) 3 (–3)
Zealot (–3)

Skills

Climbing 1
Dodge 2
First Aid 2
Hand Weapon (Bow) 2
Hand Weapon (Staff) 1
Instruction 1
Language (Druidic) 2
Myth and Legend (Celtic) 3
Notice 2
Stealth 2
Science (Animals) 2
Science (Herbalism) 2
Survival (Forest) 2
Veterinary Medicine 2

Powers/Metaphysics

Communion
Strength of Ten
Touch of Healing

Gear

Herbs, Holly, Mistletoe, Robes, Staff, Short Bow, 20 Arrows

Personality

I remember the days when the forest was peaceful, when I awoke in the misty mornings with the sounds of birds singing praises to Mother Earth, and the quiet crunch of the palug stalking its prey. I lived here, with my circle, and we were happy. We thought in our arrogance that things would always be thus.

Then the dead invaded.

It was the summer of my fifteenth year when they came, and I had just come into womanhood. I never got the opportunity to complete my rites of passage. Driven from the cities and villages by pitchfork- and torch-wielding peasants, the zombies came ravenous into our forest, bringing taint and death with them. Their disease spread quickly to the animals, who turned upon us, their druidic companions, and in the end I alone survived the slaughter of my circle. I fled from the woods into the filth of civilization. Now at the dawn of my sixteenth year, I travel alongside a would-be knight of Camelot, seeking to right what was set wrong, and restore the beauty and serenity of a forest that will never again be the same.

Quote

"When at last we discover the secret behind this mystery, this necromancer shall know the true wrath of the Goddess!"

CHAPTER SIX

The black fox crept along the compound's outer walls, an easy target for perceptive bowmen. But this was no ordinary fox. It stayed in the shadows, silent, and kept watch for any spot that wasn't as well-guarded as the rest.

Halfway down the back wall was a space where it could enjoy a moment's rest. Getting up there would require more dexterity than the animal's form possessed, which meant calling upon reserves of chi it had hoped to save. There was nothing to be done about it.

The fox crept to the opening, looking right and left. The guards were far enough away. Its limbs elongated; its tail shortened then disappeared. Its fur pulled into its skin, revealing a supple, pale female form clad in loose silken garments. The ears pulled down, slightly smaller, but retained their pointed tips, and the hair on her head grew long down her back.

The ninja swept her hair back into a ponytail, tying it with a silk scarf, and pulled a mask over her nose and mouth. She crouched low. The guards hadn't seen. A quick invisibility incantation and a wave of her hands ensured no one would. She dismissed the residual chi, a necessary evil; talismans were too cumbersome and noisy for jobs like this.

Then she was over the wall into the compound. The daimyo would be in the dojo, performing his nightly workout. This was too easy. But then, that was why the master tapped her for this job, wasn't it? She moved with speed and silence. There was a reason her clan called her Whisper.

As she climbed the inner walls, however, she felt a pang of regret at the justification of this job. Ichiro-san had been wonderful to her, even told her he loved her. She wasn't foolish enough to think a mere geisha could rise to the wife of a daimyo, but his love made her whole. Now she was destroying that, why? Honor? Duty? Not for love; that was certain.

She dropped to the ground in the inner compound and her heart skipped a beat. The guards outside the dojo moved towards her, as though they could see her. Something was wrong. They moved clumsily, slow, as though drunk. Then their stench reached her, and she understood. Her employer was right; Hamato Ichiro had to die.

Whisper launched herself high, bringing her knees tight against her, and tumbled into a flip. As she descended, she soundlessly slid her ninja-to sword free from its sheath. It would take the *kuang-shi* a moment to adjust; the hungry dead were so clumsy. She whipped the blade across just above chest level, and a neat cut appeared in the neck of one of the zombies. In a fraction of a second, its head clumped to the ground and it was a corpse again. The second zombie lumbered to face her, swinging clumsily with a katana. Whisper leapt back and sliced down, severing the thing's arm. Then she reversed her swipe and decapitated it. She hoped there weren't more.

Whisper crept into the dojo and saw Ichiro. He was unaware anything amiss had transpired. She stepped from the shadows into the room, arms folded across her chest, legs shoulder-width apart.

"Komban wa, Ichiro," she said.

He jumped, startled, and spun on her. "How did you get in here?"

She pulled the face mask down, so he could see her face. "For a kitsune geisha who knows the lay-out, it was not difficult, my love."

"Yuriko? No, this cannot be! You would betray me?"

"Like you betrayed the Three Kingdoms, Ichiro? Can you explain the two hungry dead outside?"

Ichiro's face hardened. "I made a bargain to preserve my clan. I make no excuses."

"And yet, you know your honor was questionable, or you would've made it public."

The daimyo took a tentative step towards Whisper. "Yuriko, we are connected. You love me."

Whisper's gaze softened, and a tear crept down her cheek. "Yes, Ichiro. I love you." She fell into his embrace, and kissed him, long and soft, then planted her dagger in his back and watched with a stony gaze as he fell to the floor. "But we all have our duty."

THE EASTERN DEAD

Introduction

Oriental fantasy is quite different than the fantasy of the West. While castles and kings remain, the society and culture colors the landscape. Rather than battling trolls hiding under a bridge, heroes confront wicked oni hiding in caves. Instead of oaths of fealty, the clan is the tie that binds society and honor is all-important. Ninja, samurai, and fox spirits replace assassins, knights, and elves. Wandering priests are concerned with maintaining the balance between yin and yang, positive and negative furies that must remain equal for the universe's stability. Yet certain elements remain universal—greed, love, jealousy, honor. The story of a power-crazed sorcerer seeking to usurp a kingdom is the same whether it is set in the East or the West. The difference really lies in the trappings surrounding the tale.

This chapter presents alterations to the more familiar Western fantasy to achieve an oriental feel. It is not based upon any one mythology, but is culled from sources from all over the Far East. It is as fantastical as any other Deadworld presented, and is not meant to represent the beliefs, values, history, or mythology of any country or people.

The goal of most heroes in an oriental tale is to garner honor and status. Honor is everything and reflects not only one's own behavior, but also that of the entire family. Players should constantly be concerned with *face*, or appearance of propriety and honor.

Flavor of the East

Many of the changes that must be made to reproduce an oriental feel are cosmetic—a uniquely Eastern flavor can be had just by calling certain things by different names. Below are elements of the game that should be renamed or given minor alterations to add an oriental flavor. Zombie Masters should have players mark these on their character sheets as a reminder.

Adept Heroes: Adepts are called wu jen. They cast their Invocations from talismans, scrolls that must be read and destroyed. Wu jen characters maintain a scroll library, which they use to cast Invocations. Keep a record of current scrolls, and whenever an Invocation is cast, the talisman must be re-scribed. Casting Invocations without a scroll is possible, but incurs the same penalties as Invocations cast by bound and gagged mages (p. 35) and requires a separate Dismissal Task. Necromancy is unaltered and Psychic Invokers don't exist.

Essence: Essence is called Chi (see p. 118).

Holy Order of Light Priest: These characters are demon quellers, members of an order of warrior-priests who search the land for demons and monsters to destroy.

Inspired: Inspired are shugenja, traveling Shinto priests, or Buddhist monks.

Names: In many East Asian cultures, names are given surname first, given name second.

paladin: paladin are samurai, the elite warriors and nobles of oriental society (see p. 118).

Survivors: Survivors, as presented in *AFMBE*, are bushi and represent the warrior and fighting classes of oriental society.

Swashbuckler and Ranger: These profession Qualities are generally not appropriate to oriental-style games, although korobokkuru (see p. 124) could make effective rangers.

Religion

Two of the more well-known faiths of oriental peoples are Shinto and Buddhism. Although it would take volumes to properly explain these philosophies, the basics are presented herein. It is possible to be both Buddhist and Shinto.

Shinto is an animistic religion that holds that everything from humans to rocks possesses its own spirit, or kami. When a person dies, shrines are built to her to placate her kami in the afterlife, and each person's Shinto gods are different (as they worship family members who came before). Similarly, believers venerate important nature spirits, from the kami of wind or the harvest to individual tree and lake spirits.

Buddhism, on the other hand, is not so much a religion as a complex philosophy around the belief that all life is suffering, and the only way to find release from the karmic wheel of rebirth is to realize the illusory nature of reality and find Nirvana. There are many different schools of Buddhism, each advocating various ways to achieve enlightenment—from praying to Buddha for guidance to gaining insight in the sight of a falling cherry blossom. Buddhism is especially important to samurai, who believe when they die they will be reborn again as samurai, which gives them courage to fight to the death.

Equipment

Equipment in an oriental setting remains unaltered, except for some renaming. Short swords are called wakizashi (katana can be found in *AFMBE*, p.132). Knives and daggers are called tanto, spears are yari, pole arms are bisento, and long bows are known as daikyu. Armor is unaltered from its Western counterparts, except for appearance.

New Profession Qualities

Oriental settings offer some new profession Qualities, presented below.

Ninja
5-point Quality

Prerequisite: The Gift

Ninja operate as spies, infiltrators, and assassins. They all belong to a secretive clan, from whom they learn their unique abilities, and they are expected to drop whatever they are doing when the clan calls. Those who attempt to leave their ninja clan face the wrath of the family, and are often killed, out of fear they will teach the family secrets to others. Ninja have their own code of honor and are mirrors of the samurai—while samurai fight directly, ninja attack from the shadows. Samurai revel in status; ninja remain unknown.

Ninja blend in by posing as something other than what they are, and ninja should either purchase a second profession Quality, levels in the Multiple Identities Quality, or be built with a set of skills or Character Type (such as Adept Hero or Inspired) that allows them to masquerade as something other than a ninja. The Quality provides +1 to Dexterity and Perception, two levels in Martial Arts, one level in two Hand Weapon skills, two levels in Stealth, and one level in Lock Picking (Mechanical). The character also receives the Situational Awareness Quality. On the down side, the ninja must take the three-point Secret (Ninja), the two-point Honorable, and the

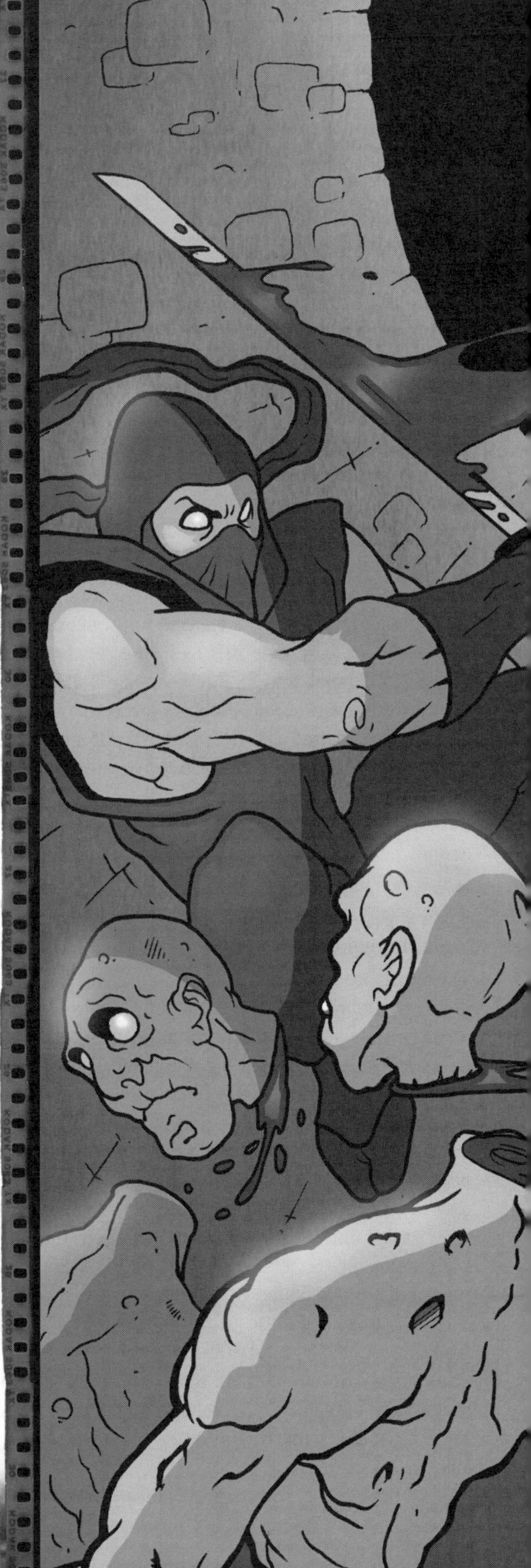

three-point Obligation (Ninja Clan) or (if ronin) the three-point Adversary (Ninja Clan) Drawbacks. The Ninja gains no points for these Drawbacks.

Samurai
5-point Quality

Honor and duty are everything to the samurai, the nobles of oriental society. Samurai are expected to put their lord above all. The samurai's immediate family is next, then clan, the Kingdom, the Emperor, and personal honor. A samurai must lay down his life without question whenever honor demands it, through seppuku or hari kiri, in which the samurai cuts his stomach open before a friend beheads him. Samurai who refuse seppuku become ronin and dishonor their lord, family, and clan; the Obligation becomes an Adversary Drawback.

Samurai gain +1 to Strength, Constitution, and Willpower, three levels of Hard to Kill (and can have up to 10 total), Nerves of Steel, one level to Hand Weapon (Katana) and Hand Weapon (Daikyu), and one point of Status. These nobles are ruthless in carrying out their duty and thus suffer from a one-point Cruel Drawback. They also have a three-point Honorable and a three-point Obligation Drawback. Samurai gain no points for these Drawbacks. Samurai cannot purchase any other profession Quality except Ninja.

Sohei Warrior Monk
5-point Quality

Prerequisite: The Gift

Sohei are monks who seek spiritual awakening through physical perfection, and often serve as defenders of their temple or monastery. They rarely use weapons, believing the body and mind are the deadliest weapons (though if they employ weapons they strive to master them as extensions of their body). The body and mind must be one for true mastery to be achieved. Eventually, Sohei must leave the monastery and search the world in their quest for enlightenment. Sohei are outside of the class structure, and are not bound by the rules that bind others. They are treated with respect by most (but are occasionally targeted by angry or drunk nobles looking for scapegoats). Sohei maintain their own code of honor that may or may not be the same as that of other members of society. This Quality provides +1 to any two physical Attributes (which can raise any Attribute to a maximum of eight), two levels of Martial Arts, Fast Reaction Time or Situational Awareness (choose one), and one level of Chi Focus (see p. 119). Sohei also suffer a three-point Obligation (Achieve Enlightenment) and three-point Honorable Drawback. The sohei gains no points for these Drawbacks.

Dual Obligations

Many oriental characters have several Obligation Drawbacks in order to represent their interlocking responsibilities. Oftentimes, characters in oriental settings owe allegiance not only to their lord, but also to family, friends, and other groups. Cast Members must clarify which Obligation comes first, and how honor plays into these obligations, particularly for samurai and ninja.

Ninja are the most important example of dual obligations, as all ninja maintain a cover identity they use to conceal their true status. Most covers maintain an Obligation to a lord, be it a sensei, daimyo, or a geisha's mistress. Whenever the obligations of a ninja conflict, he must place his clan first, even if doing so means exposure and death.

New Metaphysics

In oriental cultures, the concept of Chi replaces Essence, though the two are conceptually similar. Everything in the universe is comprised of Chi, which comes in two forms—positive and negative. Positive Chi, or yang, causes things to grow, brings good fortune, and nourishes the universe. Negative Chi, or yin, causes decay, misfortune, and death. Chi moves along particular paths, so called ley lines or "dragon veins." Specific places are said to be influenced by yin or yang by their location—low places, like a valley floor or shadowy glen, are said to produce yin, for example. Even people have their own Chi.

Cast Members, particularly shugenja, should be concerned with Chi and its flow. A place of negative energy, where zombies rise up, could be purified by encouraging yang to flow in (in other words, the Blessing Miracle), while the Binding Miracle would be said to create a barrier of positive Chi to repel zombies (who are filled with yin). Martial artists, like samurai and monks, tap their own Chi to power their awesome abilities.

Chi Focus

3-point/level Supernatural Quality

Prerequisite: The Gift

Chi Focus represents the "mind over matter" ability of martial artists. It is their ability to focus their inner strength to perform feats of combat and healing denied to normal people, and is resolved through a Chi Focus and Willpower Task. Sohei and ninja most often have this power.

Chi Abilities

All characters with levels in the Chi Focus Quality can use it in three ways: attack, defense, and self healing. A fourth use is only available to ninja. Every use of Chi Focus requires a separate expenditure of Chi (Essence). Only one power can be used per Turn and that power may only be used once during that Turn. The abilities are purchased with Metaphysics points, costing five points each. Using Chi Abilities does not require the Essence Channeling Quality; as much internal Chi (Essence) can be channeled as the character wishes.

Chi Attack

Spending five Chi and making a successful Chi Focus and Willpower Task allows for one of three things: Make a number of extra attacks equal to half the Success Levels on the Task (minimum one) at no penalty; add Success Levels as a bonus to the next attack roll; add the Success Levels to the result of the next attack for purpose of determining damage. Chi Attack can be used barehanded or with melee weapons only.

Chi Defense

Chi Defense works in a similar manner to Chi Attack, but for defense rather than offense. Spending five Chi and making a successful Chi Focus and Willpower Task allows one of three things: Make a number of extra defense actions equal to half the Success Levels on the Task (minimum one) at no penalty; add Success Levels as a bonus to the next defense roll; add Success Levels to Armor Value for one Turn per Willpower level. If the character opts to boost his Armor Value, he may not use Chi Focus in any other manner so long as Armor Value remains augmented. He can cancel the effect early with a Simple Willpower Test.

Chi Healing

By succeeding at a Chi Focus and Willpower Task, the character heals wounds equal to one Life Point per Chi spent. So a character who makes a Chi Healing roll and spends 10 Chi heals 10 Life Points of Damage instantly. This ability cannot be used on others.

Chi Vital Strike (Special)

A ninja can use her Chi Focus to inflict a devastating blow on any living or dead foe unaware of the impending attack. When making an attack against a defenseless or unaware opponent, the ninja can spend 10 Chi and make a Chi Focus and Willpower Task. If he gets two or more Success Levels, the damage multiplier for the attack increases by one.

Example: Kumiko, a ninja with Chi Focus 3 and Willpower 3, sneaks up behind a samurai and slashes him with a ninja-to sword. Kumiko spends 10 Chi and performs Vital Strike. The result of her Chi Focus and Willpower Task is 11, two Success Levels. Since slashing normally doubles, the Vital Strike means the damage is now tripled, and the samurai is probably hurting badly.

Serious Chi

For those who want more details and better conversions, we recommend Enter the Zombie. This sourcebook contains detailed rules for chi-related martial arts abilities, a Martial Artist Character Type suited to replace or supplement the Sohei Profession Quality, tables and charts of oriental weapons and equipment, and several Deadworlds that could be converted to fantasy. It's an invaluable tool for any ZM who desires to run an oriental AFMBE game, be it fantastical or modern in style.

Status

In certain Asian cultures, the people adhere to a rigid caste system. This system usually divides the social classes up by their role in society, and one born into a particular social caste have a difficult time changing. The caste system in Samguk, the fantasy setting for this Deadworld, closely follows that of feudal Japan.

Warriors: They are top of the social order because they are willing to lay their lives down for honor and duty. They have the most rights under the law, and members of lesser castes cannot challenge their word. Within this caste are additional layers—shogun, daimyo, and samurai.

Farmers: Because they produce food, an honorable profession, farmers come second on the social ladder. They have fewer rights than warriors and are subject to their whim. A samurai, for example, can enter a home and demand shelter, and can kill a man for not getting out of the way fast enough.

Merchants: These people are seen as parasites on society, for they produce nothing—only selling the wares of others. Entertainers also belong to this caste level. They have even fewer rights than farmers.

Geisha

Geisha make up an important part of society. Often they act as companions and confidantes to samurai and daimyo. A primary function of the geisha is as a professional hostess at formal gatherings, where they entertain guests through a variety of traditional performing arts. That nobles visit geisha regularly is generally accepted, though these visits should be conducted with a modicum of discretion. Open flaunting of such activities results in a severe lack of honor for the noble involved, and can even lead to death or status as a fugitive ronin. As a direct result of these common visits, however, many ninja clans maintain agents among the geisha, and they make effective assassins and spies. Geisha are considered hinin, or non-people.

Outcasts: Outcasts, called hinin, are at the bottom of the social order. They are non-people in the eyes of the other castes, and either hold jobs considered unclean (like butchers and leatherworkers) or opt out of the system altogether (monks). They have no rights whatsoever; killing a hinin isn't considered a crime, for example.

Samguk

The world of the Eastern Dead is called Samguk, or "Three Kingdoms." Until recently it was a world resembling a mix of ancient Asian cultures: Japanese, Korean, Chinese, and Vietnamese. In ancient times, groups of people and spirit folk from these various cultures were transported to a new and undeveloped realm by Amaterasu, the Shinto god of the sun and sky, and creator of worlds. Amaterasu was displeased with developments on Earth and sought to begin anew, with a select group of settlers, hand picked to develop the new world.

Unfortunately, Samguk resides in a space between Earth and Jigoku. For centuries this positioning had little effect on the inhabitants, though the strange crossing of mystical forces stunted the growth of technology. Samguk is permanently stuck in a medieval technology level.

Eventually, the three kingdoms for which Samguk is named grew into existence—the Mantis, Lion, and Dragon Kingdoms. The kingdoms continuously vie for power and status, expanding their holdings and warring with one another to gain more land or redress perceived slights. Politically, the people of Samguk employ a feudal system, with each kingdom led by a shogun, who maintains daimyo to oversee his provinces. They, in turn, maintain the samurai, who lead the bushi and oversee tracts of land rarely larger than the size of a single town, often as small as a manor or farm. In addition, independent daimyo lead various lesser clans, unaffiliated with any Shogun, but only the Three Kingdoms maintain the privilege of the Shogunate. Any lesser clan whose leader claims the title of shogun meets a swift and decisive end at the hands of the Three Kingdoms.

An emperor oversees the Three Kingdoms, and lives in the Forbidden City high in the mountains above. This emperor is thought to be the chosen of

Amaterasu, and interacts directly with her on behalf of the world. He serves for life. When the emperor dies, whichever of the Three Kingdoms possesses the greatest power and prestige installs a new emperor on the throne, and there have been times (sometimes decades) when no kingdom has been strong enough to seize the position. For the last thousand years, representatives from the Dragon Kingdom have held the throne. Recently, however, through maneuvering and intrigue, the Lion Kingdom has vastly increased its holdings. For a time, it appeared as though the reign of the Dragon would end in Samguk, as Lion Kingdom armies massed along its borders. That was before the gates to Jigoku burst open, and the dead arose.

The Rise

Jigoku, the netherworld, land of the dead and demons, is the source of Samguk's problems. No one knows how or why it came to pass, but recently the gates of Jigoku opened, and the oni (demons) gained access to the world. The first victims were the people of the Lotus Clan, a minor clan who supported the Mantis Kingdom. The Lotus Clan served as guardians of a holy burial ground where heroes of the Mantis were enshrined in death, so they might one day return to guide the Kingdom to prosperity. The members of the Lotus Clan did not expect their ancestors to return in the way they did.

It began with a quiet scratching and shuffling, and ended with a horde of zombies bursting forth from their tombs, still wearing the armor and weapons with which they had been buried. The zombies swept through the Lotus Clan villages, leaving a trail of destruction and death in their wake. The bushi, disgusted by the thought of striking down their ancestors, fell quickly to the hordes. What was worse, those killed by these kuang-shi, or hungry dead, soon rose as new zombies and feasted upon their own loved ones. Many among the peasants lamented that they must have committed some horrible sin to be punished as they were.

As the army of the dead grew, so did the gates of Jigoku open wider. More monsters from Jigoku poured forth into the world, including goblins and the bull-faced ogres called huang fei-hu, as well as the brutal, orc-like creatures known as bakemono. Universally, these evil creatures are known as oni, and have become the bane of the Three Kingdoms.

The Lion and Dragon Kingdoms, at first willing to watch the Mantis fall, quickly recognized the growing threat to all of Samguk, and have taken up arms to fight the menace. Even the korobokkuru (see p. 124) have seen their own dead rise to murder comrades-in-arms, and have sent envoys to engage in talks of alliance with the Three Kingdoms. Normally, such a united front would present unheard-of power and prosperity. Unfortunately, the taint of Jigoku fills the land, and no one can know when or where the dead will rise against the living. Jigoku has manifested physically in the world now, a Fourth Kingdom in the center of the Three. The capital, a city of jagged, obsidian spires and crooked towers, is like an acupuncture needle thrust into Samguk's dragon lines, a nexus of negative Chi corrupting the surrounding land. The anguished screams of departed souls trapped within the city fills the air. And ruling over all is the Shogun of Jigoku, a demonic being known as Yan-lo.

Several military expeditions have been sent into Jigoku, in an effort to overthrow Yan-lo and close the gates on the Dead Kingdom, but all have ended disastrously. Currently, the Three Kingdoms and the korobokkuru horde are engaged in a struggle for survival, fortifying their cities, homes, and provinces against the next incursion from Jigoku. And still, beneath it all, millennia of intrigue and warfare are not so easily quelled. The Three Kingdoms and the hordes still plot each others' downfall, seeking to be the final ruling power when the gates of Jigoku once again close. Unfortunately, this mistrust and plotting may eventually be the downfall of all kingdoms, as the taint of negative Chi spreads and leads to the eventual creation of a new level of Hell.

Unknown to the leaders of the other kingdoms, the Lion Clan, long hungry for the power held by the Dragon Clan's iron grip on the throne, called upon dark sorcerers and necromancers to make contact with forces that could give them the power they so desired. Yan-lo answered their call through lesser daimyo under his command, and once the deal was cemented, the gates of Jigoku opened. Since then, the Lion Clan has loudly debased and criticized the Dragon Emperor for his inability to suppress the zombie plague and demonic invasions. The situation is getting far out of hand, however, and the Lion Clan fears for the stability of their bargain with Jigoku. Though they realize they have made a mistake, they are in far too deep to back out now, and they work tirelessly to keep their secret. Once they hold the rulership of the Three Kingdoms, the clan reasons, they will be able to muster an army powerful enough to wage all-out war on Jigoku. Such a plan is a folly that would mean the end of Samguk.

Kuang-Shi, Zombies of Jigoku

The zombies of Jigoku are the kuang-shi, or hungry dead. These creatures are mindless animated corpses who seek only to consume the flesh of the living. The people of Samguk believe the souls of those who rise as kuang-shi are held captive and tortured in the obsidian City of the Dead, and only by destroying a kuang-shi can the soul be put to rest. Whether this is true has not been proven, but it is likely the torture part is true, at any rate. Kuang-shi rise when a person dies at the hands of another kuang-shi. Strangely, kitsune (see p. 123) seem immune to such transformations and never rise as undead when killed.

Kuang-Shi Zombies

Strength 2	**Constitution** 2
Dexterity 2	**Intelligence** –2
Perception 1	**Willpower** 2
Dead Points 15/26	**Speed** 4
Endurance Points n/a	**Chi** 7

Skills: Brawling 2, Hand Weapon (Sword) 2 [+2], Magic Bolt (Fire Breath) 3 [+3]

Attack: Claws D6 x 2(6), bite D4 x 2(4), or by weapon

Weak Spot: Brain [+6], Spine (Decapitation) [–1]

Getting Around: Life-Like [+3], Leaping [+3]

Strength: Dead Joe Average [0], Claws [+8]

Senses: Like the Dead [0], Life Sense [+2]

Sustenance: Daily [0], All Flesh Must Be Eaten! [0]

Intelligence: Dumb as Dead Wood [0], Teamwork [+4]

Special Abilities: Spew Flame [+5]; Acid Blood [+5]

Spreading the Love: Only the Dead [-2]

Power: 43

Not only are kuang-shi created when a person dies to a kuang-shi, but they can arise randomly at any time and any place. This has lead to massive deaths among the people of the Three Kingdoms. The only way to kill a kuang-shi is through decapitation or destroying the brain, and such mutilations of the dead are repulsive to those whose family members died peacefully or with honor. Chi-based attacks such as Soulfire work, but wu jen aren't common enough for this to be a practical means of battling the kuang-shi. The people slowly come to the understanding that kuang-shi are not truly their loved ones, but animated shells that once contained the souls of the departed. Unfortunately, change in Samguk comes much more slowly that is healthy, and more people die daily as a result.

While in Jigoku, kuang-shi do not need to eat (and are considered Power Level 51), though any mortals foolish enough to enter this hellish place find they are more than willing to feed, even if it's not a necessity. Kuang-shi that leave Jigoku or who rise in Samguk suffer the need to feed on a daily basis, leading to a growing plague of zombies across the land, as the people slowly adapt to the necessity of once again destroying their ancestors.

The Living

Kitsune

The Kitsune are a non-human race (though they can pass for human) and form the upper classes of Samguk. They occupy daimyo positions not only in the Three Kingdoms, but in the hundreds of lesser clans whose armies support the Lion, Mantis, and Dragon in their struggle for dominance. In millennia past, when Samguk was born, humans ruled due to their vast numbers. However, their barbaric views and resistance to natural change led humans to eventual downfall. The kitsune demonstrated a wisdom and ability to lead others that quickly raised them to prominence. That, combined with their natural affinity for magical power and their ability to change shape, lent to the kitsune an image of divinity that the spirit folk played upon, claiming to be the descendants and favored of Amaterasu. While the warmongering and intrigue continues, the kitsune have done away with the barbaric patriarchal mold established by humans, and women often hold places of power in the three kingdoms. Most notable among these is Ishada Kumiko, shogun of the Mantis Kingdom.

Kitsune use a modified version of the Elf Quality, and gain the natural ability to transform into red, silver, or black foxes. This power costs five Chi to activate; changing back costs another five Chi. They are otherwise unaltered from the Elf, though the cost of the Racial Quality (p. 22) is raised to seven due to this power.

Kitsune (Fox Form)

In fox form, the character gains Strength 1, Dexterity 5, and Constitution 5 (but loses opposable thumbs, etc.). Intelligence, Perception, Willpower, Life Points, Endurance Points, and Essence are unaltered. Speed becomes 20. Supplementing his regular skills, the character gains +2 Brawling, +3 Stealth, and +2 Tracking. The fox's claws attack for D4(2) x Strength, slashing damage and its bite does Strength, slashing damage. Kitsune also gain Enhanced Smell, Nightvision, and Walk in Shadows.

Humans

Humans make up the bulk of the population of Samguk, and many serve as samurai, bushi, and even daimyo positions under kitsune shoguns. The majority of the human population consists of peasants and commoners who work the land and run the inns and shops that keep the economy going. One can often tell the status of a human in Samguk not by their mode of dress, which remains consistent among the classes, but by the weapons, if any, that they carry. Peasants are not allowed to carry weapons, and as a result many have learned to use farm tools such as grain flails (nunchaku), threshers (tonfa), sickles, and walking sticks (bo staves) as effective means of self-defense. Bushi are not only allowed to carry weapons, they are required to. Often, members of the bushi class carry pole arms or spears (bisento and yari, respectively). On occasion, one sees a bushi wearing a katana, but never in conjunction with its wakizashi counterpart. The pairing of a katana and wakizashi is called a daisho, and is restricted to those of samurai, daimyo, and shogun classes. Daisho are a badge of office, and any who are not of the proper noble status to wear such weapons are put to death.

Korobokkuru

Korobokkuru are utterly outside of the social and political structure of the Three Kingdoms. They are considered gaijin, or alien people, barbarians without honor, privileges, or rights. They are often referred to as "the hordes," and live on the steppes far to the north, beyond the western mountains. The korobokkuru have in the past been the primary threat from outside the Three Kingdoms. Recently, with the opening of Jigoku, the korobokkuru have on occasion fought alongside units of samurai-led bushi, united against the common threat of the oni and their legions. They are vicious and effective fighters, using numbers and tactics to their advantage. They regularly engage in raids on border towns and villages. On occasion, they mount an invasion into one of the Three Kingdoms, seeking to overthrow the empire one kingdom at a time. As yet they have been unsuccessful.

Korobokkuru use a modified version of the Dwarf Quality (see p. 22). Rather than a rank and specialization in Craft, korobokkuru gain two levels in Riding.

Dragons

Dragons are as described in **Chapter Four: Dawn of a Dead Age** (see p. 83). They are not creatures to be hunted, but rare and deific beings said to control the elements. The people of Samguk venerate dragons as beneficial creatures, a symbol for strength and positive Chi.

Oni

Oni are demons from Jigoku, and supplement the hordes of zombies forming the bulk of Yan-lo's armies. There are three common types of oni.

Goblins and Orcs: Orcs are called bakemono. They and goblins are unchanged from those found in **Chapter Two: Swords, Sorcery, and Shambling** (see pp. 23, 25). Neither should be made available as Cast Members. They are oni from Jigoku, and non-evil specimens are unheard of.

Goblin Oni

Strength 2 **Constitution** 2
Dexterity 4 **Intelligence** 2
Perception 3 **Willpower** 2
Life Points 26 **Speed** 12
Endurance Points 23 **Chi** 15

Qualities and Drawbacks: Attractiveness –2, Cowardly 1, Enhanced Senses (Hearing), Situational Awareness

Skills: Climbing 2, Dodge 4, Hand Weapon (Ninja-to) 3, Notice 4, Stealth 5, Wilderness 2

Gear: Ninja-to sword D6 x 2(6), leather armor AV D6 + 1(4)

Bakemono Oni

Strength 5 **Constitution** 5
Dexterity 3 **Intelligence** 3
Perception 3 **Willpower** 3
Life Points 26 **Speed** 16
Endurance Points 44 **Chi** 22

Qualities and Drawbacks: Attractiveness –2, Cruel, Fast Reaction Time, Resistance (Fatigue) 2

Skills: Brawling 4, Dodge 4, Hand Weapon (Long Sword) 5, Intimidation 3, Running (Marathon) 2, Survival (Forest) 2

Special Abilities: Nightvision

Gear: Katana D10 x 5(25), chain armor AV D6 + 6(9)

Huang Fei-hu Oni

Strength 5 **Constitution** 5
Dexterity 4 **Intelligence** 2
Perception 2 **Willpower** 2
Life Points 65 **Speed** 18
Endurance Points 41 **Chi** 20

Qualities and Drawbacks: Acute Senses (Vision), Acute Senses (Smell/Taste), Cruel –1, Fast Reaction Time, Good Luck 2, Hard to Kill 5, Nerves of Steel, Resistance (Pain) 5, Resistance (Fatigue) 3, Situational Awareness

Skills: Brawling 3, Dodge 3, First Aid 3, Hand Weapon (Bisento) 5, Intimidation 2, Notice 2, Running (Marathon) 2, Tracking 2

Special Abilities: Damage Resistance, Infravision, Scent Tracking

Attack: Horns D10 + 5(10) and bisento D12 x 10 (60)

Huang Fei-hu

Huang Fei-hu are minotaurs, demons with a bovine head and a human body. They are the heavy hitters of the demonic legions, and thus should not be made available to players as Cast Members.

Story Ideas

Silent Blades

In this story, the Cast are all members of a ninja clan, raised from youth to act as a unit. Their master calls upon them to undertake a mission for the Shogun of the Mantis Kingdom, Ishada Kumiko, who seeks vengeance. They are to infiltrate the home of a minor daimyo in the service of the Lion clan, a man named Yamamoto Hiroshi, the loudest voice delaying the Lion and Dragon Kingdoms from coming to the aid of the Mantis. Kumiko wants him dead and his castle destroyed.

Infiltrating the castle will not be easy. If the Cast go the route of subterfuge, perhaps posing as wandering actors or itinerant wu jen looking for employment, this takes a great deal of time and effort. Hiroshi doesn't see just anyone, so the Cast has to convince numerous underlings to grant them an audience. Then comes several weeks or months spent trying to establish their cover and gain everyone's trust. Only after a long time do the Cast Members become trusted enough to gain an audience with Hiroshi. In the meantime, the Cast may pursue other adventures related to their cover story, as well as learning a great deal about Hiroshi's secret—he uses kuang-shi as servants and soldiers and appears somehow to be in league with the forces of Jigoku.

If the Cast decides to take the direct route, they must make various Strength and Climb Tasks to scale the castle walls, Dexterity and Stealth Tasks to sneak past guards, and, of course, close combat Tasks. After fighting (or sneaking) their way past bushi and samurai, they come to Hiroshi's personal guard—zombies all. These kuang-shi are never far from Hiroshi.

As ninja they cannot bring his treachery to light, for this would reveal them. It does, however, further justify their assignment and sets up future investigations into a possible conspiracy. This could lead back to other Lion Kingdom daimyo, and eventually to the sorcerers and

necromancers who originally struck the bargain with Yan-lo, which should well elevate the number of undead minions coming after the Cast. Eventually, the overall masters of the conspiracy to bring down the Kingdoms tire of the Cast's meddling, and hordes of undead are unleashed on peasant villages in retribution for each death the Cast inflicts. After a few villages are destroyed, the Cast comes to realize that fighting this battle in the mundane realms is not the way to win.

Kumiko, their employer, would be willing to fund an expedition by the ninja over the razor-sharp, obsidian walls of Jigoku. First, they must get there, avoiding or battling bakemono and goblin patrols. Second, they must find a way over the walls and into the city, no easy task even for ninja. And where to strike? During the course of their investigations, the Cast should learn about a rakshasa tiger demon named Chao-Li, Hiroshi's contact in Jigoku and a lieutenant to the dreaded Yan-lo. Killing him would significantly weaken Yan-lo and hurt the Lion Kingdom conspirators. Nothing should be as it seems, however, as the Cast discovers Kumiko's real reasons for targeting Chao-Li aren't so noble; he had her most beloved daughter murdered, and she wants revenge.

Traveling in Jigoku is survival horror at its best. There are no humans, kitsune, or korobokkuru to be found, only kuang-shi and oni, and the Cast soon finds themselves alone in the thick of a society ruled by hungry zombies.

Death on the Steppes

In this adventure the Cast should be either korobokkuru or some other kind of character outside of traditional society. They live on the steppes beyond the western mountains, the wide scrub grass plains inhabited by the horde, either because they are members of a korobokkuru tribe, or because they are fugitives or wanderers who are no longer bound by the laws of society. Ronin samurai, wandering sohei, itinerant demon quellers, and secluded wu jen would make perfect characters for a tale here.

The story begins with a raid by one clan of korobokkuru against the tent village of a rival clan. After the battle, the victors gather up the bodies of the dead for cremation, when suddenly they lunge forth and attack several living members of the tribe. The

Typical Bushi Guard

Strength 4 | **Constitution** 3
Dexterity 4 | **Intelligence** 3
Perception 3 | **Willpower** 3
Life Points 65 | **Speed** 14
Endurance Points 35 | **Chi** 20

Skills: Martial Arts 3, Hand Weapon (Katana) 4, Dodge 4

Gear: Katana D10 x 4(20), plate and chain Armor AV (D8 x 2) + 8(16)

Yamato Hiroshi

Strength 6 | **Constitution** 4
Dexterity 5 | **Intelligence** 3
Perception 2 | **Willpower** 4
Life Points 59 | **Speed** 18
Endurance Points 47 | **Chi** 24

Qualities and Drawbacks: Ambidextrous, Danger Sense 1, Fast Reaction Time, Hard to Kill 3, Honorable 3, Nerves of Steel, Obligation (Daimyo) 3, Samurai, Situational Awareness, Status (Noble)

Skills: Dodge 4, Hand Weapon (Katana) 4, Hand Weapon (Wakizashi) 4, Martial Arts 3

Gear: Katana D10 x 6(30), wakizashi D6 x 6(18), plate armor AV (D8 x 3) + 8(20)

Ishada Kumiko

Strength 5 | **Constitution** 5
Dexterity 6 | **Intelligence** 3
Perception 2 | **Willpower** 4
Life Points 65 | **Speed** 22
Endurance Points 44 | **Chi** 25

Skills: Martial Arts 3, Hand Weapon (Katana) 4, Hand Weapon (Yari) 4, Dodge 4

Qualities and Drawbacks: Attractiveness +2, Cruel 1, Danger Sense 1, Hard to Kill 5, Honorable 3, Nerves of Steel, Obligation (Emperor) 3, Obsession (Revenge) 3, Samurai, Status

Gear: Katana D10 x 5(25), wakizashi D6 x 5(15), yari D6 x 5(15), plate armor AV (D8 x 3) + 8(20)

dead walk among the korobokkuru, and it quickly becomes a fight for survival. Alternatively, for characters who are not korobokkuru, events begin several days after this attack, with a band of roving kuang-shi stumbling upon them (Tracking Tasks would be needed to follow the zombies' trail to the korobokkuru village, in order to learn the back story).

Chao-Li, Rakshasa Oni

Strength 5 **Constitution** 5
Dexterity 4 **Intelligence** 2
Perception 2 **Willpower** 2
Life Points 80 **Speed** 18
Endurance Points 41 **Chi** 20

Qualities and Drawbacks: Acute Senses (Vision), Acute Senses (Smell/Taste), Cruel –3, Fast Reaction Time, Good Luck 2, Hard to Kill 10, Nerves of Steel, Resistance (Pain) 5, Situational Awareness

Skills: Climbing 3, Dodge 3, Hand Weapon (Katana) 5, Hand Weapon (Wakizashi) 5, Intimidation 5, Martial Arts 3, Notice 4

Special Abilities: Damage Resistance, Infravision

Attacks: Claws D6 x 5(15), Bite D4 x 5(10), Katana D10 x 5 (50), Wakizashi D6 x 5(15)

A band of ravenous kuang-shi wandering the steppes would grow like a cancer in the remote area, and could endanger everyone. Thus, the council of elders who govern the korobokkuru tribe meets and decides to deal with this menace the only way they can—by hunting down the kuang-shi. The Cast Members get the job. (And the korobokkuru might seek out the assistance of any outcasts from the Three Kingdoms to aid them in this, like Cast Member wu jen and ronin). Successive adventures should chase down the trail of the kuang-shi all across the wilderness—foiling zombie attacks on remote korobokkuru tribes, saving isolated monks and sorcerers, and so on. These adventures should take some time, and keep the Cast constantly on their toes.

After the Cast has dealt with the kuang-shi on the steppes, their tribal leaders have a new mission for them—establishing an alliance with the civilized people to the south. Another way to introduce this element would be if the Cast can't contain the spread of the kuang-shi to the north, and the korobokkuru need help. Recently, the Emperor of the Three Kingdoms sent an envoy to initiate peace talks with the korobokkuru in hopes of quashing the oni menace. The leaders of the tribe have decided, after recent events, to send a return envoy to accept the proposal, and the Cast Members are selected to go. This would be especially appropriate for those Cast Members who once lived in the Three Kingdoms.

At this stage, the story becomes one of diplomacy and politics, and the emphasis should be on the differences in culture and values between the two peoples. First, any outcasts from the Three Kingdoms must overcome their status as hinin—ronin and other outsiders face discrimination and arrogance; they might have to prove themselves by completing several tasks and any number of adventures deep in the Three Kingdoms or Jigoku could take place alongside Dragon Kingdom samurai as the Cast slowly builds trust. Next, they must work to build an alliance between the Dragon Kingdom and the korobokkuru, which, of course, secret agents from the Lion Kingdom want to disrupt. Finally, once a deal has been worked out, the Cast has to return to the steppelands and convince other korobokkuru tribes to sign on.

Human Samurai Warrior

Talented Hero

Str 5* **Dex** 3 **Con** 5*
Int 3 **Per** 3 **Wil** 4*
LPs 80
EPs 38
Spd 16
Essence 20

Qualities/Drawbacks

Ambidextrous (3)
Cruel 1*
Delusions (Delusions of Grandeur) (–2)
Emotional Problems (Fear of Commitment) (–1)
Fast Reaction Time (2)
Hard To Kill 10*
Honorable 3*
Humorless (–1)
Nerves of Steel*
Obligation (Daimyo) 3*
Samurai (5)
Situational Awareness (2)
Status (Noble) 2*
Zealot (–3)

Skills

Bureaucracy 3
Dodge 2
Gambling 2
Hand Weapon (Great Bow) 3*
Hand Weapon (Katana) 3*
Hand Weapon (Wakizashi) 2
Martial Arts 2
Myth and Legend (Samguk) 2
Notice 3
Occult Knowledge 2
Play Instrument (Flute) 1
Research/Investigation 3
Riding (Horse) 3
Rituals (Shinto) 2
Writing (Haiku) 2

* Granted or modified by Samurai Quality

Gear

Daikyu Great Bow, Katana, Lantern with Oil (1 pint), Wakizashi, Plate and Mail Armor, Warhorse with Saddle Bags, 1 Week of Trail Rations

Personality

I am a man of few words.

My sword, my honor, and my liege are my life. This is the way of bushido. My sword is an extension of my will, ready to cut down whomever my lord commands. Many who speak of honor do not truly have the passion of bushido in their hearts and souls. I am not afraid to die, for I know I will be reborn again.

That is, until the gates of Jigoku opened. Now, the dead walk the land, yin given physical form. Ancestors rise from their grave to plague the living. This is not the natural order of things, but I still do not fear my own death. For to fear death is to no longer be a samurai.

When my time comes, I will face it bravely. Fear will not stay my hand. And should my body rise again, I know there will be others who will hunt me down and grant me a second death.

Now I am here, in this peasant village. The village leader petitioned my lord to protect these simple farmers from kuang-shi, and he sent me. Will I die tonight? I do not know. Life is like a lotus blossom—all things die, only to be born again.

Quote

"Duty and honor above all."

Kitsune Geisha Ninja

Adept Hero

Str 2 **Dex** 5*† **Con** 3
Int 3 **Per** 5*† **Wil** 3
LPs 39
EPs 29
Spd 16
Chi 20

* Granted or modified by Kitsune Quality
† Granted or modified by Ninja Quality

Qualities/Drawbacks

Acute Senses (Vision)*
Adversary (Various) (–4)
Attractiveness +1*
Covetous (Ambitious) (–2)
Cruel (–1)
Fear of Rejection (–1)
The Gift (5)
Hard to Kill 3 (3)
Kitsune (7)
Ninja (5)
Obligation (Ninja Clan) (–3)†
Paranoid (–2)
Secret (Ninja) 3†
Situational Awareness †

Skills

Climbing 2
Dancing (Exotic) 1
Disguise 2
Hand Weapon (Wakizashi) 3
Hand Weapon (Chain) 2†
Hand Weapon (Staff) 2†
Lock Picking (Mechanical) 2†
Martial Arts 2†
Notice 2
Science (Animals) 1*
Seduction 2
Smooth Talking 2
Stealth 3†
Survival (Forest) 1*
Traps 2

Powers/Metaphysics

Fox Transformation
Chi Focus 1
Chi Attack
Chi Defense
Chi Healing
Chi Vital Strike
Lesser Illusion 1

Gear

Backpack, Costumes (geisha, sohei, ninja uniform), Knife, 2 Ninja-to Swords, 50-foot Rope, 20 Shuriken (D4 x 3(6)) (can throw 3 at once), 5 Smoke Bombs

Personality

They say there is no way for a geisha to better her station in life. Perhaps they are correct. Perhaps my lord will never take me as his wife. This does not mean I do not strive for it. I have come to learn in my brief time here that I have the power to take what I want from this world. I have an important duty to perform, regardless of whether the officials see it.

I punish those who are without honor. Unfortunately, this may mean I have to kill my lord, soon. Truth be told, I love him and would swear my life to him, forsaking everything I now have. But he serves a daimyo who has made a pact with the forces of darkness, and in this dishonor has betrayed the Three Kingdoms. When I kill his daimyo, my lord will seek me out, and a day of reckoning will come for us both. My lord's honor, you see, lies in his service to his master, just as my own resides in the hands of my mistress and my clan.

Life would be so much simpler without honor and duty, and the zombies who now plague our land.

Quote

"You speak of duty and honor, but you know only blind obedience. I will show you what blind obedience yields!"

CHAPTER SEVEN

"Okay, make your attack roll."

Dice clattered on the table. After some quick math, Alex declared triumphantly "11!"

"That hits," Bernie said. "Now roll damage."

Alex swept up his six-sider and dropped it. He frowned. "Only four points of damage."

Bernie smiled. The party had gone precisely where he'd anticipated—down the hall to the west. There was a pit trap up ahead, one with a significant modifier to notice. And to make things interesting, he'd decided to "roll" for a wandering zombie attack from their rear. No sense making it easy on them. Then, the moment he'd been waiting for happened.

Jeff said, "My character runs down the hall away from the zombies."

"You run down the hall, in the darkness, and get twenty feet away when suddenly the ground drops away under you." Bernie said. "You take six points of damage."

"Don't I get a Notice Task?" Jeff asked.

"No, you don't. Your character is running down the hallway, in the dark. You're not moving carefully enough to notice things like pit traps," Bernie replied.

The adventure was going well. Their characters had ventured out into the wilderness, with the promise of gold from a small village. They'd made their way through the first three levels of the dungeon, and had discovered the secret base of Kaarj, an evil necromancer. Andy's character had already died in the zombie dog encounter.

Now, four zombies were attacking the party, and they were split up, with Jeff's character, Gerrad, in the pit. And Alex, who normally rolled well, had been tossing crap. It looked like it would be a good day for Kaarj the Conqueror. Bernie decided to press the attack.

"Three more zombies shamble out of the shadows."

"I cast a physical shield over the pit," George declared, grinning. "That way, we can run away from them.

"Dude, you can't use Shielding that way."

"Why not?"

"Because it doesn't create a physical barrier, it just deflects incoming attacks. It's not like an invisible wall or something." Bernie picked up his rulebook, and started flipping. Leave it to George to find a way to mess things up.

"Can I get an attack of opportunity on the zombies when they enter my threat radius?" It was Sean. And that was the third time he'd used that lame joke. Bernie ignored him.

"Dude, what happened to my character? He's down in the pit. What does he see?" Jeff got up from the table to get a can of soda.

"Two zombies. They're coming after you . . . Now George, I just reread the rules and I'm not buying . . ."

THE TOMB OF DOOM

History

The town of Skaarlev lies on the fringes of civilization, one of many small farming communities along the southern border of the Kingdom of Lerod. on the edge of unmapped wilderness. It is a bleak place of windswept plains covered in thick sod, much like the high plains of the American West. Farming is tough and the people do their best to eke out a living. The town lies on the shores of the Yan River, a main waterway for trade with larger cities. As is typical of these kinds of places, residents swear allegiance to a feudal lord, who in turn serves a king. But neither of these individuals has much impact upon the farmers' daily lives, except at tax time. On the whole, the people who make their home in and around Skaarlev are hardy and independent, just the kind of people you'd find living at the edge of the known world.

Long ago, this land was home to more than just farmers and sheep. It was once the land of barbarian horse raiders, who swept up from the south to ransack the wealthier lands of the north. Hundreds of years ago, the great barbarian king, Kelen, ruled these lands. After decades of internal warfare, Kelen united the tribes under his banner, and by all accounts he was wise and benefited his people. As was traditional for all the great warriors of his day, he was buried in a vast kaer, known by people today as a barrow mound. The people built rooms of fieldstone to hold all the things Kelen would need in the afterlife, then buried the tomb under a mound of earth.

With Kelen's death, the barbarians again fell to warring with each other over land and honor. In time, no strong leader emerged and the culture of the horse raiders died out. The more civilized people of the north migrated southward, and built towns and farms. All that remains of the barbarians are the ruins of their stone longhouses and their kaers.

But Kelen does not rest easy in his grave. For reasons unknown and unexplained, he has reanimated and intends to re-conquer his lands.

The Zombies

In truth, a necromancer lies at the heart of the zombie horde. This necromancer, Kaarj, traveled from the civilized lands to the north in order to begin building his base of power, far from prying eyes. Learned in history, he sought out Kelen's kaer and violated the sanctity of the tomb. Using powerful magics, he raised the bodies of ancient barbarian warriors along with their greatest king. He did this to disguise his hand in the zombie uprising.

The zombies under Kaarj's command come from the numerous slain warriors buried where they fell on nameless battlegrounds, as well as hapless travelers and peasants attacked by zombies and Kaarj's goblin raiders.

The basic Tomb of Doom zombie isn't especially strong, fast, or smart, though they can communicate and use weapons. They attack by lunging suddenly at their victims, biting and clawing to bring them down. Any bit of human (or elf or dwarf) flesh slakes their hunger, and they share their condition by killing their victims (who rise up in D6(3) hours)

Tomb of Doom Zombies

Strength 2 | **Constitution** 2
Dexterity 1 | **Intelligence** 1
Perception 1 | **Willpower** 2
Dead Points 26 | **Speed** 2
Endurance Points n/a | **Essence Pool** 9

Skills: Brawling 2, Hand Weapon (Various) 2 [+2]

Attack: Bite D4 x 2(4), claws D6 x 2(6), or by weapon

Weak Spot: All [0]

Getting Around: Slow and Steady [0], Burrowing [+3], The Lunge [+3]

Strength: Dead Joe Average [0], Claws [+8]

Senses: Like the Dead [0], Infravision [+2], Scent Tracking [+1]

Sustenance: Occasionally [+2], All Flesh Must Be Eaten [0]

Intelligence: Language [+1], Tool Use 1 [+3]

Spreading the Love: Only the Dead [–2]

Power: 28

Conventions Again

The Tomb of Doom Deadworld departs from the traditional way in which *AFMBE* settings are presented. A new text box is presented.

> *The text in boxes like this should be read to the players over the course of the adventure. As in other fantasy roleplaying games, this information tells the characters what they see, hear, and experience.*

A Quiet Little Town

The adventure begins with the Cast Members in the small town of Skaarlev. Who knows why they're here. They might have grown up here. Maybe they're returning from some other adventure and stop off at the town for the night. Or perhaps they come here for individual reasons, and form a party over the course of events. The ZM could play through one or two adventures prior to the start of The Tomb of Doom, with no mention of zombies, in order to convince players they're playing something other than zombie survival horror.

Of course, they're in a tavern. The ZM can stage an encounter with the usual suspects—rowdy dwarves eager to pick a fight, the talkative innkeeper, and the classic Mysterious Stranger. Give them a chance to eat, drink, wench, and gamble, to get them in the mode for dungeon delving. Let them introduce their characters and get to know each other.

Once everyone has gotten into character, and the clichés are flying fast and furious, the ZM should stage a zombie attack.

> *A shriek pierces the night, interrupting the evening's festivities. The tavern's patrons quickly bolt outside, anxious to find the source of the trouble. From out of the darkness, five figures shamble into the light of lanterns held high. One of them drags the body of a peasant woman behind him. Upon closer examination, it appears something is very wrong—the men move stiffly, their flesh pallid and bloated. Zombies! One that seems to be the leader drops its meal and advances.*

Five zombies have stumbled into town and captured a townswoman making her way home. It is she who screamed, before the zombies killed her. Like zombies everywhere, they're looking for a snack, and the Cast Members out on the street make as good a meal as any. The zombies attack. The townspeople, who were so eager to see what was going on a moment before, retreat to the tavern and barricade the door.

After the Cast deals with this threat, the townspeople from the tavern come out of hiding and thank them profusely. They receive plenty of offers of free drinks, and the innkeeper offers them a room for the night, on him. The townspeople are relieved, and begin to discuss the attack and how it fits in with recent events. With successful Intelligence and Questioning Tasks, the Cast learns that other attacks have taken place over the last few weeks. The zombies always come from the same direction—the site of an ancient, barbarian burial ground to the northeast. Other than this, the townspeople don't know much about the history of the region.

Since they performed so valiantly in this attack, the townspeople want the Cast to track the zombies to see what they can find. The town is poor, but can scrape to offer 500 silver as payment.

The Barrow

> *After a day and a night of travel, the flat plains become hilly. Numerous small mounds dot the landscape. Some of these are marked with a single standing stone carved with ancient runes. Riding further, a large rocky hill rises from the ground, this one crested by a circle of stone dolmens, which gives it the appearance of a primitive crown. At the base of the hill, three roughhewn, flat rocks form the sides and lintel of a doorway. The tomb lies open to the elements.*

Cast Members with the Tracking skill can easily follow the trail left by the zombies. They lead in a straight line from the site of the barbarian burial ground, though once among the rocks leading to the dolmens, zombie tracks are exceedingly difficult to find (four Success Levels or better to find even partial marks; in fact, the zombies enter the complex from area seven on the first level but the Cast should not learn that until they are inside). Without the Tracking skill, the Cast simply needs to travel directly south in order to find the monument.

Cast Members who possess any rune-related Craft skill can attempt to read the various standing stones with a Intelligence and Craft Task at a –4 penalty (the symbols the barbarians used are different from the contemporary style). With a successful roll, readers learn the name and deeds of the warrior interred inside the tomb. Cast Members who decide to investigate any of these lesser barrows discovers small, single room tombs. Significantly, they are empty, the bodies having disappeared without a trace (though if the Zombie Master wants, one or two zombies might occupy them). Kaarj has animated the bodies and they have long since abandoned their resting places to join his army.

The door to Kelen's tomb, a single large boulder, has been rolled out of its place and lies to the side of the doorway. Perception and Tracking Tasks reveal that dozens of creatures (with small feet, no less) rolled the heavy boulder out of place. With three or more Success Levels, a Cast Member can identify these tracks as being goblin.

1. Entrance

Beyond the gloomy doorway lies a small, roughly oval chamber. The walls are constructed of field stones stacked on top of each other, with no mortar to hold them together. The air is still and dry. Jugs and sacks have been stacked here, apparent offerings to the tomb's occupant. At the opposite side of the room is an open doorway leading deeper into the tomb.

This room holds the remains of offerings placed in the tomb for Kelen's journey into the afterlife. Whatever the clay jugs held has long since spoiled (make a Difficult Constitution Test for those foolish enough to drink or they spend D6(3) Turns retching), and the contents of the sacks rotted away long ago.

Javelin Trap: The room was previously protected by a javelin trap, which triggered when someone stepped on a flagstone in the center of the floor. The barbarians left it behind to protect Kelen's tomb from looters. The flagstone trigger can be spotted with a Perception and Notice Task, though Kaarj has disabled the mechanism and it does not work (a similar Task to notice that fact).

Once the Cast enters the room, they hear scratching and squealing. Moments later a number of rats (two per Cast Member) enter the chamber from the next room. They have been attracted by the noise and light the Cast produces, and figure its time for a snack. It doesn't help that these rats are undead, animated by the energies produced by Kaarj's Necromantic powers. Use the Attributes and abilities for zombie rats (*AFMBE*, p. 169). Unlike the original description for zombie rats, however, these monsters do not spread the love.

2. Throne Room

This room is much larger than the one previous, and is more lavishly decorated. Crude and weathered paintings cover the walls, depicting a nomadic barbarian life. A large stone chair, a throne, sits at the far end, opposite the door. Upon this sits a skeleton dressed in full barbarian regalia—a metal breastplate, a headband of gold, and the tattered remains of what must have been a fur cloak. The body clutches a sword across its lap, and its head lies slumped on his chest. Around the room wooden chests, clay jugs, and wrapped bundles lie stacked along the walls. Cobweb-covered weapons—swords, bows, spears—lean against the walls around the room, as well, perhaps placed there for their occupant's use in the afterlife.

Zombie Masters should know where this is going . . . and so should the Cast.

Once the Cast Members touch anything in the room (living characters only), the skeleton warrior seated on the throne animates in order to attack them. This is not a zombie, or even an independently intelligent creature. Rather, it is the source of a powerful Death Lordship ability granting animation to the skeleton, and was actually left behind by the people who buried Kelen (it is not Kaarj's work though he did reinforce the faded magic and is able to keep it from animating). The skeleton continues to fight for 10 Turns before the enchantment ends and the skeleton crumbles into a heap of bones. Intelligent Cast Members might think to leave the tomb and return later. The skeleton guardian does not follow them and collapses once the Invocation's duration expires. Inspired Cast Members who attempt to use The Binding to restrain the skeleton guardian find the Miracle does not work. It is not truly a supernatural being, instead an animated shell. Metaphysics that cause damage still function, however.

On opposite sides of the room, the Cast Members can locate two concealed doorways. The aged paintings do not completely hide the change in the pattern of piled stones. Cast Members can notice this with a Perception and Notice Task. It takes D6 + 1(4) minutes to clear away the debris and expose the room beyond.

Behind the throne lies a well-concealed doorway that leads to Kelen's main burial chamber. Finding this doorway requires a Perception and Notice Task with a –4 penalty. A similarly successful Task reveals the trigger latch; otherwise, the party must smash their way through. There are no other traps protecting this hidden door, which is made of thin stone and painted with a primitive battle scene. For all intents and purposes, the door looks like tomb decoration.

Treasure: Among the loot left to accompany Kelen in the afterlife, the Cast finds a total of 500 silver pieces, various household and personal items, and a barbarian luck talisman (counts as Good Luck 1 Quality). These were left by Kaarj and the goblins in order to keep the skeleton from animating.

Animated Skeleton

Strength 2	**Constitution** 2
Dexterity 2	**Intelligence** –1
Perception 1	**Willpower** 0
Dead Points 26	**Speed** 8
Endurance Points n/a	**Essence Pool** 6

Skills: Brawling 2, Hand Weapon (Various) 1

Attack: Various melee weapons (ZM's discretion)

Special: Damage Resistant

3. Treasure Room

This room appears to hold more offerings to the occupant's spirit—several crates, chests, and bundles lie scattered about. The light catches dozens of pairs of tiny rat eyes.

Once the Cast clears away the debris clogging the passageway to the east of the throne, a mass of zombie rats (three per party member) charge out of the darkness and attack (see *AFMBE*, p. 169).

This chamber holds the objects the barbarians believed Kelen would need in the afterlife. These are his personal possessions, contained in various chests.

Treasure: After the zombie rats have been dealt with, the Cast can examine the contents of the room. The chests and boxes are not locked. Inside, they find numerous gold ornaments—hair combs, rings, brooches, armbands, and the like—along with various articles of clothing, wooden plates and goblets, rugs, and the like. The entire contents of the room are worth 2,000 silver pieces if sold to historians or collectors.

4. Armory

The same crude stonework walls this room. On the surface opposite the doorway, runes have been painted in red, through their color has long since faded with age. Suits of armor and racks of weapons have been carefully placed along the rough-hewn walls.

In the chamber to the west of the throne, Kelen's people buried his weapons. As with the previous room, it takes D6 + 1(4) minutes to clear away the debris clogging the doorway.

Enchanted runes protect the contents from looters. They have been painted on the stone walls, and are obvious to anyone using a lantern or torch.

Rune Trap: When any living being enters the chamber, the runes are triggered, causing a fire blast inflicting D6 x 5(15) points of damage. Those with the Gift Quality can sense supernatural energies radiating from the runes with a successful Simple Perception Test, but cannot tell their effects. Using the Traps skill has no effect, as the runes are magical in nature.

The room contains piles of weapons and armor—short swords, leather armor, simple pot helmets, quivers of arrows, and so on. All of these are finely worked, and are suitable for a king. It is up to the ZM as to whether or not any of these are magical (see p. 48 for information on magic items).

5. Main Burial Chamber

Behind the thin stone door painted with a battle scene lies a large, rectangular room. A sunken section fills the middle. A stone sarcophagus adorned with runic inscriptions rests in that section. Four stone pillars hold up the ceiling, each with a skeleton dressed in tattered armor and clothes standing before it. Stacks of chests and bundle piles line the edges of the chamber.

This room is Kelen's final resting place, though the corpse is no longer inside. For the Cast to learn this, they must open the sarcophagus, which requires a Difficult Strength Test, or a Strength and Weight Lifting Task, with a –6 penalty. Underneath the sarcophagus lies the entrance to Kaarj's underground lair. This requires a Perception and Notice Task to discover. The sarcophagus is designed to pivot on one corner, and swings open easily by pushing on it. Touching Kelen's sarcophagus, however, triggers the four skeleton guardians protecting the room.

Like the skeleton in the throne room, these creatures are not undead in the classic sense of the word. They were left here to protect Kelen in the afterlife, and were ensorcelled by barbarian shamans long ago to attack living interlopers (they too were "recharged" and kept inanimate by Kaarj). Once the Cast disturbs anything in the room, the skeletons animate and attack. As before, they remain active for 10 Turns and cannot be affected by the Binding Miracle (though Metaphysics that cause damage remain effective). If the Cast smashes the skeleton guardians before they touch the sarcophagus, they do not animate.

Treasure: Searching the various receptacles in this room uncovers a wealth of barbarian artifacts—statues, clothing, board games, and the like. These would be worth 1,000 silver pieces to the right buyer. Kraaj left these undisturbed to fool tomb robbers into looking no further.

The First Level

This level of Kaarj's hideout holds the many zombies he has animated as part of his undead army. In general, the zombies have tunneled through the earth, so the walls are simply dirt, as are the floors.

Throughout this level, the Cast should randomly encounter bands of zombies in various numbers (roll D6(3)). These creatures wander around, awaiting orders from Kaarj, and looking for something to eat.

1. Entrance

A rickety, roughly made ladder descends into the earth, and a noisome chill wafts up from underground. The roughly twenty-foot by twenty-foot chamber at the bottom appears to be of recent construction, and simply dug out of the surrounding dirt. Two passageways lead deeper into darkness.

On a roll of 1-4 on a D10, the characters encounter wandering zombies in this room. The zombies shamble about, with no apparent purpose, though they attack any intruders.

To the left of the ladder is a secret door that leads directly to the third level of Kaarj's dungeon. This allows Kaarj to escape from the third level should he need to, and grants him access to his "fortress" without having to pass by all the zombies and goblins. In order to locate the secret door, Cast Members must say they are looking for one and must succeed on a Perception and Notice Task with a –4 penalty. Beyond the door, disguised to look like packed dirt, is a long, rickety ladder leading down to the area two on the third level (see pp. 143-144).

2. Zombie Diggers

As the Cast makes their way through this level, they come upon a zombie work gang digging their way through the earth. Kaarj has ordered them to expand the level to hold more zombies, and they're doing it the only way they know how—with their hands.

When the Cast arrives, they see four zombies clawing through the dirt. Ever eager for a snack, the zombies stop what they're doing and attack the group. If the battle lasts for more than D6 x 2(6) Turns (and every D6 x 2(6) Turns thereafter), the commotion attracts another four zombies to the fray. If they're not careful, they could end up fighting an entire army.

3. Goblin Terror

As you turn the corner,
a shriek pierces the darkness.

In this section of the dungeon, a too curious goblin has wandered into the zombie level and gotten himself into trouble. When the Cast arrives, they find the little fellow cowering in a corner while three zombies move in for the kill.

If the Cast rescues the goblin, he offers to help them find Kaarj. Although he does not know about the secret door in area one, he can take them to the entrance to the next level and provide information on number of goblins and defenses below. Although genuinely thankful for the Cast's help and truthful in his answers, at an appropriate time Jurga betrays the Cast (likely on the next level, when he's surrounded by fellow goblins).

Jurga the Goblin

Strength 2	**Constitution** 3
Dexterity 4	**Intelligence** 2
Perception 4	**Willpower** 2
Life Points 26	**Speed** 14
Endurance Points 26	**Essence Pool** 17

Qualities/Drawbacks: Acute Senses (Hearing), Attractiveness –2, Brachiation, Cowardly 1, Situational Awareness

Skills: Brawling 3, Dodge 2, Hand Weapon (Short Sword) 3, Notice 2, Riding (Wolf) 2, Stealth 2

Gear: Short sword D6 x 2(6), small knife D4(2), leather armor AV D6 + 1(4)

4. That's Right, We Said Ghost

The negative energies and suffering generated by Kaarj's activities have attracted a ghost from the Netherworld. This entity haunts this section of the dungeon and has yet to stray to other areas.

As you travel down the narrow, dirt passageway, the path becomes wider, and the temperature suddenly drops.

The ghost manifests as a human warrior who hates the living and has returned to wreak suffering on mortals. It has returned from the afterlife because of its attraction to suffering. It has no specific task to complete, no traumatic death to avenge. The ghost has no effect on the zombies who routinely pass by, and Kaarj has little to fear from a disembodied spirit (and he has plans to enslave the ghost for his own activities). The goblins have been warned to keep out of the first level entirely.

The ghost attacks the Cast Members as soon as they enter the chamber. It uses its Animate power to snatch weapons from the Cast Members and use them against the group. Cast Members currently holding their weapons can resist with an opposed Simple Strength Test. The ghost continues attacking until it runs out of Energy Essence to spend.

Ghost

Strength 3 **Constitution** 2
Dexterity 2 **Intelligence** 2
Perception 3 **Willpower** 5
Vital Essence 30 **Energy Essence** 60
Spiritus 4

Skills: Brawling 2, Hand Weapon (any) 3

Powers: Animate, Purpose (Kill the Living; +20 Essence per day when attacking living beings)

Beings of Essence: Ghosts have Vital Essence and Energy Essence Pools. Depleting Vital Essence causes the ghost to dissipate.

Channel and Tap into Essence: Ghosts can manipulate and channel Essence, and have the equivalent of Essence Channeling equal to their Willpower doubled.

Immaterial: Ghosts cannot interact directly with the physical world. They cannot be seen by normal senses, physical attacks cannot harm them, and they cannot affect material beings. Only Essence attacks can harm them (by first depleting their Energy Essence, then Vital Essence), and they attack others using their Energy Essence.

Spiritus: Ghosts can exercise control over their surroundings, measured by their Spiritus. This is the skill with which the ghost uses its abilities.

Animate: The ghost can toss objects around, manipulate things, and even attack people. Each point of Essence used gives the ghost an effective Strength 1 for lifting, pushing, and throwing. This lasts for two Turns before more Essence must be spent. Manipulating things uses the ghost's Willpower or Perception plus any appropriate skills.

Phantom Shape: By spending Essence, ghosts can make themselves partially visible. It costs five Essence points to appear translucent, and 10 Essence points to appear solid and lifelike. With 15 Essence points, the ghost can partially manifest (Strength 1; Dexterity equals Willpower). All effects last one minute, and if a point of damage is inflicted on the Phantom Shape, it vanishes.

For more information on ghosts, see the *WitchCraft* roleplaying game.

5. Zombie Snackers

In this section of the dungeon, the Cast stumbles upon a gristly scene—a number of zombies are devouring a recent kill. They grip human limbs, shredding them with teeth and claws, fresh red blood running down their chins. And with the Cast Members arriving at just the right time, they're ready for the main course.

Treasure: Searching the remains of the body, Cast Members find a belt pouch containing 10 silver coins and a Blessed dagger (+1 to combat Tasks and damage).

6. Zombie Storage

The narrow tunnel widens to form a large chamber. Row upon row of zombies stand as though waiting for something.

In this oddly-shaped chamber, Kaarj has placed the bulk of his undead army. Here, they wait for his orders to spread across the land like a zombie tidal wave. When the Cast enters the room, however, the zombies attack. As this is where the bulk of Kaarj's zombies can be found, the ZM shouldn't be afraid to overwhelm the Cast with large numbers of undead.

7. Tunnel

This rough passage was added later to provide an access point for zombies, goblins, and wolves. It slopes up to the surface, narrowing as it goes. The final ten feet must be crawled through and emerges behind a large rock (which must be climbed over). The goblins have cunningly concealed the exit with a screen of rocks. It should take an extraordinary series of rolls to enter the complex by this route.

8. Guard Post

At the end of one of the tunnels lies a locked reinforced door. If the Cast has rescued Jurga from area four, he wears a key on a chain around his neck. A curved ramp lies beyond, descending 30 feet to the dungeon's second level.

Before the Cast can get to the door, however, a final band of six zombies attacks them. They shuffle about before the door, and have been instructed to attack anyone who is not a goblin, or accompanied by Kaarj or a goblin (which means if Jurga is present the zombies let the Cast pass unmolested).

The Second Level

This level of the dungeon has been given over to Kaarj's goblin minions. Here, they sleep, eat, and brawl, when they're not following Kaarj's orders. Because they are as fearful of zombies as any other right-minded living being, there are no undead on this level.

Goblin Warriors

Strength 2 **Constitution** 2
Dexterity 4 **Intelligence** 1
Perception 4 **Willpower** 1
Life Points 26 **Speed** 12
Endurance Points 20 **Essence Pool** 14

Qualities/Drawbacks: Acute Senses (Hearing), Attractiveness –2, Brachiation, Cowardly 1, Situational Awareness

Skills: Brawling 2, Dodge 1, Hand Weapon (Short Sword) 2, Notice 2, Riding (Wolf) 2, Stealth 1

Gear: Short sword D6 x 2(6), leather armor AV D6 + 1(4)

The construction here isn't much different from the previous level—simple tunnels dug into the ground. Unlike the level above, however, wooden beams have been added to give the structure more support.

1. Passage

As you look down the long, dark, bending passage, flickering light emerges from a circular doorway in the right hand wall. A heavy animal smell, mixed with the stink of rotting flesh hangs in the air. Frequent snuffling and shuffling can be heard down the hall.

The doorway leads to a goblin lair. On the opposite side of the hall from the doorway are the unlit stables of the goblin's wolf mounts. The stench of unwashed canine and rotting food scraps fills the corridor, as the pens are open to the passageway.

The pens where the wolves are stabled are separated from the passage by low, wooden half-doors, meaning the wolves can look out onto the hallway. Unless the Cast Members have some way of avoiding detection, the wolves likely sound the alarm.

2. Wolf Pens

Three low, wooden doors separate the hallway from the stables dug into surrounding earth. Filthy straw covers the floor, gnawed animal bones lying where they were discarded. Each door leads to two large wolves.

The goblins use wolves as their beasts of burden, riding them, tying supplies to their backs, and so on. The six wolves kept in these pens alert the goblins across the hall to on-coming trouble. They bark and howl loudly as soon as the Cast comes within ten feet of the area.

Sneaking past the wolves is difficult. While a Resisted Dexterity and Stealth Task against the wolves' Simple Perception Test might succeed, it is their sense of smell that is the problem. Unless the Cast Members have some way to disguise their odor, such as Lesser Illusion, the wolves will not be caught unawares.

Wolves

Strength 3	**Constitution** 2
Dexterity 4	**Intelligence** 1 (animal)
Perception 5	**Willpower** 3
Life Points 25	**Speed** 22
Endurance Points 29	**Essence Pool** 18

Skills: Brawling 4, Dodge 2, Notice 3, Running (Dash) 1, Tracking 3

Attack: Bite D6 x 4(12)

Special Abilities: Enhanced Senses (Smell/Taste and Hearing)

3. Goblin Dormitory One

Several lanterns hang on hooks from the ceiling or rest on crude wooden tables placed around the room. Six rows of ramshackle, wooden bunk beds line the wall, a filthy, moth-eaten blanket lying crumpled on each pallet. Piles of trash, mostly cast off food scraps, litter the hard-packed earth.

This room is the barracks for a group of Kaarj's goblin servants (two per each Cast Member). They aren't particularly clean, and a litter of bones, fur, and discarded meat gives the room its pungent smell. The goblins living here do practically everything in this room—sleep, gamble, eat, fight, and so on . . . the room is a mess.

Should the wolves across the hall sound the alarm, the goblins in this room rush out to see what caused the commotion. Each is armed and ready for action. If the Cast enters without alerting the wolves, they find the goblins going about their business, and the latter must make a Perception and Notice Task to become aware of the Cast Members' presence (which means the Cast gains initiative). The sound of fighting does not attract the attention of the other goblins on this level—they're used to fights breaking out.

There is little of value in this room; most of what the goblins have is broken or of poor quality. The Cast Members might turn up D10 x 2(10) copper coins lying among all the trash. One of the devilish little monsters, however, has decided to protect his loot in an intact wooden chest he hides under a pile of filthy rags.

Poison Trap: A simple contact poison smeared on the lid protects the hidden chest, allowing it to be opened only by gripping the sides of the lid. A successful Perception and Notice Task reveals the poison's presence. Those who open the chest improperly test against the poison (Strength 3, paralysis D6 hours, contact). Inside the chest, the Cast finds a sack of six gold coins and shiny bits of metal (worthless).

4. Goblin Dormitory Two

This room is much like the first goblin dormitory, except it is separated from the corridor by crude doors constructed out of wooden planks lashed together with rope, and a short hallway. Cast Members can sneak past this room easily, if they desire.

Eating currently consumes the attention of the goblins inside. When the Cast enters the room, they find D6 + 3(6) goblins all seated around an iron pot hanging over a smoldering fire. Opening the door alerts them to the Cast Members' presence, and they quickly drop everything to engage the group.

One of the goblins attempts to sneak past the Cast Members during the melee to warn the other goblins and Kaarj. This should be handled as a Dexterity and Stealth Task opposed by the closest Cast Member's Simple Perception Test. Otherwise, as before, the sound of fighting does not alert the other goblins on this level.

Now would be a good time for Jurga to betray the Cast Members. As soon as the goblins attack, Jurga joins the fight on the side of his fellows.

Treasure: The goblins in this room have fared a little better than their fellows in the first goblin dormitory, and have a bit of loot between them. The total take consists of D6 x 2(6) silver coins and D6 x 20(60) copper coins (hidden under filthy mattresses, under trash heaps, and in small hidey-holes).

5. Cold Storage

Venturing down the corridor, the stench of death hangs heavy in the air. The path ends abruptly at a roughly dug room. Rotting corpses lie heaped like cordwood around the room.

Here, the goblins keep the bodies of any people they've killed, where they wait until Kaarj requires more bodies to animate. Although the Cast might fear a massive undead uprising at any moment (something the ZM should encourage with false Perception and Notice Tasks), the corpses here are well and truly dead.

If Jurga remains with the Cast Members, he really doesn't want to go down the hall and into this room. When questioned, he's up front about it—he doesn't like all the dead bodies. He should be unhelpful about their status as zombies, however, to keep the Cast guessing. In truth, he doesn't know if they're dead or undead.

At the Zombie Master's discretion, there may be normal, living rats making a meal of the bounty of death the goblins have provided. These rats scurry away when the Cast first enters the room, though disturbing the bodies (to search for treasure, perhaps) results in an attack. There's no treasure left on the bodies—they've been picked clean by the goblins.

Rats

Strength 0 | **Constitution** 1
Dexterity 4 | **Intelligence** –1 (animal)
Perception 3 | **Willpower** 0
Life Points 5 | **Speed** 10
Endurance Points 20 | **Essence Pool** 8
Attack: Bite D4 – 1(1)

6. Chieftain's Room

Opening the wooden door, a noxious stench assails your nostrils. The rough, packed earth cave is littered with the bones of small animals and rotting carcasses. In the middle of the room, a fat goblin reclines on a pile of animal skins, being fed raw rat intestines by scantily clad girl goblins. Upon being disturbed, he leaps up, snarls, and charges.

The chief of the goblin tribe occupies this room, and it is he who acts as the tribe's connection to Kaarj the necromancer. Being bigger and stronger than everyone else in the mob, he believes he should get better treatment. He lives in his own private den, serviced by the tribe's few female members.

Kagga, Goblin Chief

Strength 4 **Constitution** 3
Dexterity 4 **Intelligence** 2
Perception 4 **Willpower** 2
Life Points 47 **Speed** 16
Endurance Points 32 **Essence Pool** 19

Qualities/Drawbacks: Acute Senses (Hearing), Attractiveness –2, Brachiation, Covetous (Ambitious) 3, Cowardly 1, Hard to Kill 2, Situational Awareness, Status (Chief) 3

Skills: Brawling 3, Dodge 3, Hand Weapon (Mace) 4, Intimidation 3, Notice 2, Riding (Wolf) 2, Stealth 2

Gear: Small mace D8 x 4(16), leather armor AV D6 + 1(4)

Kagga, the tribe's chief, doesn't attack the party alone. His female serving girls are all armed and dangerous, and willing to fight on behalf of their meal ticket. Use the game statistics for goblin warriors (p. 139), but substitute Hand Weapon (Knife) for Hand Weapon (Short Sword). They are armed with small knives.

The sound of a commotion coming from this room attracts the attention of Borga, the tribe's shaman, and the guards from area seven across the hall. They arrive quickly to see what is going on, with Borga lending his Metaphysical support to the fight.

Kagga is an ambitious goblin, and has hitched his wagon to Kaarj because he hopes to one day have a great deal of power in the necromancer's empire. He's delusional, to say the least, and the Cast can capitalize on this. Should they have the opportunity to talk to Kagga (by restraining him somehow, for example), they could either convince him of the flaws in his logic ("Necromancers don't share power.") or to switch sides ("If you join us, we'll make you a king."). This should be resolved as an Intelligence and Smooth Talk Task resisted by Kagga's Simple Intelligence Test. If they succeed, Kagga can muster any remaining goblins to help the Cast assault the next level.

Most important, Kagga wears a rusty key on a string tied around his neck. This key opens the door to area two of level three and disarms the trap on it.

Treasure: Kagga believes strongly that the tribe exists for his personal benefit, and takes the lion's share of the booty they have amassed. Contained in a sack hidden in a hole covered by a canvas tarp (Perception and Notice to locate), is the tribe's wealth: D8 x 10(40) gold coins, D12 x 10(60) silver coins, D4 x 100(200) copper coins, and various jewelry (value determined by ZM). Unfortunately, Kagga protects this stash from his "loyal" followers with a pet snake, discoverable only with a Perception and Notice Task with a –6 penalty after the tarp is lifted. If not discovered, the snake strikes automatically when the treasure is moved.

Trap: Poisonous Snake (Strength 6, corrosive, injection).

7. Shrine to Zork

Toward the far side of the room stands a small wooden pallet covered with animal hides. The skulls of various animals lie in a pile next to the bed, stacked neatly like some kind of trophy rack. Behind the alter, a golden idol stands in an alcove carved into the wall, surrounded by guttering candles. The idol depicts a naked goblin clutching a tiny spear. Before the pallet is a tiny, bloodstained altar made of stone.

Two goblins guard the doorway, while a wizened old goblin clutching a rattle kneels before the shrine.

In this room, the goblins have erected a shrine to their god, Zork. Not much is known of Zork, other than that the goblins revere him as an icon of goblin behavior. A goblin shaman, Borga, attends to the goblins' spiritual needs (whatever those might be). Most of the time, he spends his time contemplating the greatness of Zork and sacrificing small animals.

When the Cast enters, the goblins immediately attack. The two guards try to keep the Cast Members occupied while Borga hides in the shadows and fires arrows (using his Mystic Targeting Quality). If things go badly for the goblins, Borga switches to Invocations, notably Elemental Fire blasts. If Kagga switches sides and joins the Cast, Borga goes along with his chief. Under no circumstances do the guards run to down to the next level to alert Kaarj.

Treasure: The golden idol of Zork is worthless aside from the value of the thin metal coating (100 silver coins).

Borga

Strength 2 **Constitution** 2
Dexterity 3 **Intelligence** 3
Perception 4 **Willpower** 3
Life Points 26 **Speed** 10
Endurance Points 26 **Essence Pool** 17

Qualities/Drawbacks: Acute Senses (Hearing), Attractiveness −2, Brachiation, Cowardly, Essence Channeling 5, The Gift, Mystic Targeting, Psychic Invoker, Situational Awareness

Skills: Brawling 3, Dodge 2, Hand Weapon (Short Bow) 3, Intimidation 2, Magic Bolt 3, Notice 2, Occult Knowledge 2, Riding (Wolf) 2, Stealth 3

Metaphysics: Elemental Fire 3, Farsight 2, Lesser Curse 2

Gear: Short Bow D6 x 2(6), quiver (15 arrows), leather armor AV D6 +1(4)

Notes: Borga does not actually have a connection with Zork because goblins cannot be Inspired. However, he is an exception to the rule that goblins cannot be Gifted, and has learned Invocations. With his Psychic Invoker Quality, he does not require gestures or incantations, making it appear as though his powers are of divine origin.

The Third Level

The third, and final, level of Kaarj's underground hideout employs different construction from those above. The walls throughout have been reinforced with stone blocks. These are more uniformly cut than those used in the construction of Kelen's tomb, though dwarf characters who make a successful Simple Intelligence Test can tell the quality is shoddy and unprofessional.

1. Zombie Hounds

A twisting passageway winds its way down to a roughly triangular chamber dug into the earth. Two iron floor sconces provide light from either side of a wooden door banded with iron. The room is chilly and smells earthy. Four pairs of dead, animal eyes stare out from the shadows of the two opposite corners, glinting in the firelight.

As soon as the Cast Members enter the room from the level above, four zombie dogs attack them. Kaarj animated them to guard the entrance to his level, as he did not trust the goblins to actually follow orders. Use the Attributes and abilities for zombie dog (see *AFMBE*, p. 169), though they share the love in the same way as The Tomb of Doom zombies. The zombie dogs are incapable of raising the alarm, since they're dead (and don't have vocal chords). Kaarj has found a way around this problem, by magically enchanting the door.

Screaming Trap: Cast Members with the Gift Quality can sense supernatural energies radiating from the door with a successful Simple Perception Test, but have no way of knowing their effect. Kaarj has inscribed it with a rune and powered it to warn him of intruders; any living person other than he triggers a piercing scream. The key around Kagga's neck disarms the alarm (see p. 142).

2. Work Room

This large, rectangular room radiates an aura of evil and fear. Mystic symbols have been inscribed in a circular pattern on the floor, daubed in what appears to be blood. Red and black candles flicker from sconces placed around the room, with two flickering on a stone slab embedded in the west wall and fitted with iron restraints. A mysterious stain darkens the floor around the slab. The south wall holds a massive wooden table, cluttered with the tools of the magician's trade—beakers, books, scrolls, jars, a human skull, and much more.

During daytime hours, Kaarj splits his time here and in the library (area five). There is a 40% chance (1-4 on a D10) of him being here, working on animating zombies. A Warding circle, the mystic symbols covering the flagstone floor, is intended to keep zombies *in* while Kaarj works on them. The Ward has Strength Rating 5 (see p. 44).

If the Cast triggers the alarm on the door to this area, Kaarj expects them (no surprising him). Like many evil sorcerers, he's a coward and depends on his undead to do the fighting for him. Four flesh-eaters occupy the room, standing guard at the doors opposite the entrance. Kaarj bolts from the room, through the door on the right-hand wall, to get to his library and the Kelen zombie. He leaves his zombie guards to delay the Cast.

In addition to the zombies, Kaarj has left a little surprise for intruders. The west door has been enchanted so that anyone living who touches it triggers a Lightning Bolt Invocation.

Lightning Trap: When the door is opened by anyone other than Kaarj, it discharges a lightning bolt that inflicts D6 x 3(9) points of damage. Inspired Cast Members can sense supernatural energies radiating from the door with a successful Simple Perception Test, though they cannot identify the precise nature of the spell.

The east door does not emanate magic and has no traps.

Underneath the heavy worktable laden with magical gear lies a hidden trapdoor leading to Kaarj's warren of escape tunnels. Kaarj does not use this route himself because he does not want to give the existence of the tunnels away, and wants to lead the group through the lightning trap. Particularly crafty Cast Members could take the opportunity to cut Kaarj off at the pass, so to speak. Locating this trapdoor requires a Perception and Notice Task with a –4 penalty.

Zombie Guards

These zombies are older, raised during Kaarj's initial wave of zombie raising, and he has spent his time crafting them using the Enhance Zombies power.

Strength 4	**Constitution** 2
Dexterity 2	**Intelligence** 1
Perception 1	**Willpower** 2
Dead Points 34	**Speed** 4
Endurance Points n/a	**Essence Pool** 12

Skills: Brawling 2, Hand Weapon (Spear) 3 [+3]

Attack: Bite D4 x 2(4), claws D6 x 4(12), or spear D6 x 4(12)

Weak Spot: All [0]

Getting Around: Life-Like [+3], Burrowing [+3], The Lunge [+3]

Strength: Strong Like Bull [+5], Damage Resistant [+5], Claws [+8]

Senses: Like the Dead [0], Infravision [+2], Scent Tracking [+1]

Sustenance: Occasionally [+2], All Flesh Must Be Eaten [0]

Intelligence: Language [+1], Tool Use 1 [+3]

Spreading the Love: Only the Dead [–2]

Power: 42

3. Pit Trap

Kaarj, like many of his kind, is extremely paranoid. He doesn't expect anyone to come down to his level without his permission, so he's left a pit trap for unsuspecting intruders. He never uses this passageway.

Pit Trap: This location is a covered pit that opens when a person stands on it. The lid resets itself in two Turns. The pit is twenty feet deep (see *AFMBE*, p. 108 for falling damage). The bottom of the pit is larger than the opening suggests, to accommodate the four zombies Kaarj keeps down here to deal with trespassers. They haven't eaten in a week.

4. Lair of the Necromancer

This room appears to be a bedroom of some sort. A simple wooden pallet piled high with animal furs is located to the right, with a crude nightstand standing next to it. Tapestries hang on the walls in an effort to keep out the chill. Two intricately worked chests sit in an alcove to the left, covered with discarded robes.

Kaarj makes his home here, and has tried to give it all the amenities he believes appropriate to a future ruler of the world. The room is as lavishly furnished as he can manage so far from civilization (and it's not easy to get nice furniture underground).

Kaarj is here 90 percent of the time during the night, often sleeping (though the alarm in area 3.1 wakes him). After waking, Kaarj dashes to the secret door in the southwestern corner of the room. Depending on how long it takes for the Cast to pursue Kaarj, they may not have any idea where he went, and must succeed on a Perception and Notice Task with a –2 penalty to find the door (disguised to blend in with the surrounding stone wall).

The chests in the room contain Kaarj's personal effects—mostly necromancer robes decorated in a skull motif. One of the chests is trapped.

Trap: Anyone who opens the chest without using the key (or noticing and disarming it) gets sprayed in the face with poison (Strength 6, corrosive, contact).

Treasure: Kaarj's trapped chest contains a sack of 300 gold coins, a Blessed dagger (+2 to hit and damage), and an amulet of healing (+10 Life Points, two times a day). If given enough time, Kaarj will gather these things before fleeing.

The other chests contain treasure looted from the burial mound: 2,000 silver pieces, jewelry worth a total of 1,000 silver pieces, and a small sack of gems (total value 800 gold pieces).

The Shadow

Kaarj has used his necromantic abilities to trap a shadow, a being of negative energy, and uses it to guard his bedroom. He has commanded it to attack any intruders.

Strength 5	**Constitution** 10
Dexterity 4	**Intelligence** 3
Perception 5	**Willpower** 3
Vital Essence 50	**Energy Essence** 80
Spiritus 5	

Skills: Brawling 4

Being of Essence: Shadows have Vital Essence and Energy Essence Pools. Depleting Vital Essence causes the ghost to dissipate.

Channel Essence: Shadows can channel one Essence point per Turn for each level of Willpower and Intelligence, which it uses to power the effects of the Elemental Cold (use Elemental Fire effects, but with cold damage instead of fire) at normal Essence costs and an effective Invocation level equal to their Spiritus.

Essence Drain: With a Simple Spiritus Test opposed by a Simple Willpower Test by the target, a shadow can drain six Essence points from anyone it touches (Dexterity plus Brawling for the shadow, Dexterity plus Dodge for the victim). Half the Essence absorbed goes to replenish its Vital Essence. The victim's body temperature drops and he pales noticeably during such an attack.

Immaterial: Shadows cannot be affected by physical attacks, as they do not possess corporeal bodies, nor can they interact directly with the physical world. Only Essence-based attacks and magical weapons can harm them (first depleting Energy Essence, then Vital Essence).

Shadow Form: By spending Essence, shadows can make themselves partially visible. It costs five Essence points to appear as a two-dimensional outline that lasts one minute, and if a point of damage is inflicted on the Shadow Form it vanishes. In this form, the shadow can inflict five points of cold damage to anything it touches.

5. Library

The walls of this L-shaped room are lined with wooden bookshelves that hold numerous leather-bound volumes and parchment scrolls. A small reading desk occupies the center of the chamber, with books and scrolls piled around the base. A glass lantern illuminates the room, casting shadows in the corner.

Kaarj spends a great deal of his day sitting in this room, performing research and drawing up his plans for world conquest. If the Cast ventures down to this level during the daytime, there is a 60 percent chance of Kaarj being here (1-6 on a D10). In this case, when the Cast triggers the alarm in area one, he gets his pride and joy—the Kelen zombie—and makes his way towards the source of the trouble. If the Cast pursues him from area two, and he makes it to the library, he fetches the Kelen zombie. Together, they confront the Cast.

Kaarj's first action is to cast Shielding, creating a physical shield (see p. 42) with AV 10. On the second Turn, he invokes Lesser Curse, inflicting Ill Luck on the most powerful looking Cast Member; the total bad luck pool is three, costing nine Essence. He continues to curse Cast Members while they battle the Kelen Zombie. Should the Cast attack Kaarj directly, he alternates between recharging his physical shield and fighting. Once he runs out of Essence, Kaarj attempts to escape.

The animated body of the once proud barbarian king occupies a small cell hidden behind a wooden door. Kaarj keeps the zombie bound inside a Warding circle (Str 8) so it cannot wander around aimlessly. The zombie hasn't eaten in a few days and is very hungry.

The bookshelves hold various tomes of blasphemous knowledge, such as *Rotgar's Manual of Death*, the *Book of a Thousand Screams*, and the *Necronomicon*. Characters who take the time to examine all the books and scrolls locate D6(3) Invocations among all the theory and diagrams. These books can substitute for a teacher for the purposes of learning these Invocations, but experience points must still be spent as normal to actually acquire them.

The Kelen Zombie

Kaarj has lavished attention on his undead barbarian king, since he's supposed to be the front man for Kaarj's insane grab for world domination. He has made extensive use of Enhance Zombies (Death Raising 4) to provide additional Aspects.

Strength 7 **Constitution** 2
Dexterity 3 **Intelligence** 1
Perception 2 **Willpower** 2
Dead Points n/a **Speed** 18
Endurance Points n/a **Essence Pool** 17

Skills: Brawling 4 [+2], Hand Weapon (Sword) 5 [+5]

Attack: Bite D4 x 7(14), claws D6 x 7(21), or bastard sword D10 x 7(35)

Weak Spot: None [+10]

Getting Around: The Quick Dead [+10], Burrowing [+3], The Lunge [+3]

Strength: Monstrous Strength [+10], Claws [+8], Flame Resistant [+1]

Senses: Like the Living [+1], Infravision [+4], Scent Tracking [+2]

Sustenance: Occasionally [+2], All Flesh Must Be Eaten [0]

Intelligence: Language [+1], Tool Use 1 [+3]

Spreading the Love: One Bite and You're Hooked [+2]

Special: Nest [+5], Noxious Odor [+5]

Power: 82

Kaarj the Conqueror

Strength 2 **Constitution** 3
Dexterity 3 **Intelligence** 5
Perception 3 **Willpower** 4
Life Points 30 **Speed** 12
Endurance Points 32 **Essence Pool** 70

Qualities/Drawbacks: Attractiveness –2, Covetous (Ambitious) 3, Delusions (Delusions of Grandeur) 3, Essence Channeling 10, Fast Reaction Time, The Gift, Increased Essence Pool 10, Paranoid, Resistance (Pain) 3

Skills: Craft (Rune Carving) 3, Dodge 4, Hand Weapon (Staff) 2, Hand Weapon (Sword) 5, Intimidation 4, Myth and Legend (Human) 3, Occult Knowledge 3, Research/Investigation 3, Riding (Horse) 2, Rituals (Necromancy) 2, Science (Anatomy) 2, Trance 4

Metaphysics: Elemental Air 2, Lesser Curse 2, Shielding 2, Warding 3, Necromancy 6, Death Lordship 5, Death Speech 5, Death Raising 5

Gear: Robe, Cloak, Leather Armor AV D6 + 1(4), Horned Helmet, Blasphemous Amulet, Broadsword D8 x 2(16), Skull-topped Staff

Notes: Kaarj dresses in the manner of the typical fantasy necromancer—long black cloaks adorned in a skull motif, a helmet sporting big, curved horns, and a skull facemask.

Depending on how things are going and how tough the Cast appears, Kaarj may use the secret door here to escape the complex. Reluctantly, he will leave the Kelen zombie to keep the Cast occupied.

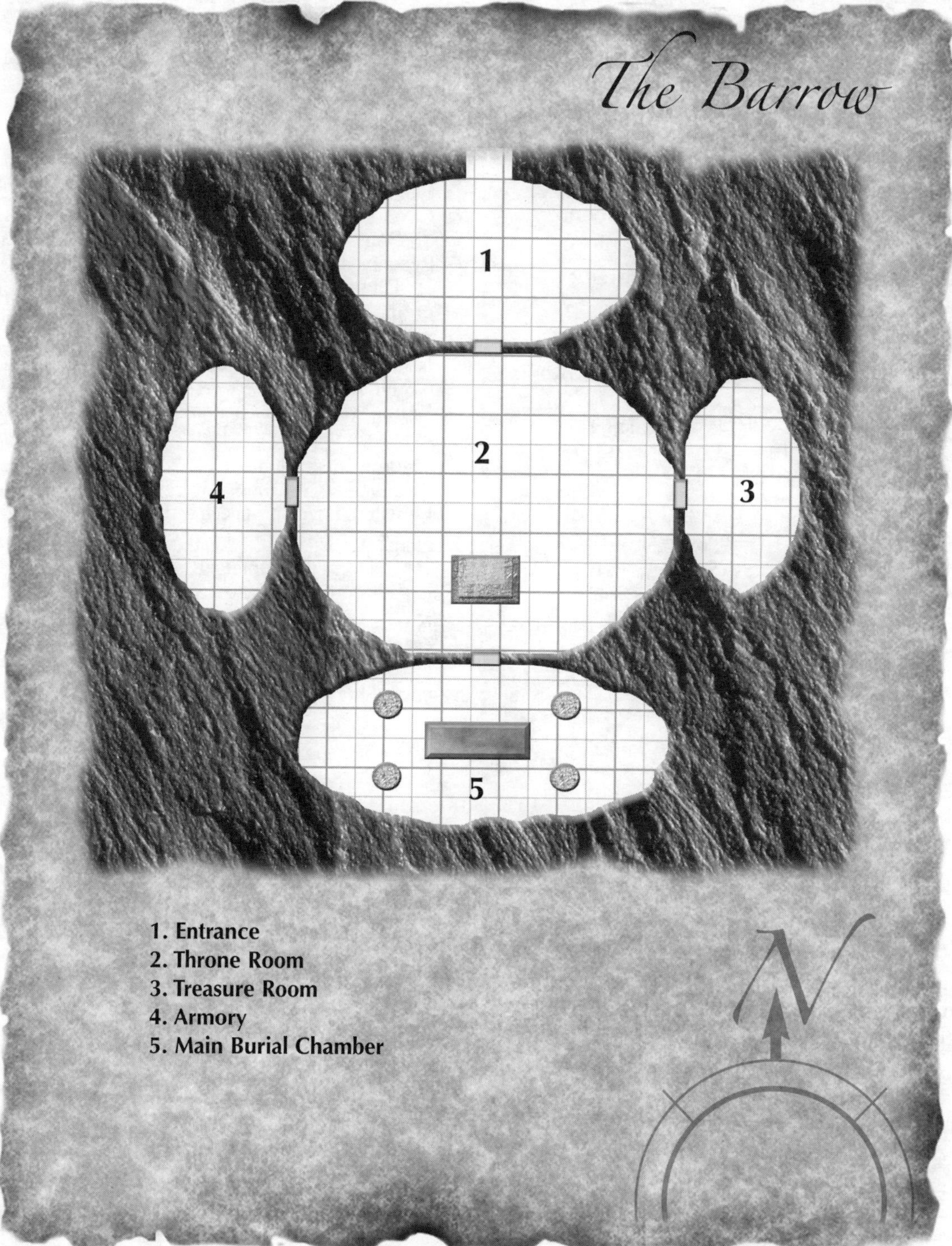
The Barrow
1
2
3
4
5
1. Entrance
2. Throne Room
3. Treasure Room
4. Armory
5. Main Burial Chamber
N

The First Level
1
s
5
4
6
2
3
8
7
1. Entrance
2. Zombie Diggers
3. Goblin Terror
4. That's Right, We Said Ghost!
5. Zombie Snackers
6. Zombie Storage
7. Tunnel
8. Guard Post
N

The Second Level
1
2
3
4
5
6
7
1. Passage
2. Wolf Pens
3. Goblin Dormitory One
4. Goblin Dormitory Two
5. Cold Storage
6. Chieftain's Room
7. Shrine to Zork
N

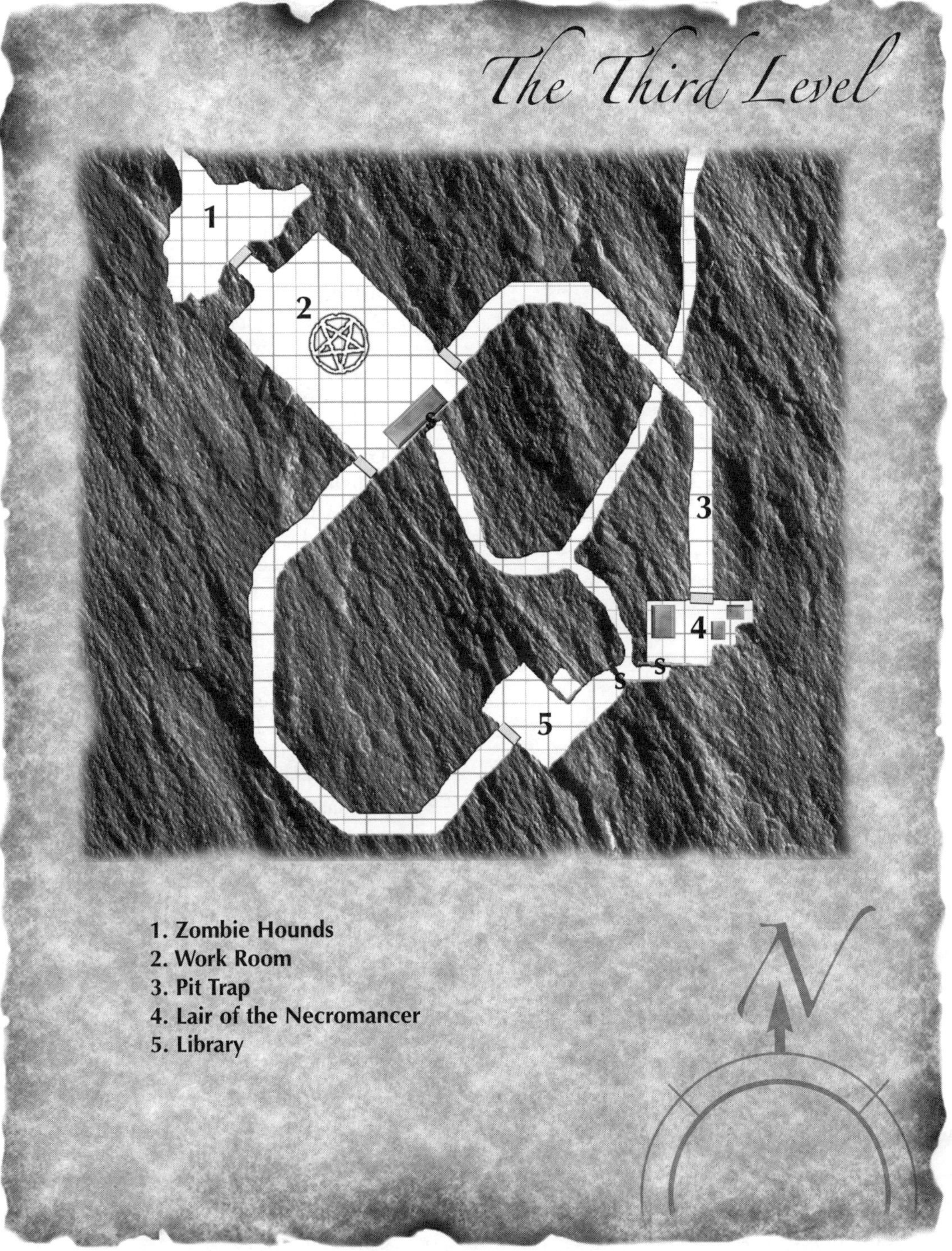
The Third Level
1
2
3
4
5
S
S
S
1. Zombie Hounds
2. Work Room
3. Pit Trap
4. Lair of the Necromancer
5. Library
N

Charts and Tables

Expand Your Game!

UNISYSTEM

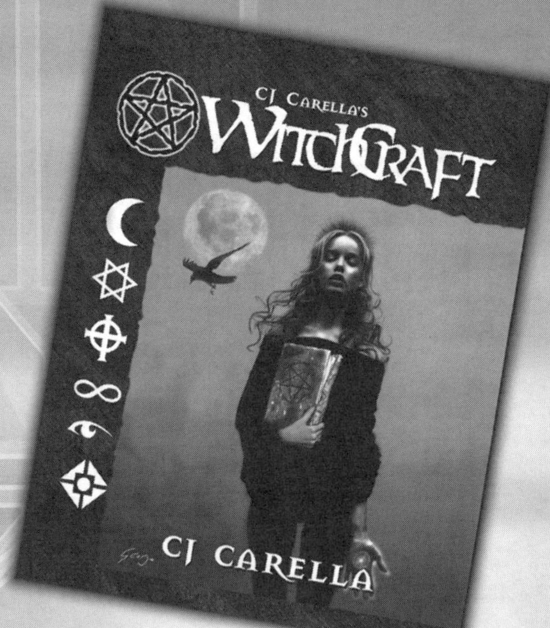
CJ Carella's
WitchCraft
CJ Carella

Army of Darkness
Roleplaying Game

Buffy
the Vampire Slayer
roleplaying game
Core Rulebook

Angel
Roleplaying Game
Corebook

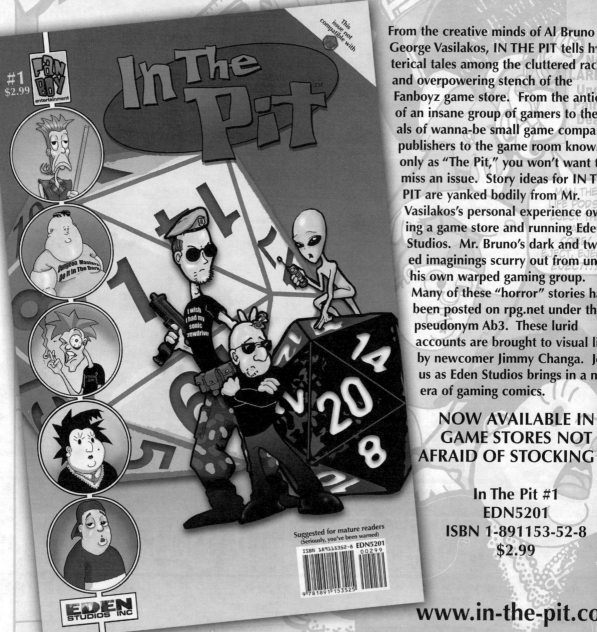